PUBLIC ENEMY

A SAM POPE NOVEL

ROBERT ENRIGHT

For my girls,

CHAPTER ONE

Something didn't feel right.

As the grey clouds gathered above the City of London, Henrietta Sarratt looked out from the eighth floor of the Bloom Enterprises' office and felt a sense of failure. It was quarter to seven in the morning, fifteen minutes before the meeting was due to begin, and she could feel her stomach turning with anxiety.

And she always trusted her gut.

It's what had made her such a tremendous police officer for fifteen years, and, paired with her intuition, had seen her steadily rise through the ranks of the Metropolitan Police Service where she served as the commissioner. It had been the opportunity of a lifetime when she was offered the role, but there had been a nagging sense of injustice in how it came about. Her predecessor, Bruce McEwen, had been a mentor to her, and as she'd served as his assistant commissioner, she'd fallen under his wing and watched as he'd led the Met with intelligence and nobility. His stout refusal to bend the rules for the rich and powerful soon saw him make powerful political enemies, which meant he was forced towards an early retirement.

Sarratt had been groomed to take the role, but there was an underlying view among certain political figures that she was nothing more than a stopgap. Optics wise, it helped the Met as an organisation to have a black woman leading the way, but the rumours were beginning to swirl that her tenure was under the microscope.

It was why she'd taken the meeting.

It was why she didn't feel quite herself.

'Good morning, Commissioner.'

The well-spoken voice snapped her from her gaze, and she turned as Piers Bloom stepped through the door being held open by his put-upon assistant. As the CEO of the biggest engineering company in the country, Bloom walked with the power and panache befitting a man of his position, and as he strode towards her, he extended his left hand.

'Good morning, Mr Bloom,' Sarratt said with a forced smile, and shook his hand firmly.

He winced with pain.

Although his left arm was moving freely, his right arm was still strapped across his expensive three-piece suit, the sling holding it in place. It had been nearly two months since Sam Pope had put a bullet through it, when the vigilante had accosted Bloom and two of his associates in an exclusive restaurant in the heart of the city. Bloom tried to hide the pain, but Sarratt clocked it.

Her eye for detail was second to none.

'Our guest will be joining us shortly...' Bloom spoke as he approached the polished oak table in the centre of the room and pulled out a few of the leather chairs. He gestured to one. 'Please sit.'

'I'm fine, thank you,' Sarratt replied. Petty, but she needed to fight the nagging sense that she wasn't in control of the situation. Bloom blew out his cheeks and took one of the seats.

'As you wish. Can I get you a drink? Tea? Coffee?' He snapped the fingers in his good hand, and his assistant stepped forward like an obedient pet.

'No, I'm fine thanks.' Sarrett waved it off. 'I try not to depend on caffeine in the morning.'

'Well, I can admire that,' Bloom said, his grey beard stretching across his face as he smiled. 'I, on the other hand, do not possess that strength.'

As Bloom turned and placed his order with his assistant, Sarratt turned and looked back out over the city. The depressing cold of January had set in, and the headlights of the steadily building traffic were filling the roads below. The city was just waking up, yet she'd spent the whole night awake, wrestling with the idea of walking away from this meeting.

With following her gut.

But as her husband, Jordan, had said, *'Sometimes, you need to do what is sensible as opposed to what is right.'*

It didn't sit well with her, but she saw the sense in his words. The vultures were circling above her, especially after the events in November that had seen three police officers murdered and a sizable amount of gold taken from the national bank. Although the breadcrumbs had been scant and quickly swallowed up by the press, all evidence pointed towards an inside job that Sam Pope had foiled.

People were killed.

A good man, DS Connor Vokes, had been left fighting for his life and had thankfully pulled through.

DS Jessica Sutton, as ferocious a detective Sarratt had ever seen, had decided to transfer to the Department of Professional Standards.

Sarratt's own confidant, Chief Inspector Mary Dummett, a woman she'd considered a friend, was now serving time in a heavily protected wing of one of His Majesty's Prisons.

The press was still pulling at threads to determine the cause and effect of those events, and with no clear figure of blame, the narrative of an unruly police force and a weak commissioner was starting to gather pace.

This meeting could help change that.

That was what their guest had pitched to her.

As Bloom's assistant scampered from the room, the powerful CEO turned his attentions back to Sarratt.

'Beautiful, isn't it?' he said confidently, as he pushed himself from the seat gingerly, and stood beside her. 'I take great pride in the things I've done for this city. As you do, I would assume?'

'We do our best.'

'You are too humble,' Bloom said with a grin, the halogen lights above gleaming off his bald head. 'The people who walk these streets, or drive on those roads, or work in these buildings, they all rely on you to keep them safe. To do the right thing.'

'And is this the right thing?' Sarratt said dryly, looking up at him. 'Because I feel like the right thing for me to do would be to ask why Sam Pope shot you in the first place?'

'Wrong place, wrong time,' Bloom said with a forced smile.

'Really? Because all the evidence suggests Sam Pope doesn't really make mistakes.'

For just a split second, the edge of Bloom's mouth twitched with anger, but he caught it and forced it into another grin.

'Read the reports,' Bloom said with a wave of the hand. 'Bakku was just a front for some illegal activities, and Peter Grant was unaware of this when we booked the meal. Like I said, wrong place, wrong time.' The door to the meeting room flew open again, and Bloom turned to face his fast-approaching assistant. He pointed to the table, and as the assistant placed the coffee down, Bloom lowered himself into the chair and looked up at her. 'I'm sensing you're a bit uncomfortable, Commissioner.'

'Really?' Sarratt responded. 'You should be a detective.'

'Well, I am the leading engineer in this country.' Bloom gestured for her to sit. 'Tell me, if you think I have some ulterior motive, please…enlighten me.'

'I don't think that will be necessary.'

The booming voice cut through the room, and both Bloom and Sarratt snapped their heads to the door where Admiral Nicolas Wainwright stood. Despite his advancing years, he moved with the agility of a man half his age, and he barged past the assistant and into the room. The young man shot a sorrowful glance to Bloom, who just waved him away as he stood. Wainright stepped with purpose, his back straight, and his shoulders set as he regarded them. As the Chief Defence Staff for the United Kingdom, Wainwright was one of the most powerful men in parliament, with rumours persisting that if he chose to pledge his allegiance to any political party, he'd be a shoo-in for Downing Street. But as a strict and proud military man through and through, Wainwright had little interest in the squabbles and petty shade throwing of the Houses of Parliament. He was in charge of keeping the country safe, and as he approached Sarratt, he nodded his approval to someone who held similar responsibilities.

'Commissioner,' he said with a warm smile. 'It's lovely to see you.'

'And you, Admiral.' Sarratt stood to attention, and immediately felt like she'd handed the power over to him.

And he knew it, too.

'Please. Call me Nicolas.' Wainwright stared at her for

a moment before turning to Bloom. 'Piers, my old friend. How's the shoulder?'

'Still on the mend,' Bloom said as he shook Wainwright's hand. 'Shall we?'

'Yes. Let's sit.'

Wainwright's voice was jovial, but the command was stern, and as Bloom returned to his coffee, Commissioner Sarratt tentatively took the seat opposite him. Wainwright, as a show of power, took the seat at the head of the table.

'Now, Commissioner…' Wainwright began.

'Henrietta is fine.'

Wainwright smiled.

One-one.

'Henrietta…' he continued. 'I think it's safe to say that something needs to be done about the current situation.'

Sarratt looked to Bloom and then back to Wainwright.

'I don't follow, sir.'

Damn.

Two-one.

Wainwright leant forward, looming large towards her.

'Suffice to say, your reign as commissioner is not being perceived as a success. Now, before you cut me off, I want you to know that I was fully behind you when McEwen stepped away, and I remain fully behind you now.'

'Thanks?' Sarratt looked confused.

'But the optics don't look good. Sam Pope was a problem Commissioner McEwen failed to address, and that ended in an international episode with the French that had us on the brink of conflict. Now, two months have passed, but someone still needs to be taken to task for what happened in this city.. Forget the gold. People want a name for the deaths of those police officers. *Your* police officers.'

The accusation was clear, but before Sarratt could respond, Wainwright continued.

'And right now, your name is on the docket. But it doesn't have to be…'

Wainwright's tone lightened, and Sarratt could once again feel her gut trying to speak out.

She drowned it out with her husband's words.

'Sometimes, you need to do what is sensible as opposed to what is right.'

'What are you suggesting?'

'I'm suggesting we start up the Sam Pope Task Force again.' Wainwright leant back in his chair triumphantly. Sarratt looked to Bloom who nodded his agreement and then shrugged.

'That was years ago. And even then, it was just a political move by a mayoral candidate and besides, we don't have the funding—'

'That's where I come in,' Bloom finally spoke.

'Yes, you see my good friend Mr Bloom here, one of the biggest philanthropists this country has ever known, has experienced first-hand the dangerous reality of allowing Sam Pope's quest for justice to continue. Thankfully, the bullet only hit his shoulder, but how long will it be before a stray bullet hits an innocent child?'

'Even so, and even with the extra funding, the Met isn't equipped right now to go after such a target and—'

'I have a team,' Wainwright cut in, and Sarratt could feel the final strands of authority leave her grip. 'With Mr Bloom's generosity, we'll hire experts who will be able to bring the Sam Pope matter to an effective and more importantly, legally sound conclusion. This is your opportunity, Henrietta. If you give this your backing, you nail your flag to this mast, *you* will be the commissioner who finally stopped Sam Pope. All those whispers about your competence, all those rumours about your position… they'll all disappear.'

Despite the promises of acclaim, Sarratt knew she was

being backed into a corner. The two men who had their eyes locked on her held considerable sway with the right people, and turning down their offer was tantamount to career suicide.

When she'd taken on the job, she'd promised herself she'd make a difference.

She hadn't so far.

And if she was to be removed, and painted as a failure, she'd never be able to.

There was still so much to achieve, and so many vital changes to make.

Swallowing her guilt along with her pride, Sarratt let her husband's words filter through her mind once more and then stood.

'Okay,' she said with a firm nod. 'I'll get the ball rolling.'

'Fantastic,' Wainwright said, his grin verging on mocking. Sarratt regarded him coldly.

'And what do you get out of this?'

'Excuse me?' Wainwright sat back in his chair, his hands resting on the table.

'What's in it for you?'

'Young lady…' He began condescendingly. 'I've spent over forty years of my life fighting for the safety and freedom of this country. Far be it from me to tell you how to do your job, but it's high time this violent man was brought to justice. A safer country. That's what's in it for me. I'll be in touch.'

The finality of his words caused a shimmer of unease through Sarratt's body, and as she turned to leave, she gave one more dismissive glance to Bloom, before she stormed from the office. As the door closed behind her, Bloom waited a few moments before turning to Wainwright.

'Do you think she bought it?'

Wainwright chuckled.

'It doesn't matter. She knew what would happen if she didn't agree.' He drummed his fingers on the oak. 'That's the problem with today's world. Peel back enough layers, and people will always put themselves first. Balikov understood that. It's why he wanted to change things.'

The mention of their fallen potential leader filled the room with an eerie silence, and as he sighed, Bloom broke it with a question.

'And what about Sam Pope?'

Wainwright's face went blank. Slowly, he turned to Bloom, his eyes filled with murderous intent.

'Sam Pope is a dead man.' Wainwright stood, fixing his waistcoat as he readied himself to leave. 'He just doesn't know it yet.'

CHAPTER TWO

The war was never over.

As he watched another aeroplane cut through the clouds above Luton Airport, Sam Pope wondered if his fight would ever end. With his hulking frame wrapped in a black puffer jacket, Sam's eyes followed the plane as it lowered down beyond the airport terminal and out of sight. The aircraft was most likely filled with families and couples, all returning from their winter sunshine and back to the bitter, dreary winter of the United Kingdom.

All of them returning to their normal lives.

But to him, this was normal.

For nearly five years now, Sam had been waging a one-man war against crime and corruption, spanning from the UK to North America, from Berlin to Budapest. He'd gone toe to toe with mercenaries, French politicians, biker gangs, arms dealers, even the head of the British Armed Forces.

He'd been shot.

Stabbed.

Tortured.

Left for dead on numerous occasions.

But here he was, braving the cold January evening, and

as the bitter wind gnawed at the edges of his ears, he pulled the thick woollen hat down over his short brown hair. He shuffled a little on the spot, his bearded jaw grimacing at the pain that still throbbed in his left calf. It had been two months since he'd been at another London Airport, fighting Dominik Silva's team, and stopping the dangerous hitman from making off with millions of pounds worth of gold. He'd left half a dozen bodies in his wake, but Sam had paid the price for it.

As he always did.

Thankfully, the bullet had only grazed his calf in the wild shoot-out in the warehouse, but Silva had targeted it during their own face-to-face confrontation. Despite the pain, Sam had walked away, and he was certain that Silva himself was locked away inside the darkest hole in the country.

But Sam hadn't walked away from the fight.

He couldn't.

The previous summer, he'd been sent into the bowels of hell itself to stop a murderous oligarch who was planning on pulverising the western world and rebuilding it in his image. Sent into a brutal underground fighting tournament by a covert government operation and one of the dearest people to his heart, Sam had fought with every fibre of his being to stop the incoming attacks.

But it wasn't over.

The head of Directive One, a man known as Blake, had handed him the intel on all the powerful UK players involved with the sinister plot, and although he'd handed that over to DS Jessica Sutton to do things by the book, there were names on that list that she'd never be able to get.

Men who were too rich.

Too powerful.

But not to Sam.

He pulled the sleeve of his coat up and checked the time, and then kept his eyes peeled on the exit of the terminal. Michael Hartson was due through those doors any minute now, and Sam was under no illusion that what he'd planned would be tricky. As a former minister within the government's cabinet, Hartson had been building a successful post-political career as a mediator between large-scale companies. He'd overseen three major takeovers in the past few years and was widely regarded as one of the most influential men in the business world.

He was also on the list Blake had given Sam.

Some of those takeovers had included the likes of Peter Grant and Piers Bloom, men who had already experienced Sam's wrath and now it was time to bring Hartson down as well.

But Sam wasn't there to kill him.

He was there to expose him.

Sure enough, through the throngs of scattergun families and irritable dads doing their best to direct the luggage trolleys, a well-dressed, middle-aged man emerged, flanked by two suited men who screamed military. Over the course of the past half a decade, Sam had come across numerous army men who'd found that private security was a lot more lucrative than serving their country.

Sam needed to be quick.

And they might be a problem.

The two men formed a barrier around Hartson, showing little regard for the civilians as they barged through the group, directing him towards the luxury taxi waiting for him in the no-parking zone. Whatever fine the airport issued would be chump change to a man like Hartson, and as he approached the black vehicle, the driver stepped out and hurried to the back of the car, leaving the driver's door open.

Sam made his move.

One of the security detail had opened the back door to the car, and Hartson was lowering himself in, as the other watched over the driver while he placed the three suitcases into the boot. Sam kept his head down, the wind now carrying the dampness of incoming rain, and as he stepped briskly towards the vehicle, his hand reached inside his jacket, his fingers expertly sliding over the grip of the Glock 17. As Hartson pulled the door closed, Sam stepped out towards the car and drove the point of his elbow into the security guard's temple. The man went limp before he'd even hit the car, and the thud drew the attention of the second guard, who stepped around the back of the car, only for the steel grip of the handgun to connect viciously with the bridge of his nose. As the man stumbled back, and a few civilians gasped in horror, Sam swung his foot into the back of the security guard's leg, sweeping him off his feet and letting him crash onto the solid concrete curb.

'Down,' Sam ordered the driver, aiming the gun squarely at his forehead. The driver trembled with fear, and Sam felt a twinge of guilt as the man struggled to his knees and the surrounding onlookers began to raise the alarm. The armed police who roamed the airport would be there in seconds. Sam swiftly raced round to the driver's door, dived in, and slammed the door shut. He spun, aiming the gun at Hartson who was fumbling with the handle.

'Leave it,' Sam commanded angrily, and Hartson sheepishly lifted his hand away from the door. Sam hit the auto-lock on the dashboard, and then pulled the car away, amid a wave of panic as the armed police and medics appeared in his rear-view mirror. With his foot pressed to the metal, Sam guided the car through the weaving traffic lanes that surrounded Luton Airport, the speed building as he whizzed past a few buses packed with travellers who'd parked offsite a few miles away. Within minutes, they'd cleared the airport completely, and although the place would soon be swarmed by the police, Sam knew they were in the clear. By the irritated sigh from the backseat, Hartson did, too.

'What is it?' Hartson said with a hint of annoyance. 'Money?'

'Just keep quiet,' Sam responded, keeping one eye on the road as he shot a glance in the rear-view mirror.

'This is all quite embarrassing,' Hartson snapped with disgust. 'Tell me how much you want and then let me out of the fucking car.'

Sam approached the lights that led down the country road to the neighbouring village, and as they flashed to amber, he slammed his foot down once again. The luxury car burst forward through the rain, racing through the now red light, and all Sam heard was the furious honking of horns and the screeching of tyres. The sudden propulsion had sent Hartson forward, crashing face first into the back of the passenger seat. He flopped backwards, his nose bleeding and broken as he groaned in pain.

'Put your seat belt on,' Sam said with a wry smile.

'Now listen here, you fucking rat, I'll see to it that…'

Sam hit the brakes again.

Hartson's face was reacquainted with the back of the chair.

As he flopped back into his seat, his face a bloodied mess, Sam calmly restarted the car and then half a mile down the country road, he turned off down a dirt track. The only light was from the headlights of the car, and it illuminated the surrounding trees that arched over the road like a tunnel, protecting them from the rain. After a few moments, Sam pulled the car into a mud covered clearing and killed the engine. Behind him, Hartson was trying to breathe through the pain of a shattered nose, and Sam stepped out into the bitter winter evening. The faint sound of sirens echoed in the distance, a useless call for him to return his prisoner.

They wouldn't find them.

Not until Sam allowed them to.

With his boots squishing through the mud, Sam yanked the back door of the car open, and Hartson tipped out, crashing hard onto the ground and letting out another yelp of pain. With little regard for the man's pain threshold, Sam snatched the back of Hartson's collar and hauled him up, before sending him sprawling into the front of the car where he collapsed in the blinding beams of the headlights.

'Please.' Hartson's tone had dropped to a whimper. 'Please. Whatever you want.'

'I want the truth,' Sam said as he stepped over him. Hartson looked up with confusion. Sam made a show of the Glock in his hand, sending the panic spreading through the corrupt businessman once more.

'What are you talking about?'

With the blood trickling from his nose and across his lips, Hartson began to push himself up onto his knees, only for Sam to drill his boot straight into Hartson's chest, sending him sprawling back into the mud. Hartson coughed and spluttered as he rolled onto his front, and as he slowly pushed himself back to his knees, he froze in horror as he felt the gun press to the back of his head.

The tears began to fall from his eyes.

'Please don't kill me,' he begged.

'I'm going to ask you some questions,' Sam said coldly. 'If I think you're lying, then I will pull the trigger. Do you understand?'

'Yes.' Hartson managed, his breathing escalating.

'Is your name Michael Hartson?'

'Y-y-yes.'

'Did you serve as the Minister for the Civil Service?'

'Yes. For two years, about seven years ago.'

Sam pressed firmly against the back of Hartson's skull, pushing him forward, and drawing another gasp of terror.

'Were you aligned with Vladimir Balikov, and complicit in a terrorist plot to destroy this country?'

The accusation clearly held merit, as Hartson heaved with fear, as if his darkest secrets had just been poured out on the ground before him.

The torrential downpour had broken through the resistance of the trees, and was now hammering down upon them, clattering on the roof, and windshield of the parked car.

'I-I-I…' Hartson stammered.

Sam pressed harder.

'The truth,' he said forcefully.

'Yes. Yes, I was. Okay? Please…just don't kill me.'

Sam stepped forward and pulled what Hartson believed was the gun from the back of his head. He held it out, revealing to Hartson that it was a recording device, and Sam made a show of ending the recording. Hartson's fear swiftly turned to a rage-induced panic as he spun on his knee.

'What the fuck do you…'

Sam drove his elbow into the side of the man's skull, and Hartson collapsed into the mud. Sam pocketed the evidence he needed and then squatted over Hartson's motionless body and rummaged through his pockets until he retrieved his phone. He dialled the emergency services who answered pretty swiftly.

'Nine-nine-nine, what is your emergency?'

The voice was female and very calm.

Sam looked down at the motionless man at his feet, the rain sliding down his nose and dripping to the mud below.

'This is Sam Pope. I've got a Michael Hartson here needing some medical assistance. Trace this call.'

Before the woman could respond, Sam tossed the phone back into the car and then pulled his hat down over his ears once more. With the engine still running, the headlights illuminated the wooden gate and a few feet of the field beyond, before nothing but darkness awaited. He looked down at the treacherous man at his feet, shook his head, and then placed both hands on the wooden fence. With one push, he leapt the entire thing, and after a few feet, he was swallowed by the darkness.

The police would be there soon.

They'd look for him.

But he'd be long gone.

And as he checked the recording as he walked, Sam knew he'd taken another name off his list.

And only added to the shitstorm that would soon be coming his way.

CHAPTER THREE

OVER A DECADE AGO…

'Murray. Murray. Receiving.'

Amongst the wreckage of his Jeep, Corporal James Murray could hear the robotic voice of Sam Pope echoing from the radio. He turned back to Private Griffin, who was going into shock as the blood loss from his severed arm was beginning to snatch away his life. A few hundred yards away, he could hear the panicked cries of the ISIS patrol that had blasted his Jeep from the road and had set about murdering them all in cold blood.

Until Sam Pope had intervened.

Somewhere along the cliff faces that overlooked the Afghan terrain, the deadly sniper was shrouded in cover, raining death from above on the soldiers who had tailed Murray and the rest of 'Alpha Unit' from their mission. They had expected some resistance, but with two of his squadron dead, another on his way, and two more severely injured, Murray knew he was only moments away from being KIA.

'I'll be right back.' He promised Griffin, who was clawing at him with his only hand, the fear evident in his eyes.

'Don't leave me…' Griffin gurgled.

'I promise I'm not going to leave you,' Murray said firmly, as another explosion echoed from the cliff face above, and Murray whipped his head just in time to see the expert shot from Sam obliterate two more of the ISIS crew. The remaining members had taken cover behind their vehicles, and as Murray kept low, he used the fiery remains of his own as cover. With his skin covered in a mixture of his and his men's blood, he adjusted his SA80 Assault Rifle in one hand and reached into the front of the Jeep for the radio.

'Pope. You crazy bastard.' Murray chuckled in the face of certain death. 'Not looking good here.'

He looked back to the men he'd hauled from the destroyed convoy, keeping them within the cover of the remains of the vehicle. But they were sitting ducks, and if the entire opposition set upon them, there was no way Pope and he could keep them all alive.

'Do you have any grenades?' Sam's voice came through loud and clear.

'Negative,' Murray responded and peeked over the smoking vehicle to see a few soldiers starting to shimmy to the side of their vehicle. He adjusted his grip on his rifle.

Time was ticking.

'Any ammo?'

'Just one box with seventeen magazines,' Murray said, looking at the spilled ammo on the floor beside him. 'Get your arse out of here, mate. Just promise me you'll find Becky and tell her what happened.'

Murray's thoughts immediately went to his beloved wife, knowing their plans to start a family were now nothing more than a pipedream. Sergeant Pope was a hell of a shot, but if Sam stayed any longer, they'd level the entire cliff face to eliminate him.

He didn't want another person to die because of him.

The remaining few minutes he had left on Earth were already designated for the dying men behind him.

'Listen to me.' Pope's voice came through with urgency. 'Cover that ammo in fuel and throw it as far as you can. Do it now.'

Murray was smart enough not to question it. There were literally seconds before his cover was compromised, and as good as Sam Pope *was behind the scope, not even he would be able to reload fast enough to stop an avalanche of bullets ripping through him and the remains of Alpha Unit. With the Jeep on its side, Murray drove his combat knife into the petrol tank, and the warm petrol flowed through the hole, drenching his hands and the ammunition in fuel. Then, with a silent prayer to a God he'd never reached out to before, he hurled it over the fiery remains of the overturned vehicle towards the oncoming enemy.*

He dived and took cover as a shot echoed from the cliffs above.

The explosion told him it was a direct hit.

As the ringing in his ears began to subside, and his vision stopped shaking, Murray pushed his battered body to his feet and glanced across at the fiery remains of one of the Jeeps, along with the scattered remains of the ISIS soldiers. Despite the pain that echoed through his body, he hauled his men to the remaining Jeep, putting a bullet in one of the ISIS soldiers who tried to reach for a gun through the wreckage.

As he pulled away, he knew some of his men probably wouldn't make it back.

But he'd give everything to give them a fighting chance.

Somewhere in the cliffs beyond, Sam Pope was lying in wait, covering them before making his own route to a designated extraction point.

With death still following them, Murray couldn't help but chuckle as he guided the Jeep back across the rough terrain.

'Pope.' He scoffed to himself. 'You crazy bastard.'

It wasn't often James Murray thought about Sam Pope.

Over the years, the haunting memories of that near death experience in Afghanistan had begun to fade away, and when he finally left the military as a well-respected major, they'd been filed in the deepest reaches of his mind. In the years since his departure, Murray had set up his own private-security firm, which had soon blossomed into one of the most profitable contract services in the UK. Having served under General Ervin Wallace, Murray had seen how the man had used Blackridge for financial gain and had applied a number of the same ruthless tactics to ensure that Guardian picked up the pieces.

Unlike Wallace, however, Murray never gave the illusion that his outfit was there for the benefit of the country. They were, in essence, an elite military team for hire, and although Murray held somewhat of a moral compass, that had begun to lose its focus over the years. Contracted work out in the middle east, the place where he'd almost met his maker, had put their profits in the millions, and the twenty-strong roster of soldiers he had at his disposal were all living lives way beyond the means of the actual military.

The work was usually easy, overseeing shady deals between nations, or 'high-end' shipments from powerful players in the black market.

Some of whom had been shut down by Sam Pope himself.

The Kovalenkos.

Slaven Kovac.

Vladimir Balikov.

And when that news had filtered through to him, Murray would always think back to that afternoon under the harsh Afghan sun, and remember that were it not for Sam Pope, he'd have long since rotted in the sand.

It was funny how things came full circle, and as he sat in the waiting area of Bloom Enterprises, in a well-fitting, tailor-made suit, a part of him hoped the job spec wouldn't be what he'd predicted.

'Mr Murray?'

A young, anxious personal assistant appeared in the doorway, and Murray stood, towering over him. As he approached his late forties, Murray had begun to see the signs of age creeping in. His dark hair was now almost completely grey, along with the neat beard he'd trimmed on a weekly basis. His impressive physique was still visible, but the effort to maintain it was growing by the year. The assistant led him up the elevator to the top floor, and guided him through to a plush office, where a day before, Bloom and Admiral Wainwright had forced the Commissioner of the Metropolitan Police into their plan. Now, she remained seated as they both stood to greet Murray, both assured that this would go much smoother.

'Major Murray,' Wainright said with a smile.

'Not for a long time, Admiral.' Murray shook the man's hand firmly.

'Piers Bloom.' Bloom introduced himself and received a firm nod and handshake. 'Please sit.'

Sarratt looked appalled, realising she'd been relegated to the fourth voice around the table, but Murray did offer her a nod as he took his seat. The other two took their seats as the assistant bumbled in with a jug of water. Bloom's thanks were nothing more than a glare. As Murray poured himself a glass, he rolled his shoulders and sat back in his chair.

'Nice office.'

'Thank you.'

'So, you want to tell me why you're going after Sam Pope?' Murray said, cutting to the chase. Bloom looked a little taken aback, but Wainwright just offered a warm smile and then looked to Sarratt, who sighed, and leant forward.

'Because it's high time somebody reinstated what the law actually meant.'

Murray smiled to himself and then fixed Wainwright with a sceptical look and sipped his water once again. He looked to Bloom, who seemed triggered into agreement.

'Exactly that. I was in the wrong place at the wrong time and am still feeling the effects of it.'

He motioned to the sling wrapped around his wiry

frame, and Murray smiled, finished his drink, and placed the glass back down.

'Thank you, all, but if you're just going to insult my intelligence, then I think this meeting is over.' Murray stood, fixing the bottom button of his jacket. Bloom shot a worried look to Wainwright, who straightened up.

'Fine.' Wainwright motioned for him to sit again. 'I should have known better than to bullshit you, James. How many times have you worked for me now?'

'Never. I don't work *for* people.'

'Semantics.' Wainwright waved it off. 'How many contracts has Guardian fulfilled on behalf of the UK military? Half a dozen?'

'Seven,' Murray stated with a nod.

'And you and I both know, on each and every one of them, the reason I require an off-the-books team isn't important. So, answer me this, before I answer your question. Why does it matter?'

Murray held Wainwright's stare, refusing to budge. It was a clear power play, and Murray knew that despite forging a reputation as the antithesis of his predecessor, there were several similarities between Wainwright and Wallace. There was a reason the commissioner of the Met wasn't the one making the decisions, after all. After a few tense moments, Murray leant forward, and poured himself another glass of water and took a sip.

'Sam Pope saved my life,' Murray finally spoke. 'Admittedly, it was a long time ago. But things like that, they usually carry a little bit of weight.'

'I see,' Wainwright said insincerely. 'Will this be a problem for you?'

'Not if we're on the level,' Murray snapped back. 'The brief was to run the Sam Pope Task Force on behalf of the Metropolitan Police, right? So that means you're giving me free rein to bring him in and he'll get a fair trial?'

'That's the plan.' Wainwright smiled.

Murray squinted. He didn't buy it.

'And you're on board with this?' Murray turned to Sarratt.

'Yes,' Sarratt said grudgingly, before Wainwright interrupted.

'She'll be announcing it this afternoon, along with the Met appointed representative as discussed.' Wainwright seemed bored. 'Does that suffice?'

'It should do,' Bloom piped in. 'We're paying you enough.'

'For Sam Pope?' Murray chuckled. 'You aren't paying half of what this will take. But you didn't answer my question. Why are you going after him now?'

Wainwright leant forward, the calm façade slipping slightly.

'Because he *needs* to be stopped. Understood?'

The question was a poorly disguised threat to not press any further, and Murray once again regarded Wainwright with a fixed stare. Eventually, he necked the rest of his water and stood, gesturing for both men to stay seated.

'We'll report in tomorrow morning. As requested, we'll need access to all files and footage and—'

'Already done.' Wainwright also stood, ignoring Murray's request, and took a step forward and extended his hand. 'Just don't fuck this up. Or there will be consequences.'

Murray smirked at the challenge, and as he took Wainwright's hand, he shook a little firmer than usual.

'Trust me, if we fuck up with Sam we're all dead men, anyway.'

Murray relinquished his grip, offered a curt nod to Bloom, and then marched out of the office. As he headed down the stairwell, he was already tapping away on his phone, sending a list of requirements to his second in command, Fabian Jensen, who would wrangle up his squadron to take down Sam. With every word he typed out, he felt dirty with betrayal, but the world had conspired to put them on different sides of the agenda.

This was what James Murray did.

Time had laid to rest the day Sam Pope had saved his life in the excruciating heat.

Now, they walked two separate paths, one a path of righteousness, and the other a path paved with extreme wealth and respect.

The very fact their paths were colliding was simply business, and Murray knew that.

It wasn't personal.

It was just business.

As he sent the message, he stepped through the revolving automatic door to Bloom Enterprises and out into the bitter cold of the winter's day, the grey clouds making the City of London a more depressing labyrinth than usual. The wheels were in motion, and in less than twenty-four hours, he would begin his contract to take down the most dangerous man in the country.

A man who had saved his life.

If the opportunity came to repay the favour, Murray would do his best.

But this was business.

And Murray was the ultimate professional.

Back in the office, Bloom was standing by the window, looking down at Murray striding down the street with his phone in his hand.

'Do you think he'll get the job done?' he asked, not looking back to the desk.

'He should do,' Wainwright said confidently. 'He's the best there is.'

'And he *will* report in to me,' Sarratt stated, trying her best to stay in a conversation that had been pulled away from her.

'Of course,' Wainwright said unconvincingly. 'But the bottom line is, we need to stop Sam Pope. And Murray is the best option we have right now.'

'The public won't like it,' Sarratt said with a shake of her head. 'A private security firm working on behalf of the Met? It's bad optics.'

'Which is why we need the right person to relay the importance of it all,' Wallace said with a grin and then motioned to Bloom. Instantly, Bloom leant across and held down a button on the conference phone in the middle of the desk.

'Send her in.'

Sarratt looked between both men, confused.

'Send who in?'

Wainwright grinned.

'The face of the Sam Pope Task Force.'

Before Sarratt could probe further, the door flew open, and Wainwright stood with his arms open. Sarratt's mouth dropped, the shock of seeing a remnant from the past.

The hair was longer, and any attempt to hide the greys had long been abandoned.

The skin was wrinkled.

Gaunt.

The eyes were just as dark as simmering as she remembered, when she feared the woman she'd eventually replace.

Commissioner Sarratt stood, and with a sigh of disbelief, greeted the woman who had marched back into her world.

Ruth Ashton.

CHAPTER FOUR

Three years was a long time for a hatred to build.

Ever since that fateful night outside the University College Hospital London, Ashton had been mourning the demise of a life she'd spent decades building. Back then, she'd been the Assistant Commissioner of the Metropolitan Police Service, a role she'd adored and proudly fulfilled with every fibre of her being. The preceding career had been one filled with accolades, with commendations for bravery, along with heading up multiple CID task forces that had taken down some of the biggest criminal syndicates the country had ever known.

She'd done it all by the book.

By the law that she so vehemently upheld.

But the country had fallen in love with a vigilante.

When the name Sam Pope first came across her desk, she didn't believe the rumours. A troubled ex-soldier, who was mourning the loss of his son, had been shovelled away in the Met archive offices, picking off criminals for his own amusement. It seemed preposterous, but after the assault on the well-known Frank Jackson and his alleged High Rises, Pope uncovered collusion among senior police officers that set off a chain of events that would ultimately define Ashton's downfall.

She was put in charge of the Sam Pope Task Force, with her stellar record for results making her the obvious candidate. As she made political moves to eventually usurp Commissioner Stout and take the top job, she wisely moved a woman of ethnicity into the forefront of the team.

DI Amara Singh.

That was another name that made her skin crawl.

As the hunt for Sam had intensified, and bodies began to pile up, the rumours of Sam became legend among the public.

Corrupt politicians.

Bent coppers.

Sex traffickers.

Drug dealers.

These were the targets of Sam's one-man crusade of justice, and soon, in the eyes of the public she'd sworn to protect, Sam Pope was seen as a more effective deterrent than the police force themselves.

It had made her sick.

Soon, she felt surrounded by traitors, as the likes of DI Singh and the revered DI Adrian Pearce were clearly aiding Sam. She just couldn't prove it. The task force fell apart when, through collusion with Sam, DI Pearce uncovered corruption inside the political push behind it.

Ashton was under pressure and at the end of her rope.

Then she met General Ervin Wallace.

As the Chief of Defence Staff for the United Kingdom, Wallace was a legendary figure within the British Armed Forces, and commanded such fear and respect, Ashton found herself drawn to the man instantly. Despite the rumours that swirled around Wallace, she found his obsession with stopping Sam Pope as powerful as a magnet, and soon found herself falling in love with the man. Their affair was physical and at times, primal, and while he treated her coldly in the aftermath, she felt, on some level, that he cared for her, too.

It would also mean she'd be a shoo-in for the top job, as Wallace alluded to wanting an ally in such a powerful position.

But then he was killed.

Brutally slaughtered and dumped from the top of a building by Sam Pope, who had the audacity to deny it.

But Ashton saw through it, and her blind hatred mixed with grief saw her overlook a glaring mistake, and after Sam had infiltrated and then escaped from a maximum-security prison, the then commissioner, Michael Stout, accused her of forging his signature for her own benefit.

She'd been set up.

And somehow, although she could never prove it, she knew that Sam Pope had been the cause of it.

After that, Ashton lost everything.

Her position as the Assistant Commissioner.

Her future prospects.

All the respect and reverence from her peers.

Ervin Wallace.

All of it gone. Buried six feet under by a man who willingly broke the law and was championed by the people for doing so. Somehow, despite being a loyal, and upstanding servant to the public and to the Metropolitan Police Force, Ashton had been discarded, and painted as the villain, while Sam Pope was given the chance to walk away.

It had pushed her to the brink.

For two years, Ashton tried to bury her pain and loss in the bottom of every bottle she could find, but kept finding that the bottles were endless. The thought of harder drugs, or even just ending it all, often danced through her mind, before a moment of clarity struck her when she heard about the incident surrounding Jasper Munroe and the fall of one of the UK's most powerful businessmen.

People didn't want to burn their heroes.

They wanted to bury their villains.

To do that, she needed to make the world see what she already knew.

That Sam Pope was the most dangerous criminal the country had ever known.

It soon became an obsession. Although her path back to the Met may have been shut off, Ashton still had powerful friends in high places, and it didn't take more than a few phone calls to gain access to the ever-growing archives they had on the man. As someone who had spent the final stages of her police career hunting Sam Pope, she knew about the people he put away.

What she was after now was the collateral damage he left in his wake.

The armed police officers he'd shot.

The anarchy at the Port of Tilbury.

The impact of shutting down London Liverpool Street Station.

The death of a well-respected journalist.

The list went on.

The obsession grew and grew, and soon, Ashton was reaching out to her perceived victims of Sam's crusade, and the more she dug, the bigger the list grew.

The public didn't care about the criminals or the corrupt people Sam Pope either killed or put behind bars. But paint the picture of the honest, hard-working civilian having their lives ruined because of it, and the paradigm would shift.

That was what she pitched to Admiral Nick Wainwright, a man she respected but who'd stepped into shoes that were just too big to fill. He was the polar opposite of Wallace, who had commanded every room he walked into with his impressive stature and sheer force of will. Wainwright was more reserved, and although his exemplary military record commanded just as much respect, he certainly acted like a man in the latter stage of his life. On account of her years of service to the country, he'd granted her a meeting, but her proposals fell on deaf ears.

Wainwright just didn't seem interested.

Dossier after dossier.

Pitch after pitch.

She sent countless reports to his office, but never once received a courtesy *thank you*.

But that all changed after Piers Bloom and a couple of other well-known businessmen found themselves in Sam's crosshairs. Ashton knew better than to ask for the reasons, but suddenly, her angle on bringing down Sam Pope was now top of Wainwright's list of priorities.

And it moved quickly.

Within weeks, the idea of a new Sam Pope Task Force was pitched, with Piers Bloom happy to fund the initiative, along with the outside contractors Wainwright had already selected. Ashton was invited to meetings with the two men, walking them through her extensive research to build the narrative of the cost of Sam Pope's war on crime on the innocent people who had declared him a hero.

Then Wainwright gave her the opportunity she hadn't even hoped for.

To be the face of it.

'The public need someone they can trust. Someone who has been in this from the start and someone who can deliver this to them with clarity and commitment.'

For the first time in years, Ashton had felt useful again.

And now, as she walked into the office, she extended her hand to a shell-shocked Commissioner Sarratt and smiled.

'Commissioner,' she said respectfully. 'I must say, I am so proud of how far you've come.'

Sarratt looked around the room, slightly confused, and then took the hand.

'Thank you,' Sarratt said with a forced smile. 'But I don't understand what's going on?'

'Ruth Ashton may no longer be with the Met, Commissioner, but she is still held in high regard by a number of politicians and higher-ups. The dossier she's compiled on Sam Pope is, quite frankly, one of the greatest pieces of detective work I've ever seen, and so I believe that she is best placed to deliver this to the country.'

'But she isn't a police officer,' Sarratt said firmly, and then turned to Ashton. 'No offence.'

'None taken.' Ashton smiled. 'But the admiral is right. People will ask questions, and I can answer them. Besides, if this doesn't work, then based on what the admiral has told me, your position cannot afford to take that hit.'

Sarratt glared at her.

'And what exactly does that mean?'

Wainwright stood, seizing control of the conversation.

'It means, putting it bluntly, that people want you out, Henrietta. So, this can go either one of two ways. Either we go ahead with the plan and bring Sam Pope in quickly and efficiently under your guidance, or it backfires, and Ashton and Guardian take the blame.' He shrugged. 'All I'm trying to do is protect your position.'

'Really?' Sarratt scoffed. 'Because it feels like a number of decisions about the Met are being made without my input.'

Wainwright smiled, once again taking his seat and pressing his fingers together.

'Decisions are being made to *protect* your position within the Met.' Wainwright smirked. 'Now, I hate to be blunt, but you can either get on board, or get off. Either way, Sam Pope will be brought in, and you can either do what your predecessors couldn't, or you can join them on the scrap heap. The choice is yours.'

Sarratt held Wainwright's unwavering stare, before shooting a quick glance towards Bloom and Ashton, who were watching intently. There was no fight to be had. The wheels were already in motion, and Sarratt once again fell back to her husband's wise words.

She needed to be sensible.

Even if, in the pit of her stomach, she knew it was a mistake.

As the silence grew into a tense stand-off, Sarratt finally sighed.

'Fine,' she said curtly, trying to show some authority. 'But I want my eyes over *everything*. Do you understand?'

'Of course.' Wainwright smiled victoriously. 'I wouldn't have it any other way. We'll need the announcement to be made first thing in the morning. I trust you can arrange that.'

Sarratt placed both hands on the table and leant forward, her frown threatening to pull her forward even further.

'I am not your fucking PA.'

Wainwright smirked.

'Not if you play along.'

Sarratt stood, processing the clear threat, and then smarted her jacket. She straightened her shoulders, trying hard not to regurgitate her swallowed pride.

'I am still the Commissioner of the Metropolitan Police. You'd do well to remember that.'

With that, Sarratt scowled at both Bloom and Ashton, before marching out of the office, slamming the door behind her. Bloom blew out his cheeks and turned back to Wainwright, who seemed unphased.

'You think she's actually on board?'

'I think she's scared,' Ashton said.

'It doesn't matter what she is. Right now, we have the go ahead. Tomorrow morning, Ruth, you'll announce the start of the task force. Do you have everything you need?'

Ashton nodded.

She had three years of grief and hatred locked and loaded.

'Yes, sir.'

'Good.' Wainwright waved his hand. 'Then I'll be in touch.'

Dismissed from the room, Ashton left abruptly, leaving Wainwright to ease himself from the chair and stride to the window, peering out over the City of London. Bloom stayed in his seat, his eyes on the door that Ashton just left through.

He looked shaken.

'Are you sure about this?' he eventually asked.

Wainwright didn't look back.

His eyes were focussed on the horizon as he gazed over the capital city of the country he'd vowed to protect.

'One hundred per cent.' Wainwright spoke with little emotion. 'It's the only way people will actually listen.'

CHAPTER FIVE

Sam couldn't remember the last time he'd had a dream.

As he pushed himself up from the bed of his studio apartment in East London, he allowed the quilt to slide down his battle-scarred torso. Despite being in his early forties, his strict fitness regime still kept him in peak physical condition, although his sculpted muscles were covered with scars. The two that adorned his chest, courtesy of two point-blank bullets from Ervin Wallace, should have ended his life, but in truth, had been the seed where his quest for justice grew.

The death of his son had been the catalyst.

And while the years of grief had subsided into a peaceful acceptance; Sam was relieved that his sleep was something he no longer dreaded. In the years following Jamie's untimely death at the hands of a drunk driver, Sam's guilt manifested in haunting apparitions of his son, his twisted body pleading with Sam to save him.

He couldn't.

Over the years, as more blood was shed, Sam was often visited by visions of his deceased friend Theo, along with the gallery of criminals he'd put in the ground.

It was all driven by guilt.

Sam could have stopped Miles Hillock from getting in that car that faithful night, but he'd failed to intervene.

To do the right thing.

And it had cost him everything.

With a gentle groan, as his ageing and beaten body fought against him, he lifted himself out of his bed and strode to the bathroom, and moments later, he was standing under the pressure of the shower as it rained down over him. He scrubbed himself with soap. The scarred skin from stab wounds and bullet holes were constant reminders of how far he'd been willing to push himself.

How close to death he was willing to walk.

For a long time, Sam had felt like a lost soul and a man with nothing to lose was a dangerous one. But over time, as he peeled back layers of corruption within the British institutions that had been built to keep the country safe, he'd found a new sense of purpose.

A new reason for being.

And with it came an acceptance that he no longer had a son, but he held onto a memory that would always keep him going.

Keep him pushing forward.

Stepping from the shower, he looked at himself in the steamy mirror as he brushed his teeth, his eyes darting from scar to scar, bringing flashes of violence through his mind.

His fight to the death with Oleg Kovalenko.

The brutal battle with Slaven Kovac.

The myriad of assassins sent his way by Dana Kovalenko.

Mr Hudson.

Laurent Cisse.

And most recently, Dominik Silva.

All of them had left a lifelong mark on Sam, and as he stared at his own personal tapestry of pain, his mind fell to Mel Hendry. A woman who'd loved him not for what he'd been, but for who he'd become. For six blissful months, Sam had lived in the centre of Glasgow, spending his time working at the local scrap yard and building a new life with Mel and her outspoken teenage daughter, Cassie.

For a short period, Sam had felt human again.

But the inherent need to do good put an end to that, as Sam's moral compass directed him to a billionaire's son, and brought his world crumbling down. Mel and Cassie had been threatened.

The scrap yard was turned into a graveyard.

And Sam said goodbye to a chance of happiness.

There wasn't a day that went by that Mel and Cassie didn't enter his mind, and on a weekly basis, he resisted the urge to hop on a train to Glasgow, push open the door to Mel's business, the Carnival Bar, and whisk them both up in his arms. But time had moved on, and a woman like her wouldn't be shy of suitors.

Nor would she want a beacon of danger around her daughter.

It was just another road closed to Sam, and like the passing of Jamie, was just another painful pillar that held up his mission.

The mission to expose the truth of what he'd stopped.

Sam had handed the list of names to DS Sutton months ago, but nothing had come of it. No breaking news articles about the British elite funding a global terrorist network.

No repercussions for the men and women who'd tried to bring about a continent-wide massacre, which would have been rebuilt in the image of Vladimir Balikov.

It meant DS Sutton had been silenced, and with her transfer to the Department of Professional Standards swiftly approved, it meant she'd effectively been squirrelled away to the same cupboard that Adrian Pearce had been.

Those in power only wanted the truth if it benefitted them.

He'd leant on the former police commissioner, Bruce McEwen, for any information, but he'd been blacklisted by the Met. McEwen had his suspicions that his replacement and friend, Commissioner Sarratt had nothing to do with it, and all fingers pointed towards Admiral Wainwright who had been on Sam's list.

Was still on Sam's list.

Sam knew he could storm the offices of all the powerful names who'd bet against the country, put a bullet between their eyes, and the world would be a better place.

But nothing would change.

He'd still be painted as a crazy veteran with a vendetta, and from the mud he left behind, more weeds would grow. He wanted the truth to be exposed, for the right people to do it through the right channels. Sutton had been silenced, which was why he'd sent the recording of Hartson's confession to one of the few people he truly trusted in the world.

Lindsey Beckett.

The tenacious reporter had built her career impressively and was now the chief political reporter for the BBC. With her striking looks, appealing Northern Irish accent, and commitment to the truth, Beckett had broken through as one of the most trusted voices within the BBC.

She would believe him.

After all, he'd saved her life.

It had been nearly two years since Sam's friend, Sean Wiseman, had been beaten to within an inch of death. Having started a relationship with Beckett, he was a target for one of her persons of interest in a bid to stop her from exposing their lies.

Sam had fought back.

In fact, it was what had drawn him from a life of peace and violence and showed him the truth.

The country needed him.

Someone had to fight back.

Having dressed in his usual jeans and black T-shirt, Sam took to the modest strip that comprised the kitchen on the far wall of his one-bedroom apartment and chuckled at what Etheridge would say if he saw him. A firm believer in Sam's one-man war, Etheridge had forged Sam a new identity and left him a small fortune to fund it before he went dark.

But Sam couldn't bring himself to spend that money on needless luxuries.

All he needed was a roof over his head, a semi-decent bed, and the basics of a well-balanced diet.

And copious cups of tea.

As he poured boiling water on the tea bag in his mug, Sam wondered if Etheridge was still able to track him. The identity he'd built for him, Jonthan Cooper, had been compromised in his mission to take down *Poslednyaya Nadezhada*, but Directive One had built him a new one. As *Ben Carter*, Sam still had access to his fortune, and he imagined somehow, Etheridge would have been able to trace the money.

At least he hoped so.

Sam pulled out the small table that was fitted to the wall, slid a stool underneath, and took a seat, shovelling spoonfuls of porridge into his mouth as the radio played behind him. As always, the morning presenter was overly excited, trying his level best to hype people up for another day ahead, his tiring shtick interspersed with similar sounding pop songs.

Sam was waiting for the hourly news update, hoping that the first signs of Beckett's progress would come through. Hartson had a political legacy, and his collusion against the very government he'd served would be headline news.

But again, nothing.

Beckett had been silenced.

Just as DS Sutton had been.

Once again, the truth only mattered when there was a benefit to be had.

Frustrated, Sam tuned out from the rest of the news bulletin, his mind racing as he pondered his next step. Maybe doing things the 'right way' was wrong? Maybe the only way to seek justice against those who'd funded and colluded with *Poslednyaya Nadezhada* was to put them down. Then maybe the news outlets would investigate the reasons Sam had targeted them in the first place.

As the news reporter spoke jovially about a new social media craze, Sam took his final mouthful of porridge and then stood, taking the bowl to the sink for a quick clean.

Then he heard something that caused him to freeze.

'And now finally, the Metropolitan Police had released a statement pertaining to the wanted vigilante Sam Pope.'

Sam dropped the bowl and turned and stared at the radio.

'A press conference has been called later this morning, where we understand the previously named Sam Pope Task Force, which was started a few years ago, will be relaunching with a renewed focus on bringing Pope to justice. We'll have more information as the press conference unfolds.'

The radio cut back to the usual host, who irritatingly focussed on the social media craze, so Sam stepped forward and turned the radio off.

They were coming for him.

Clearly, the frequency with which he was targeting the elite had startled them into action, and as the true power behind the country, they were now pushing the Met to bring him in. It didn't bother him as such, as they'd been after him for nearly five years, but Sam knew it was a dangerous road to go down. A renewed focus meant more resources, which meant quicker responses.

It meant more honest, hard-working officers would be sent his way.

It meant that those higher up, were scared.

Which meant he had to push forward.

He had to keep going.

Sam glanced outside at the bitter, winter morning that was breaking over the City of London, and he threw on his coat, before tucking his Glock 17 into the back of jeans. He needed to know what was going on, and there were only a few people who'd be able to help him.

One of those people was Lindsey Beckett, and if he knew her as well as he thought he did, she'd already be at the BBC offices, thumping on doors to find out what was going on. It wasn't just a coincidence that hours after his abduction of Hartson, Sam was now top of the list of priorities again.

Lynsey would want the same answers he did.

He just hoped she'd have them.

As he stepped out into the cold, Sam pulled up his hood, stuffed his hands into his pockets, and marched into the rain. It was a long walk to West London where the offices were, but he could do with the fresh air.

As he headed into the city, he didn't realise that plans were already in place to turn it against him.

CHAPTER SIX

'This is fucking bullshit, Tom. And *you* know it.'

Lynsey Beckett was standing in her editor's office, hands on her hips, and the familiar ice-cold glare of someone who wouldn't give something up without a fight. Her editor, Tom Alderson, rubbed the bridge of his nose and sighed, knowing full well that the issue wouldn't go away.

'First off, please watch your language. I'm still your boss,' he said as firmly as he could. 'Second, my hands are tied. The word's come from higher up.'

'But this is news, Tom.' Lynsey slammed her hand on his desk, causing a few of the reporters in the open plan office to turn in their direction. 'So why the fuck are we not reporting it?'

Swiftly, Tom leapt from behind his desk and shuffled to the door of his office, slamming it shut to keep the interested ears out.

'The hell if I know.' Tom shrugged as he retook his seat.

'We are the BBC. We are paid for by the British public.'

'Don't start.' Tom waved her off.

'Oh, I'm sorry?' Lynsey's sarcasm cut deeper thanks to her thick, Northern Irish accent. 'Should I stop finding the truth about what's going on in this country?'

Tom tipped his head back in frustration.

'Christ's sake, Lynsey. You have to be the biggest pain in the arse in this place.'

'I'll leave if you want?' She threatened, her words laced with sincerity. 'I'm sure there's a long list of news outlets that will run with it.'

'Don't be so childish,' Tom snapped back. Lynsey had worked for Tom for a number of years, and these outbursts were par for the course of having such a brilliant reporter on his team. 'You know how it is. If we dig too deep, someone higher up will always step in. It's the way it works.'

'But it shouldn't. And the public deserves to know that we're only telling them what we're allowed to tell them.' She took a deep breath and shook her head. 'Did you listen to it? The recording?'

It had been over twenty-four hours since a padded envelope had been delivered direct to her desk, with a recording device inside. The playback was of Michael Hartson, the former Minister for the Civil Service and one of the more well-known politicians in the country. Since then, he'd forged a lucrative career in the business world, but the recording laid bare a more sinister side to the man.

Involvement with terrorists.

Collusion against the very country he'd served.

It was headline news.

With a resigned sigh, Tom leant across his desk.

'Yes. I did.'

'And…' Lynsey's piercing eyes bore through him.

'And it's pretty damning,' Tom agreed. 'But it was under duress.'

'Necessary duress.'

'Is there such a thing?' Tom chuckled. 'Look, mate. You and I both know that any confession given under such circumstances is going to be dismissed.'

'But it proves that there *is* something bigger going on, right?' Lynsey finally took a seat, seemingly calmer. 'We had the reports of a silencing job within the Met Police a few days after the gold was stolen. Rumours of a list of well-known names. Names of people involved and then suddenly, nothing.'

'You think they trod on it?' Tom asked, his chin resting on his clasped hands.

'Abso-fucking-lutely I do,' Lynsey replied. 'And we need to report on that, Tom. We owe it to our profession and to the people.'

Her boss blew out his cheeks, clearly exhausted. As he rubbed his eyes with the balls of his hands, he sat back in his chair and fixed her with a look.

'You know we can't. If the Met and the government have told the higher-ups that it's off limits, then it's off limits. You know the line they take when it comes to Sam Pope. And well—'

'Well, what?' Lynsey spat instantly.

'Let's just say that I've had more than a few conversations with them about your position on *that* matter.'

The message was clear.

Ever since Sam Pope had saved her life from the despicable Daniel Bowker, she'd found herself championing his cause. Whether that was pushing for his story to be presented in a more compassionate manner, or just by honouring it by pushing for the right thing.

Sam Pope may have been a criminal in the eyes of the law, but he had an unwavering sense of justice.

The man had risked life and limb to protect her and avenge the men who had beaten her fiancé, Sean Wiseman to the brink of death. He had told her then that he'd stepped away from a life of violence, but she knew the type of man Sam Pope was.

He couldn't walk away from the fight.

What scared her most, was he would die trying.

But the rumours around the office had swirled about her links to Sam, and although Tom had fought her corner, she knew certain avenues had been closed off to her, and when the opportunity arose to become the Chief Political Reporter for the BBC, Tom had warned her there were some pretty serious objections to her appointment. With the spread of misinformation across social media platforms, every news broadcaster in the country was tightening down on what could and couldn't be reported, and Lynsey had been given express instructions about her political reporting.

She could report the truth.

Within reason.

And this didn't fall within reason.

The silence began to grow uncomfortably, and Tom leant forward in his seat and offered her a warm smile.

'How's Sean?'

It was the personal touches, along with his impeccable eye for a good story, that made Tom such a great boss. Even if he did tow the political line at times.

'He's good.' Lynsey smiled. 'Back working three days a week.'

'That's great. Set a date yet?'

Lynsey looked at the engagement ring on her left hand and felt a little surge of love.

'Not yet,' she said bluntly. 'Too much to do.'

'I've been married for over twenty years,' Tom said, sitting back in his chair. 'Trust me, there's always too much to do.'

Lynsey pushed herself off the chair and stood straight.

'So long and short of it, they've killed the story?'

'Afraid so.' Tom shrugged. 'Like you said, bullshit. But we still have a lot of news to report and—'

Knock knock.

Both Lynsey and Tom turned their focus to the door, where through the shutters, they could see Morganna Daily. Before Tom could offer an invite the feisty reporter had pushed open the door and stepped in, excusing herself as she did. After the roaring success of her interview with Olivier Chavet for British News Network, Morganna had become one of the hottest properties in their profession, with her social media following exploding. She was relatable to the younger demographic, and combined thoughtful, measured questioning with stunning good looks. It meant she could be a conduit between the broadcasters and the younger generation who were looking elsewhere for their news, and soon she had every network reaching out to her.

Tom had insisted on bringing her in, telling Lynsey that she could blossom under her learning tree.

Lynsey wasn't so sure.

Perhaps it was that Morganna's persistence and lack of tact reminded her too much of herself, but Lynsey didn't appreciate the way Morganna carried herself.

She knew she was a big deal.

And acted like it.

'Sorry to interrupt,' Morganna said insincerely. 'But there's been an interesting piece added to the breakfast news.'

'On TV?' Tom said, picking up the remote control for the flatscreen TV on his wall.

'No. Breakfast radio.'

Lynsey and Tom frowned with confusion, and Morganna rolled her eyes and turned the volume up on her phone, as the cheery, Scottish voice of the newsreader was enjoying his five-minute interruption of the usual morning radio nonsense.

'And now finally, the Metropolitan Police had released a statement pertaining to the wanted vigilante Sam Pope...'

All of them listened intently, and Lynsey could feel the muscles tightening in her body. The news briefing ended and Morganna shut her phone off.

'Did you know about this?' Lynsey shot an accusing look at Tom, who returned in kind.

'No, I did not,' Tom said, lifting his own phone in frustration. 'I need to make some calls, but we need someone down there in the front row. And I mean an hour ago.'

'I'm on it,' Lynsey said with a reassuring nod.

'Not you,' Tom said in exasperation. 'Do you honestly think they'd let you report on Sam Pope?'

Lynsey went to say something, but Morganna stepped forward.

'I'll do it,' Morganna said with a confident smile.

'Fine,' Tom agreed before Lynsey could interject. 'Take whoever you need, then get your arse back here pronto.'

'Thanks, boss,' Morganna said, before flashing a wry smile at Lynsey who forced one of her own. As Morganna left, Lynsey watched her ambitious protégé dash down the corridor before she turned back to Tom.

'Whatever this is, it's in response to what Sam sent us.'

'Just let it go, Lynsey,' Tom said, flicking through his contacts. 'I need to make some calls.'

'Sam Pope is not a public enemy,' Lynsey stated. She turned to leave. 'This is bullshit.'

'It always is with you,' Tom called after her, but she cut him off by closing his door. It was over ninety minutes until the press conference was to take place outside New Scotland Yard, and it was going to take every bit of her self-control not to go down there.

The seconds felt like minutes.

Minutes felt like hours.

She tried to busy herself by clearing down her inbox, but when she looked up, only half an hour had passed. Just as Lynsey was contemplating pissing off every single one of her bosses, her phone buzzed with a text message.

An unknown number.

Outside. To the left.

A smile spread across Lynsey's face.

Swiftly, she threw on her coat, collected her bag, and headed down through the enormous BBC office. As she stepped through the automatic glass doors at the front of the building, the private courtyard felt abandoned. With its own private arcade of shops and restaurants, the BBC had cultivated a 'mini street' for its employees. A stone's throw down the road was the dilapidated stadium for Queens Park Rangers Football Club, and opposite her work building, was the enormous, modern, Westfield Shopping Centre.

Two contrasting London institutions, either side of one of the country's fundamental pillars.

The rain and cold had turned the usually vibrant area into a ghost town, with a few employees huddled under umbrellas as they headed towards the building. Lynsey hunched her shoulders and turned her back to the cold, protecting the flame of her lighter as she lit her cigarette.

Then she headed left.

After a few hundred meters, she passed through one of the side streets into a restricted parking area, and a hulking figure stepped into view.

'Been a while.' She smiled, allowing the smoke to filter from her nostrils.

'How's Sean?' Sam asked in his surprisingly gentle voice.

'Everyone asks that. It annoys me that he's so liked.'

Lynsey joked as she took another puff. 'He's good. Almost there.'

Sam nodded with a smile. They both knew the severity of her fiancée's injuries, and the enormous struggle he'd faced to come back from them. As the rain fell, Lynsey looked around, and then back to Sam.

'So, what's up, Sam?' she asked. 'Not to be rude, but this is bordering on career suicide for me.'

'I know.' Sam held up a thankful hand. 'But I just wanted to know what was going on?'

'With what? The task force?' She stubbed her cigarette out on the wall. 'I take it you heard?'

'Yeah. Is it to do with—'

'The recording you sent me. I can't prove it, but the fact they shut down the story instantly and then now have redoubled their efforts to find you, makes me think you might have rattled the wrong cage.'

'Story of my life.'

'Ditto.' The two friends shared a warm smile in the cold rain. Lynsey then blew out her cheeks in exasperation. 'Keep that number. I'll message you if I find anything.'

'Thanks. I owe you one.'

'I know you do. In fact, you owe me a lot of ones.' She sighed. 'This might have to be the last one.'

It was regrettable, but Sam knew she was right. Despite her assistance and commitment to his cause, he knew he was putting her career in danger.

It wasn't her fight, and he refused to let her be affected by it.

'I think so, too,' he agreed, and then lifted her chin with his finger. 'Just make sure you keep doing what you're doing.'

Sam then squeezed her shoulder, stuffed his hands into his pockets, and then headed back through the alley.

Lynsey, feeling her heart break slightly with guilt, lit another cigarette, and called after him.

'Be careful, Sam.'

He carried on walking.

He didn't look back.

'Always.'

With his final word echoing against the narrow walls, he disappeared around the corner, and as Lynsey blew a plume of smoke into the bitter, cold wind, she knew it was a lie.

Sam Pope would do what was necessary.

Whatever the cost.

CHAPTER SEVEN

With a few deep breaths, Ruth Ashton tried her best to settle the butterflies in her stomach. For three long years, she'd dreamt of a moment to get back at Sam Pope, not only for the death of her career but also for the man she loved.

Ervin Wallace.

Despite his insistence, she knew he was responsible for the death of a hero and knowing that in the final moments of his life, as he hurtled from the top of the abandoned High Rise, Wallace was dealing with the pain of having his throat slit. All that anger and grief had manifested itself in her mission, and now, as Police Commissioner Sarratt spoke just a few feet away from her, Ashton had never felt closer to having her voice heard and her message understood.

Sam Pope was no hero.

He was the most dangerous man in the country.

The journalists had gathered in an excitable mob outside the New Scotland Yard building, and Ashton could sense the excitement levels rise as eyes landed on her. It was good for her ego, as her mere presence seemed to send a shockwave of intrigue through the group and even as Sarratt began her introduction, most eyes were on Ashton. It was good for her ego, and she now appreciated the fresh haircut and brand-new black pantsuit that she'd treated herself to. Almost as much as she appreciated the downpour to disappear moments before she was due in front of the cameras.

This was her ticket back to prominence.

Maybe not with the Metropolitan Police, but she was certain that a man like Admiral Wainwright would find use for someone as diligent and as focussed as she was.

All she had to do was bring in Sam Pope.

With her mind wandering, Ashton snapped her focus back to the present moment to catch the tail end of Sarratt's speech.

'Injustice isn't something we can abide by. Nor can we condone the steps taken by people to battle it themselves.' Despite her best efforts, Sarratt was struggling for enthusiasm. 'For years now, Sam Pope has taken a noble stand against crime and corruption, but to a cost that many of you do not understand. Some, not all, have even glorified his actions, claiming him a hero who's needed. Well, I say, as the leader of the greatest police service in the world, he is a criminal who must be stopped. Which is why, effective immediately, the Sam Pope Task Force has been reformed, with substantial funding and backing to bring this criminal crusade to a swift and lawful conclusion.'

Murmurs of discontent echoed through the crowd, and Ashton tried to scout any journalists who seemed to agree with the notion. They would make great allies for her future endeavours.

Sarratt ploughed on, ignoring the hands that had risen.

'I will not be taking questions,' she stated. 'I understand a number of you will want answers, and for those watching at home who believe in Sam Pope's mission, you may want reasoning. So now I will hand you over to a woman who dedicated over two decades of her life to protecting this city and this country, and someone I have had the pleasure to work under and learn from. So please welcome, the primary consultant on the Sam Pope Task Force, former assistant commissioner, Ruth Ashton.'

Ashton felt a twinge of anger at the perceived jibe at her former position, and she offered a curt smile to Sarratt as she approached the podium. As she turned to face the journalists, Ashton felt another surge of anger, as she half expected a round of applause for her triumphant return.

'Ladies and gentlemen. The good people of this nation. My name is Ruth Ashton, and as the commissioner said, I proudly served this country for over twenty years, eventually serving as the Assistant Commissioner of the Metropolitan Police Service. During that time, I led numerous operations that tackled organised crime to high levels, leading to the arrests of several prominent criminals. In fact, during the last few months of my tenure, we shut down the operations of Harry Chapman, one of the biggest importers of drugs into this country. But never, in all my years, did we face a threat quite like Sam Pope.'

Ashton could sense she had them. They were listening.

Finally.

'There have been numerous theories around Sam Pope's crusade, with countless, unconfirmed stories pertaining to corrupt police officials and slanderous lies painted against well-respected political figures. Yes, there have been issues within the Met, and these issues were swiftly dealt with by the likes of Commissioners Stout, McEwen, and our current commissioner, Henriette Sarratt.' Ashton turned and offered Sarratt a smile and a nod. 'And while it is within the remit of our journalists to paint pictures for the public, above all, it is their duty to report the facts. The truth. And the truth is, the reality, and cost of Sam's one-man war has never been told. Until now.'

Ashton had to contain the smile that was threatening to crack across her face. All eyes were on her.

Every ear was turned in her direction.

This was her moment, and not even the slight drizzle being carried on the cold winter's breeze could take it from her.

'During Sam Pope's first acts as a vigilante, a well-respected, innocent therapist was taken hostage by him, and in doing so, he left behind two dead bodies and two assaulted police officers. This was not reported by the media. A car chase during which Sam Pope willingly drove on the opposite side of the motorway caused a three-car collision, where five innocent members of the public were treated for injuries. Five people, including an eight-year-old boy, who were just going about their lives.' Ashton shook her head. 'These are the stories of Sam Pope that do not make the news sites.'

Ashton's tone was almost accusatory as she stared out at the reporters.

'Theodore Walker, a man who served this country as a combat medic with distinction, and a pillar in his community of Bethnal Green. A man who, after dedicating his life to serving our brave soldiers in the heat of battle, dedicated it to helping under-privileged kids. A man who served alongside Sam Pope in the army, and a man who had death delivered to his door by Sam Pope. Again, another story that you failed to report to the people.' Ashton shook her head in disgust as she turned the page on the podium. 'Three armed police officers attending a call at a residential home in Farnham, all shot in the legs by Sam Pope as he made his escape, with one of them retiring from active duty due to the complications. Another two assaulted, both receiving concussions, while another was thrown down the stairs and suffered a broken collarbone as a result. All thanks to Sam Pope, who proved he was willing to do *anything* to avoid arrest.'

The crowd were beginning to stir. Ashton had always been able to read the room, and although they were standing out in the open, she could sense the mood changing.

They were beginning to really listen.

'How about the death of Helal Miah, a well-respected name within the journalistic world, who was murdered by a terrorist in his hunt for Sam Pope? While you reported his death at the time, you omitted the fact that this innocent man was tortured and then hanged.' Ashton let the brutality of Miah's death register with them all. 'General Ervin Wallace, a man who served this country and this government with distinction and honour, who tried his best to reach out to a soldier who'd lost his way and was then brutally attacked and killed by Sam Pope.'

Out of the corner of her eye, Ashton could see Sarratt contemplating stepping in, as if Ashton was skirting a little too close to the line. Beyond her, Admiral Wainwright nodded his approval.

'Three years ago, a man held an entire ward of the University College of London Hospital hostage, strapped with a bomb, to pull Sam Pope out of hiding. Days before, after breaking out of prison, Sam Pope instigated a riot within the cells that cost the lives of six guards and seven inmates. Six men, earning a decent living, who were beaten to death in their workplace. Shall I go on?'

Ashton scowled over the podium. Her hatred for Sam Pope was overflowing, and she knew she was one step away from making it personal.

It was to her.

But for the country to agree, she needed to keep it professional.

'These are just half of the examples on my list, ladies and gentlemen. I have the impact of Sam's actions shutting down London Liverpool Street Station for an entire afternoon, and the effect it had on commuters and businesses alike. I have the heartbreaking accounts of a small, family run business in Derbyshire being devastated by Sam's fight. A scrap yard in Glasgow that was turned into a war zone, and an innocent, family-orientated businessman now under investigation for collusion. Millions of pounds' worth of criminal damage, that will be covered by the law-abiding taxpayers of this great country. The very people who Sam Pope claims to protect.'

Ashton took a breath.

Everyone was hanging on her words.

All microphones and cameras pointed towards her.

This was the moment. The moment the country final saw Sam Pope for what he truly was.

'As someone who has spent many years within the police service, I know the troubles that many people are facing. Times are hard, and in those moments, when the structures put in place don't seem to have the answers, people look for hope wherever they can find it. To a vast many, Sam Pope was that figure. A man who seemed to be fighting for the good of the people. And I'm not going to stand here and say that he hasn't been instrumental in the downfall of a number of criminal organisations that had polluted this great nation with drugs and weapons. I do believe that Sam Pope set out to do the right thing, but somewhere along the way, he lost sight of what he was doing it for. Over a hundred people dead. Countless injured. The impact this has on their families and their quality of life. These are not the actions of a hero, but of a man who is without a shadow of a doubt, the most dangerous man in the country. And if Sam Pope truly cared about right and wrong and about keeping this country safe, then he would hand himself in. But he doesn't. In fact, we have strong evidence to connect Sam Pope to the gold-bar heist of the Bank of England a few months ago. Tell me, what justice is there in him robbing this country of money?'

Ashton flicked a glance to Sarratt, who was scowling at the fabrication.

But it seemed to work.

'So, with all that to process, I want to extend a warning to the good people of this city and of this nation. Sam Pope is *not* to be approached. If you have any information as to his whereabouts, please contact the dedicated Sam Pope Task Force. We want to rebuild the trust between this institution and the people we serve, and to do that, we need to stop one of the most dangerous and violent crime sprees this country has ever seen.'

Ashton leant forward, glaring into the camera for effect.

'And for Sam Pope, this is an opportunity to do the right thing and turn yourself in. Otherwise, we will leave no stone unturned to find you. Thank you, all, for your time.'

An explosion of noise erupted before Ashton, as the sea of reporters all yelled out their questions that she ignored. As the cameras flashed and the reporters called out to her, Ashton approached Sarratt, who greeted her extended palm with a firm snatch. As they posed and smiled for the cameras, Sarratt spoke through gritted teeth.

'A few embellishments there, Ruth.'

Sarratt shook hard, jolting Ashton's shoulder, who responded in kind.

'Someone has to get the job done, Commissioner.'

Sarratt pulled her hand back, casting her eye over the ambitious woman who smirked back at her. Ashton then strode confidently to Wainwright, who was flanked by a sturdy man with neat grey hair and a beard. The admiral shook her hand and watched as Ashton walked with a few other officers back towards the glass doors of the New Scotland Yard building. As she disappeared from sight, and the swell of excitement from the reporters began to fizzle, Commissioner Sarratt also marched past him.

'I hope you know what you're doing,' she spat accusingly, before making a beeline for the office herself.

She had every reason to feel undermined. Because that was exactly what Wainwright had done, and although his promises of protecting her position seemed to have worked, he knew that pushing for her removal once Sam was dealt with would be the most beneficial. As he processed everything, Murray sighed.

'Are you sure about this?' Murray asked. He didn't seem to be concerned. More put out.

'Yes,' Wainwright said without looking at him. 'It's the only way they'll turn on him.'

'And it has to be her?' Murray said, his hands in his pockets. 'It could get messy.'

Wainwright scoffed and then turned to Murray with a sinister smile.

'Good.'

CHAPTER EIGHT

Sam watched on from the table of the small café he'd pitched up in and could feel his anxiety building. A narrow establishment, with rows of tables and plastic chairs affixed to the ground, the café was jam-packed with local tradesmen and residents, who all had turned their attentions to the TV that clung to the wall above the counter.

Ruth Ashton was standing, braving the elements as she scowled and snarled her way through her space.

Sam had faced many ghosts from his past. She was certainly the most surprising.

As had often been the case, Sam had hidden in plain sight, with most people either turning a blind eye to his presence or in some cases, a few respectful nods.

But he could sense the mood changing with every word she spoke.

And in fairness, every truth she laid out.

"I have the heartbreaking accounts of a small, family-run business in Derbyshire being devastated by Sam's fight. A scrap yard in Glasgow that was turned into a war zone, and an innocent, family-orientated businessman now under investigation for collusion. Millions

of pounds' worth of criminal damage, that will be covered by the law-abiding taxpayers of this great country. The very people Sam Pope claims to protect."

A few heads turned in Sam's direction, where he was seated at the table nearest to the window that overlooked the rain-soaked street. Beyond that, a large building was coated in plastic sheets and scaffolding, and just as Ashton had begun her character assassination, a burly man decked out in a high-vis jacket and hard hat had marched in for his morning coffee. Now, he was standing in the queue, his heavily tattooed arms folded, and his eyes glued to the TV screen.

Ashton had already rolled off a number of the people who'd lost their lives because of Sam.

Some of whom had been dear to him.

Others, not so much.

But after every few sentences, the construction worker shot a glance over to Sam, muttering under his breath and through his thick beard.

"Over a hundred people dead. Countless injured. These are not the actions of a hero, but of a man who is without a shadow of a doubt, the most dangerous man in the country."

Ashton was putting on a hell of a performance, and Sam sipped his coffee, keeping his eyes on the rest of the room as more glances were shot his way.

Gone were the respectful nods.

Now, it was a mix of fear or disgust.

Just as Ashton had clearly intended.

"Sam Pope is not to be approached. If you have any information as to his whereabouts, please contact the dedicated Sam Pope Task Force. We want to rebuild the trust between this institution and the people we serve, and to do that, we need to stop one of the most dangerous and violent crime sprees this country has ever seen."

Before even placing his order, the construction worker

turned on his heels and marched back through the narrow café, and Sam clenched his fists ready for the attack. But the man hauled open the door and strode out into the street, jogging across the road to the construction site, and casting a few glances back in Sam's direction.

Time to go.

But then the TV grabbed his attention, and he glanced up into the cold, furious eyes of Ruth Ashton and could feel the venom in her voice.

'And for Sam Pope, this is an opportunity to do the right thing and turn yourself in. Otherwise, we will leave no stone unturned to find you. Thank you all for your time.'

Everyone in the café turned on their seats, offering varying looks of fear and concern at him, as one of them slid their phone out of their pocket. Sam finished his coffee, and just as he went to stand, the door flew open once more and the bearded construction worker returned, along with three of his colleagues, all of them glaring at Sam with a bloodlust and unearned confidence.

'Get the fuck up,' the bearded man demanded, clearly high on the idea of being a public hero. Sam rolled his eyes.

'Walk away,' Sam said calmly, as one of the construction workers shuffled around to the front of the table. Sam looked up at him, easily spotting the instant effects of the cocaine that was pumping through his blood. 'That's the only warning you boys will get.'

Sam could feel the cold metal of his Glock against the base of his spine, but pulling it out on the public would only pour fire on the bonfire that Ashton had created. Hurriedly, the owner of the café stepped out from behind the counter.

'Please. I don't want any trouble in here,' the man begged, and Sam sighed once again.

'Not in here.' He relented, and the construction workers stepped to the side as Sam stood, sliding his coat from the back of his seat and then followed two of them out of the café, with the bearded leader, and his coked-up friend following behind. This needed to be quick, as Sam was certain that at least one phone call would have been made as to his whereabouts, and based on the warning from Ashton, he expected the boys in blue to be there in minutes.

As they walked towards the tarped-off construction site, the bearded ringleader shoved Sam in the back to keep him moving.

'People like you make me sick.' He spat.

'What? Intelligent?' Sam retorted, and one of the other members chuckled, drawing an angry retort from the leader.

'Just get the fuck in there so we can fuck you up.'

Sam shook his head slightly and obliged, following the two men through the rain-soaked tarp and into the clearing between fence and building. The concrete had been ripped up, and his boots squelched on the wet sand beneath his feet. A cement roller stood stationary to the side, alongside a stack of thick, grey slabs, and another pile of scaffolding poles. As they entered, the bearded man shoved Sam forward, as the four men fanned out, surrounding him. Sam shot glances towards all of them, working through his mind the best pattern for attack. The one who'd clearly taken a bump was shaking with adrenaline and would be the easiest first target. One of the men had a reluctance, which meant he was unlikely to jump in if Sam struck first, but the other two would be the problem. Like the bearded leader, the other man was bulky, but mainly through overindulgence, and Sam knew that if he could get him off his feet, he'd be easy to keep down.

It was four on one.

But Sam fancied his chances.

As the four men circled him like a pack of wolves, Sam slid his arms into his coat and rolled his shoulders.

'Last chance to not do this, fellas.'

The bearded man laughed out loud.

'This fucking guy.' The smile dropped. 'Fucking do him.'

As if his command was a starting pistol, the coked-up follower launched towards Sam and threw a reckless right hook. Swiftly, Sam ducked underneath, and as the fist flew over his head, Sam swung his elbow up, drilling the man in the nose. The impact shattered it instantly, and before the man could even reach for it, Sam drove a boot into his attacker's shin, knocking his leg out, and sending him crashing face first onto the sand.

Three on one.

Sam looked at all three men before him, enjoying the sudden trepidation in their stance, as they traded worried glances among each other. As the rain lashed down, the instigator charged forward, slamming his body into Sam and trying to lift him off his feet. Sam dropped his bodyweight forward, digging his heels into the sludge beneath, and drilled an elbow down into the man's spine. Despite the howl of pain, the bearded man refused to let go, allowing the other member of his gang to catch Sam with a right hook. Sam swung to the side but blocked the follow-up punch with his forearm. He drilled his fist into the man's throat before driving his elbow down into the leader's spine once again. As his grip relented, Sam stepped back, and then thrust his knee into the man's face, splitting his lip, and sending a spray of blood down his bearded chin. As soon as he turned, the other man swung another wild right, but Sam ducked, then exploded with a furious right hook to the gut and then brought a crushing elbow down onto the back of the man's skull.

He hit the ground.

Lights out.

Two on one.

Sam looked to the hesitant fourth man, who in the face of the inevitable battle, had frozen in fear. As Sam stepped towards him, the man's eyes shot to just behind Sam, who spun just in time to see the lead pipe swinging towards his skull. With a bloodcurdling roar of anger, the bearded man swung to kill, but Sam thrust his hands into the incoming wrists, catching it just before the metal crashed into his skull. As the two men struggled for control, Sam released one hand and drove a hard punch into the man's bicep, and as he dropped the lead pipe, Sam then caught him with a sickening headbutt, sending the man crashing to the floor.

Somewhere in the distance, the familiar wailing of sirens filled the air, starting the internal countdown in Sam's mind.

The patrons of the café would have seen them enter the building site, which meant he needed to get out of there. Sam turned back to the bearded man, who was slowly rolling himself onto his back, looking up at Sam, his eyes peering through the blood that covered his face.

'Fuck you, Pope,' the man said, and then spat a mouthful of blood in his direction.

Sam took a calming breath and then shook his head. The man had instigated everything, drawing Sam into a situation where *they* wanted to hurt *him*. Despite two of his friends being unconscious, the man was seemingly unwilling to admit defeat, so Sam lifted the metal pole from the sand with the express purpose of making him.

As he took one step towards him, a hand fell on his shoulder and he spun, ready to strike.

It was the hesitant man, whose face had drained to a sickly pale at what he'd witnessed.

'He isn't worth it,' the man stammered quietly, and Sam felt the horror in the man's eyes. Sam turned back and looked at the damage he'd caused.

Two men lying motionless in the mud.

A third, wheezing for breath through his broken nose, and a face plastered with his own blood.

Sam dropped the pole and turned back to the last man standing, who cowered with fear.

'I'm not the bad guy.'

As the feeble man nodded in agreement, the bearded man on the ground let out a sickened laugh.

'Tell that to my kids,' he said as he sat up. 'Tell that to all of our kids.'

For a split second, Sam felt a twinge of remorse. Despite them instigating the fight with him, they were just a bunch of guys who'd bitten off more than they could chew. Hard-working men, just trying to make a living and in the aftermath of Ruth Ashton's call to arms, were doing what they believed to be the right thing.

Just doing the same thing, in essence, as he was.

Stepping up for what they believed was right.

The sirens grew louder, no more than a few streets away, and Sam turned on his heel and marched towards the gap in the plastic sheet, and as he emerged back onto the road, he could see a group of faces at the café window, all of them staring in his direction.

They all knew what had happened.

And as the flashing blue lights came into view at the end of the high street, Sam pulled up his hood and picked up the pace as he headed to the nearest side street, hoping that the endless, concrete labyrinth that comprised the City of London, would swallow him up.

The police would be informed.

Word would spread.

And Sam Pope knew what would happen next.

The country would be begging for his arrest.

With the sirens wailing and the blue lights signalling the arrival of the police, Sam turned off into the rain-soaked alleyways and wondered how the hell he was going to make this right.

CHAPTER NINE

With his muscular arms stretching the sleeves of his jacket as they folded across his chest, James Murray stood at the back of the meeting room in New Scotland Yard. The third-floor window gave a tremendous view across the Thames, and he gazed out, wondering where Sam Pope was at that very moment, and if he had the good sense to get out of town.

He already knew the answer.

The team before him were doing their level best to paint Sam Pope into the villain of the story, but there was one thing they could never portray him as.

A coward.

On the way to the briefing, Murray had linked up with his trusted right-hand man, Jensen, who was champing at the bit for his shot at Pope. After Project Hailstorm disbanded, Murray had taken the young private into his squadron, and after one tour together in Iraq, Murray had ensured he took Jensen when he started up Guardian. Men who were willing to die for you were worth their weight in gold, but men who were willing to kill for you?

Priceless.

Jensen was a fine soldier, and combined his ruthlessness with expert hand-to-hand combat. In fact, the only marksman Murray knew who was more accurate behind a scope than Jensen, was the man he was hunting. As he glanced to his right-hand man, Jensen returned a cruel grin. His hair, as always, was shaved to the scalp, and his greying beard was thick but neatly trimmed.

But it was the eyes.

The eyes told him that to Jensen, this was more than just another job.

This was a chance to prove his superiority.

It was why he was battling a slight taste of guilt in the back of his throat. Sam Pope had saved his life, and here he was, about to take point on the most expensive and far-reaching manhunt that the Metropolitan Police had ever initiated. They had unlimited funding thanks to Piers Bloom, and with Admiral Wainwright driving it behind the scenes, it wasn't a case of *if* they caught Sam.

It was when.

And the more Murray spent time with Wainwright and Bloom, the more he realised that bringing Sam Pope to justice wasn't really the goal. As was always the case with any job undertaken by Guardian, Murray never asked for the finer details. As far as he was concerned, the less he knew, the better. It made pulling the trigger and collecting the money a whole lot easier, and when he went home to his wife and kids, it allowed him to step away from the realities of his job.

But this felt different.

Sam Pope was the reason he even had the life he now cherished, and he knew there was going to come a time in the near future where he would have Sam at gun point.

And he was certain that Wainwright would demand he pull the trigger.

It seemed to be a sentiment shared by the commissioner, as Henrietta Sarratt was seated at the table before him, making little effort to hide the disdain in her eyes as Wainwright and Ashton looked over the footage. Murray had already seen it, and judging from the ecstatic smile on Ashton's face, and the more calculating expression across Wainwright's, her speech had had the desired effect.

'This is excellent,' Ashton said, sitting back in her chair triumphantly.

'Is it?' Sarratt scowled. 'Because after your little speech yesterday, it would appear that four people decided to take matters into their own hands and put themselves in harm's wa—'

'Four concerned citizens.' Wainwright interrupted.

'Excuse me?' Sarratt's scowl now fell upon the admiral, who stood and clasped his hands at the base of his spine as he moved towards the window.

'Four concerned citizens who were just trying to do the right thing. They tried to restrain a violent criminal who used his expertise and training to beat three of them within an inch of their lives to evade capture.' Wainwright turned back with a grin. 'That's what I see.'

Murray scoffed at the man's gumption. Sarratt, however, looked furious.

'You can't be serious? We have eyewitness accounts that these men accosted Sam in the café and marched him across to the site. We have CCTV footage from the streets that shows this happening.'

'That can be…altered.' Wainwright grinned. 'What we have right here, Commissioner, is an opportunity to pour gasoline on the fire. Yes, it might stray a little from the truth, but it will do exactly what we set out to do.'

Sarratt shook her head as she stood.

'I did not agree to lie to the people of this city.'

'No.' Wainwright's voice rose with authority. 'But you did agree that this task force was necessary. Ruth did a stellar job yesterday in stoking those flames of doubt in Sam's nobility with the public. This here, this is an opportunity to prove her right.'

'But it's illegal. Tampering with evidence.' Sarratt pressed her finger down on the table. 'Just remember who I am.'

'And just remember who you could be,' Wainwright threatened. 'The people believe more in Pope than they do your ability to keep them safe, Henrietta. We've been over the options if this fails, and believe me, *you* do not want this to fail.'

The two of them locked eyes, neither one daring to break the stare first. At the back of the room, Jensen folded his meaty arms across his chest as he chomped on a piece of gum, and he nudged Murray with his elbow to signify his enjoyment. Murray rolled his eyes, sighed, and stepped forward.

'If I may interrupt?' Murray spoke as he approached the table. 'I find in search and restrain operations that the quickest solution is often the best. The more we allow this to escalate, the more volatile either the public gets, or worse, Sam. Now, we have the opportunity to control this narrative from the get-go, and I would hazard a guess that you'd rather that than any videos being posted online by some fuckwad looking for clicks?'

Murray shrugged, and Sarratt grudgingly broke the stare, drawing a smirk of victory from Wainwright. She turned to Murray and gestured for him to continue.

'All I'm saying is my team has now been assembled. We are prepped and ready to go at the next sighting of Sam Pope. Chances are, if we spin this the way that's been discussed, not only will idiots not try to take him down themselves, but more people are likely to be afraid. And if they're afraid—'

'They'll call it in,' Sarratt finished for him with a

disgusted shake of the head. After a brief pause for thought, she looked back to Wainwright. 'I don't like it.'

'You don't have to like it,' Wainwright said as he once again took his seat. 'You just have to sign it off. Like I said, Henrietta, it's your flag nailed to this mast.'

All eyes were on Sarratt once again, and not for the first time, she felt completely helpless. As someone who wielded such power over such a fundamental institution, she'd never felt more out of control. Although she couldn't see them, she could feel the strings attached to her limbs, and Wainwright was as conniving a puppeteer as she could have imagined.

There had to be more to it than just keeping the country safe.

The man was obsessed with catching Sam Pope.

But why?

As her mind tried to connect dots that she couldn't see, Ruth Ashton took her opportunity and leant forward.

'Put me out there this morning,' she demanded eagerly, and checked her watch. 'Its eight thirty right now. We could have a conference at ten. Really get this rolling.'

'It's too soon,' Murray insisted.

'Didn't you say the quickest solution is the best one?' Ashton challenged. 'We show how Sam is willing to hurt innocent people to keep his freedom, then the message will hit harder. I can spin it. After yesterday, they'll eat up anything I say.'

'Fucking Meryl Streep over here.' Jensen piped up from the back of the room, and all eyes turned to him as he arrogantly chewed with his mouth open.

'And who are you, exactly?' Ashton spat angrily.

'Fabian Jensen.' He introduced himself as he pushed himself off the wall and took his place next to Murray. 'I'm basically Guardian's secret weapon.'

'Well, can we keep him a secret?' Ashton quipped.

'Enough,' Sarratt demanded. 'When you say you can act quickly…how quickly is that?'

Murray rubbed his thick stubble.

'Let's face it, Sam isn't going to run. We know that much. Injustice is like catnip to him, so we give him a reason to come looking and go from there. And considering we have the backing of the Met Police, meaning they can shut down an area before we get there, and we can run as many red lights as we need to.' Murray weighed it up and then turned to her with a stoic look on his face. 'So to answer your question…pretty fucking fast.'

The disrespect was just another sign that Sarratt had no say over the situation. The entire operation smelt like a cover-up, and the further the group pushed her to the side, the more she wanted to pull on the thread. Wainwright was happy to threaten her position, wield his influence with senior figures to remove her if needed, just so she would sign off on it.

To keep things above board.

But the limitless backing from the absent Piers Bloom.

The military outfit with the sterling reputation.

A ghost from Sam's past to be the face of it.

Wainwright had positioned all his pieces exactly where he wanted them.

In front of him.

He was squirrelled away, just far enough so none of it would come back on him. Instead, he'd shifted all the responsibility and potential blame onto her.

She needed to play along. Not just for the good of her career, but to hopefully give her enough time to figure out what was really going on.

'I'll brief the PR department that we're holding another briefing at ten,' Sarratt finally said. 'Do whatever you have to with the footage.'

'There's a good girl.' Wainwright smiled patronisingly.

'Quickest resolution is the best,' Sarratt said, shooting a glance to Murray who squinted with suspicion. 'So, let's just get this wrapped up, shall we?'

With that, Sarratt turned, and marched from the office, slamming the door firmly behind her. Ashton chuckled, almost giddy at the thought of once again outshining the woman who took her seat in the Met hierarchy. Wainwright turned back to the laptop with the footage on, when he looked up at Murray with an eyebrow raised.

'Everything okay?'

Murray kept his eyes on the door. He was certain he'd sensed a moment of clarity within the commissioner.

'Yes, sir,' he eventually responded. 'I think we need to keep an eye on her.'

'Who? Sarratt?' Wainwright waved him off. 'Once this is over with, she'll be lucky if they don't throw her in prison.'

'Why's that?' Ashton asked, looking up from her phone screen where she was already working on her speech.

Murray and Wainwright shot a glance to each other, before Wainwright fixed Ashton with his slimy grin.

It made Murray's skin crawl.

'Just politics, my dear.' He pointed to her phone. 'Make sure you say what needs to be said. It's crucial that *you're* in front of those cameras to let the world see who Sam Pope truly is.'

The confidence rushed through Ashton like a drug, and she smiled, and stood abruptly.

'Will do, Sir.' She nodded to all three of them. 'Wish me luck.'

'Good luck,' Jensen said mockingly, and then perched himself on the edge of the table. Murray watched Ashton hurry through the door, and as it closed, it bothered him that he didn't feel anything.

No remorse.

No guilt.

Not for her.

'Are you sure about this?' Murray asked, his eyes still fixed on the door. 'About her?'

'Of course,' Wainwright said coldly. 'She's the perfect choice.'

Murray shrugged, and Wainwright turned to Jensen, who offered him a mocking smile.

'And you?' Wainwright didn't even bother to disguise his disappointment. 'You're as good as he says you are?'

Jensen looked to Murray, and then back to Wainwright, before pointing at the admiral with his finger and pretend shooting.

'I don't miss.'

Wainwright rolled his eyes at the theatrics and returned his focus to the laptop.

'Make sure you don't.' He didn't look up. 'Now go. You have less than ninety minutes until the press conference. Something tells me it's going to be a busy day.'

Murray approached the door and yanked it open, allowing Jensen to stride through first, and as he followed, he couldn't help but agree with the admiral.

It was going to be a long day.

It was also going to be messy.

CHAPTER TEN

The nerves from the day before were gone.

With almost double the number of reporters gathered in an eager mob outside the New Scotland Yard building, Ruth Ashton gazed out from behind the glass entrance doors, allowing the adrenaline to shake through her entire body.

They were there for her.

She was now not only the face of the operation, but the voice of trust. Despite the undignified way her career with the Met had come to an end, she'd always wanted to be a beacon of trust and safety for the people of her country. It was why she'd wanted to bring Sam Pope down before he'd even got going. Had people like Mark Harris not wrapped himself up in corruption, or weak-minded people like Amara Singh and Adrian Pearce not fallen under Pope's spell, so much chaos could have been avoided.

All the bloodshed.

All the death.

Had they backed her then, Sam Pope would have spent the last few years behind bars, and she could have had a life with Ervin Wallace that would have undoubtedly seen her in Sarratt's seat.

But now was the chance to put things right.

An opportunity to not only rally the country behind her, but to also show the likes of Wainwright and other powerful political players that the organisation needed someone of her strength and conviction.

And it was a chance to put Sam Pope in the deepest, darkest hole they could find and then cover it with cement.

As she peered out through the glass, beyond the few droplets of drizzle that spattered against the pane, she took a deep breath. Unlike the day before, she wasn't immaculately presented. The sudden urgency to get ahead of Sam's brutal attack on the public meant that she was sacrificing her own appearance to the public. One of the Met's PR team offered that it would benefit her likability with the nation, that she has been hard at work and putting the mission first.

But Ashton didn't pay it any mind.

She didn't need some snooty woman half her age telling her how to address the public, all because she did a crummy media degree and had an understanding of TikTok.

This was a serious matter.

And it needed to be addressed.

Ashton turned to step towards the automatic door, and stopped as both Wainwright and his consultant, Murray, approached. Commissioner Sarratt stood to the side, making it clear that their association was a loose one.

'Ready?' Wainwright asked.

'Yes.' Ashton nodded. 'Have you processed the footage?'

'We have. But we won't play it until after you've finished.' Wainwright assured her. 'We want your words to be the focal point here. The tone. The severity. All of it rests on your shoulders, Ruth. We can let the networks scramble for the footage afterwards.'

Ashton nodded her understanding.

'Try not to be too sensationalist,' Sarratt chimed in. 'This is a police investigation. Not an awards ceremony.'

The comment drew a smile from Murray, and Ashton glared at them both.

'I know how to do my job,' Ashton spat as she stepped to the door. 'If you knew how to do yours, then maybe I wouldn't be needed here.'

Swiftly, she exited the building, not allowing Sarratt the opportunity to reply, and a wave of excitement swept across the press as she approached the podium. Murray stepped in line behind her, walking with the power and poise of a trained killer, and he took up a position a few feet to her right. Further back, Wainwright and Sarratt lingered off camera.

All eyes were on Ruth Ashton once again.

And it took every fibre of her being not to crack a smile.

A hush fell over the street.

Ashton looked up and planted her stare deep into the camera.

'One day.' She began. 'It took only one day for Sam Pope to show his true colours. You may have already been privy to the news that four men were assaulted yesterday in East London. Four honest, hard-working construction workers, who set out that morning like any other, to do an honest day's work to provide for their families. Four men, who despite our warnings, still tried to do the right thing.'

She took a beat. Her delivery had been flawless.

'One of the men, who we can identify as Tom Butler, went to the local café, as he did every morning to buy a round of coffees for his team. There, he saw our public announcement. There, unfortunately, he also found Sam Pope.'

Ashton flicked a look back to Wainwright and Sarratt. Wainwright, however, was looking at Murray.

'As a father of two, Mr Butler understood the danger he was putting himself in, and upon identifying Sam, he and his team tried to provide a public service and restrain the vigilante until the police arrived. Not wanting to put the other customers in danger, they tried to restrain Sam across the road in their construction site, where Pope proceeded to savagely beat three of the men to escape.' Ashton paused for effect and then continued. 'Are these the actions of an innocent man? Two of the men are in hospital, being treated for broken bones and concussions. Another has suffered severe damage to his spine. For what? Trying to protect their fellow citizens? Whatever you believe, the facts are undeniable. Sam Pope is a menace to this country, and for too long, he has been allowed to hide in plain sight by a public who thought he was a hero. But for those three men, who needed medical care, and are unable to work today, is he a hero?'

Ashton slammed a dramatic fist down on the podium, causing a few reporters in the front row to jump slightly.

'We implore you to be vigilant. We implore you all to see the truth. Sam Pope has spat in the face of law and order for years, and now, with the net tightening, even honest, hard-working civilians are in danger if they get in his way. We have a dedicated task force, ready to act at a moment's notice. So, if you *do* see Sam Pope. Please, do not approach. Please, do not try to be brave like Tom Butler and his colleagues. Sam Pope is a highly trained, highly decorated soldier, with over a hundred recorded deaths to his name and most likely, hundreds unaccounted for. The man is a stone-cold killer, and has proven that the police services, the armed forces he so proudly served, and even the public, are fair game if they get in his way.'

Ashton had them.

Her words were being lapped up by the reporters, and she allowed herself a split second to wonder how many people were glued to their TV screens.

'And like yesterday, I have a message for Sam Pope.' Ashton leant forward, glaring into the camera. 'You are *not* above the law. And I will *not* stop until you face the full might of it.'

Before Ashton could bask in the glory of her speech and accept the adulation, the sound of metal cutting through the air began to grow rapidly. It was closely followed by the terrifying crack of a rifle, and before anyone could react, a bullet collided with Ashton's forehead. In a matter of milliseconds, the sharp, metal round burrowed through her skin and her skull, ripping through her brain and exploding through the back of her head.

The blood spatter burst into the drizzling rain as her lifeless body snapped backwards and fell to the ground, and amid the horror and panic that erupted instantly, every live camera feed went to black.

But the moment was captured forever.

Live on TV, across every news network in the country, former Deputy Commissioner Ruth Ashton had been assassinated.

The rifle was still in good condition, but that was hardly surprising to Jensen. Sam Pope's legend existed long after he'd exited the military, and although Jensen had never crossed paths with the man, he still held the name in awe. One of the things Jensen had been told from his infrequent dealings with General Wallace at the tail end of Project

Hailstorm, and by Murray who he'd followed out of the army and into contracted work, was how Sam became one with his weapon. Years of training had turned Fabian Jensen into one of the most lethal marksmen the country had ever known.

But not it's deadliest.

So, when the plans were put in place, Wainwright ensured that Murray and Jensen were given 'off the books' access to all the evidence accumulated on Sam Pope over the years. During the first round of the Sam Pope Task Force, they'd raided a number of stashes he had across the city, confiscating an entire arsenal of weapons.

Yet Sam had still pushed on.

Still remained effective.

Lethal.

One of the weapons confiscated was the Accuracy International Arctic Warfare bolt-action sniper rifle that had been secured at the Port of Tilbury many years ago. Sam had used it to fire a shot that saved the then Detective Inspector Amara Singh from the clutches of Andrei Kovalenko, detaching the man's arm from his body with one swift shot. When the police had traced the location of the shot, they found the rifle, droplets of blood to indicate an injured Sam had made his escape, and the dead body of Oleg Kovalenko suspended from a metal hook that hung from the roof.

Lethal.

Murray had been assured that anything missing from the evidence wouldn't be traceable, and it was the perfect way to accelerate the man hunt.

Painting Sam as a threat to the public and police was one thing.

Proving it was another.

After Murray and Jensen had left Wainwright that morning, they'd returned to their van, where the rifle was, and Jensen did another quick check of the weapon to ensure its readiness for use. Carefully stripping it with gloved hands, he examined the parts before reassembling the rifle with expertise and respect.

The only fingerprints they wanted on it were the ones Sam had left years ago. Murray had then driven Jensen to an office block eight streets away from the New Scotland Yard building, and by using his Met-issued pass, navigated the paltry security with ease.

'Do your thing.' Murray had said as he left him in the stairwell. Jensen could sense the apprehension in his friend's voice, but he understood. Murray had only told the story once, but Jensen was aware of how Sam Pope had saved his boss's life.

Guilt was not a feeling Jensen experienced.

The world was a cruel and vile place, and men with his skill set could thrive within it. The military had beaten out any compassion for human life a long time ago, and nowadays, he enjoyed the wealth he'd earned by putting his skills to more lucrative jobs. There was always some rich, conniving bastard looking for a gun for hire, and Murray had the long list to ensure a very healthy income.

All Jensen had to do was point and shoot.

It took him a few minutes to find the perfect spot on the roof of the building, and in the distance, he could see the ever-growing crowd of reporters flocking outside the police headquarters. The wind was pretty heavy, carrying with it a cold and uncomfortable drizzle. Jensen could make the required adjustments in his head, taking into account the speed and direction, but it was hardly the longest shot he'd taken in his career.

He may as well have been point blank.

He placed the black sports bag on the ground and unzipped it, and then carefully lifted the bulk of the weapon out. He loaded a bullet into the bolt-action chamber, and then lowered himself onto one knee by the edge of the building. He drew the weapon up, resting one elbow on the brick, and then drew the scope to his eye. It took him a few quick scans of the crowd to find his bearings before he locked his sight onto the podium, just as Ruth Ashton was approaching the microphones.

His training kicked in.

Every muscle in his body tightened, locking him into position.

His stare became unblinking.

His breathing calmed.

Every calculation raced through his head, and he slightly adjusted his position to account for them.

He waited.

Ruth Ashton seemed like a confident woman, one driven both by her career and her clear detest of Sam Pope. That didn't make her guilty.

It just made her unfortunate.

As he watched her performance, his gloved finger gently stroked the trigger.

She slammed her fist down on the podium.

Jensen took one more deep breath.

Then he squeezed.

He felt the entire weapon jolt in his arms, and he watched with pride as a second later, he watched the top of Ashton's skull turn to red mist. He could hear the rising hum of panic, and then rocked back on his heel, before ejecting the casing of the bullet onto the ground.

He left Sam's rifle beside it.

Without even a hint of guilt, Jensen pushed himself up, and hurried back through the door to the maintenance stairwell, bounding down the steps two at a time. As he reached the bottom floor, he pulled out the burner phone and called the emergency services.

They eventually picked up.

With a well-rehearsed panic in his voice, he stammered that he heard the shot, and then saw Sam Pope leaving the building. The woman tried to calm him down, and he smiled as he gave the address, hung up the phone, and then crushed it under his boot. The armed response unit would be swarming the place within minutes, and they'd find the rifle.

They'd find the bullet casing.

And pretty soon, the entire country would believe that Sam Pope had publicly executed a senior police figure.

With a spring in his step, Jensen headed as far away from the chaos as possible, eager to see what would happen next.

CHAPTER ELEVEN

The shockwaves of the assassination were relentless.

Every phone in New Scotland Yard was on a constant ring, and the streets surrounding the building had been locked down, with armed response units sweeping through a one-mile radius, all in search of Sam Pope. It hadn't taken long for the shooter's location to be found, with a team of armed officers sweeping through the building and retrieving the sniper rifle and the shell casing that had brutally ended Ruth Ashton's life.

Sarratt felt sick to her stomach.

As she sat behind the desk in her office, she knew that even shutting the blinds to the outside world didn't stop all eyes from falling on her.

They were looking to her for guidance.

For a response.

But deep down, she knew she'd given the entire operation the green light. Strong-armed by the threats to her own position, she'd agreed to sign off on the new Sam Pope Task Force, even against her better instincts. Admiral Wainwright was a formidable man, but his cruel nature was only trumped by the power he wielded within the country's governance.

He was untouchable.

And he'd made it very clear that Sarratt was not.

But now, just a few hours removed from one of the most shocking events in recent memory, Sarratt sat her desk, her eyes glued to the TV screen on the wall, and the relentless barrage of updates on the news channel. The footage was gruesome, but thankfully, the network had decided to block out the moment Ruth Ashton's skull was turned to paint and dust.

Sarratt wished she could do the same.

The return of a woman she'd worked under had given her cause for concern, and although Sarratt would never speak ill of the dead, Ashton had never been a woman she could warm to. Steadfast in her own self-belief, Ashton was the blueprint for playing the political game, rising through the Met Police thanks to her admittedly stellar career, but also her ability to lick the right boots when needed. She'd never extended any opportunities Sarratt's way, and at times, had done her best to lift the ladder with her.

Having her forced into the task force had been a curve ball from Wainwright, but the idea that Sarratt herself shouldn't be the face of the operation had held merit. It would have shown her authority in her position at the top of the food chain, and also reinforced the notion that she was willing to reach out for expert help to bring Sam in.

Now, it would appear, she was merely a sacrificial lamb.

Sarratt had given her approval for the entire operation, which had seen an innocent and respected woman assassinated on live TV and she would undoubtedly need to peddle the narrative that Sam Pope was the man behind the trigger.

She had her doubts.

There was more to all this than just keeping the country safe, and the more time Sarratt had spent in the closed rooms with Wainwright and Murray, the more she felt there was more at hand. James Murray was what they were paying for. A tough, soulless mercenary with the means and the capabilities to bring down Sam Pope and anyone who stood in their way.

But Wainwright had more skin in the game.

Of that, Sarratt was certain.

And that was the reason, despite the rolling news warning the nation that Sam Pope was at large, and that he'd just murdered the former deputy commissioner in cold blood, Sarratt's attention had turned elsewhere.

She was digging into Wainwright.

After the events at Gatwick a few months ago, where DS Sutton had pulled Chief Inspector Dummett from the fire and then explained to Sarratt what had been going on, the young detective had decided to move to the Department of Professional Standards. She'd passed on a list of names, a who's who of the most powerful people in the country, and all of them with supposed links to terrorism.

The list had never made it to Sarratt.

In fact, the list had mysteriously vanished.

And Sarratt wanted answers.

Because if her gut was as good as it had been her entire career, then she was certain what name she'd find on it.

Right on cue, the door to her office opened, and her immediate, angry response at being disturbed was curtailed by the frown of Admiral Wainwright.

'What a mess,' he said forlornly, slamming the door behind him. As always, he was dressed immaculately, the picture of power and authority. 'We need you out there, Henrietta.'

'What we need, is the press to keep that poor woman

out of the headlines.' To Sarratt's disgust, Wainwright chuckled. 'I'm sorry, sir, is this situation funny to you?'

Wainwright didn't wait for an invitation as he lowered himself onto the sofa pressed against the far wall of Sarratt's spacious office. Calmly, he poured himself a glass of water from the jug on the centre of the coffee table and took a long sip. Finally, he turned to her.

'I find it funny that you think the news would do such a thing.' He took another sip. 'Ruth Ashton was a fine woman who served this country with respect and grace. Her murder needs to be acknowledged.'

'That's what you think this is? A murder?'

'Don't you?' Wainwright locked his eyes on her.

'I think she was assassinated.'

'Assassinated. Murdered.' Wainwright waved it off. 'Same difference.'

'Not really. Not when an assassination is arranged.' Sarratt could feel her temper boiling below the surface, and Wainwright seemed to read the room and placed his glass down. He stood slowly, a rare showing of his advancing years, and he adjusted his glasses before he spoke.

His voice was low.

Threatening.

'I'd say we should all be on red alert.' He warned. 'Because what would possibly stop Sam Pope from targeting another pillar of the Metropolitan Police?'

He locked eyes on her.

The message clear.

Sarratt held his stare, refusing to back down, and she took a deep breath and Wainwright smiled, nodded, and then headed to the door. Before he pulled it open, he turned back to address her once more.

'I think a statement should be made. A joint one. You

and I united in the horror of Sam's actions.' Wainwright's tone made it clear it wasn't a suggestion. 'But let's not lose sight of who's *really* in charge here.'

Sarratt didn't respond.

She didn't move a muscle.

Wainwright pulled open the door and headed back out into the chaos of the building, slamming it shut once more. The second the noise was shut out, Sarratt exhaled, only then realising her rage and disgust had trapped the air in her lungs. With Wainwright's threat still echoing in her ears, she rushed back to her desk, opened her laptop, and started working on two things at the same time.

She wanted to do some digging on Guardian and their potential links to Wainwright.

And second, she needed to get in touch with DS Sutton.

The same pandemonium had swept through the BBC headquarters. Every reporter worth their salt was fighting tooth and nail to get their voice heard on the matter, all of them hoping that their pitch or their spin on the assassination would see them given the story of their career. Tom Alderson had shepherded them all into the biggest conference news he could find and demanded they all calm down.

The story wasn't who was going to report on the death.

The story was the death itself.

A few ambitious reporters pitched in first, adding a sensationalist spin on the murder of Ruth Ashton, with one of them even going as far as to pitch the headline *A nation under attack*. Tom beat it back, saying the last thing he wanted was to spread panic and that, in turn, led to another session of shouting.

It was big news.

A well-known, highly respected public figure had just been executed live on their network.

Tom was impatiently waiting for Morganna to return from the front line, knowing full well that having her input would help steer the conversation into something meaningful. Hopefully, Morganna would solve the problem for him by having some exceptional footage and first-hand details that meant the conversation would be a quick one.

She was there.

She should run with it.

But until she returned, Tom had the arduous task of calming down a room of excited, hungry journalists, who were already posting their condolences and theories on social media.

He needed to nip that in the bud.

'Right. First things first, any more posting on social media and you'll be reporting on the high level of dog shit on Wimbledon Common,' he said firmly. 'And second, let's not lose sight of what has actually happened here. It's easy to let your journalistic nature lead you into theory instead of fact. But the fact is, Ruth Ashton, the former deputy commissioner of the Metropolitan Police Force, and face of the Sam Pope Task Force has been killed. Let's not lose that as the seed of this story.'

'Killed by Pope,' a voice piped up, followed by agreeable murmurs. Tom shot a glance to the back of the room, where Lynsey Beckett stood, arms folded across her slight body, and her piercing eyes overlooking the group of journalists with disappointment.

'We don't know that,' Tom said, holding up a finger. 'And like I said, we need to deal with the facts. That's our job, people.'

Lynsey scoffed at the back of the room.

Tom planted his hands on his hips, trying to convey his authority as he addressed her.

'You got a problem, Lynsey?'

'No, no.' She shook her head. 'It's all about the facts.'

He could detect the sarcasm in her voice but turned back to the other journalists.

'I want to know everything that led up to this moment. Every meeting in her calendar, every call she made. We need to paint the picture of her final acts and what could have led to this disgusting crime.' Tom looked back to Lynsey. 'Morganna will be best placed to piece today's events together, so I want you all digging into the last twenty-four hours, last week, hell, last three years since she left the police. I want to know who Ruth Ashton became, and every step she took to get to this unfortunate day. Understood?'

The speech seemed to work, and his team of journalists enthusiastically nodded before scarpering from the room like excitable teenagers.

All except one.

Lynsey Beckett.

Tom sighed and rubbed his temples.

'Not now, Lynz,' he said. 'We've got too much to do.'

'I know. Apparently, we need to build the story of this heroic woman and her apparent murder by Sam Pope.'

'I didn't say that.'

'But you think that's what's going on, right?'

'I deal with facts, Lynsey,' Tom snapped. 'And right now, the woman who came out leading the charge against Sam Pope just had her fucking head blown off live on our network. Now, I know you have some bizarre past with Pope that you've continued to keep from me, but right now, I'm just following the facts, and there is only one person who would benefit from Ruth Ashton being dead.'

'Think about it, Tom,' Lynsey protested. 'How do you

get the country to turn on this man? You list all the shit he may or may not have caused, and then you double down by making him seem more dangerous than he is.'

'You don't think Sam's dangerous?' Tom stepped back, a little shocked. 'Seriously? He has over one hundred confirmed kills across both his career and his crusade. Confirmed, Lynsey. I know you might paint him like some kind of white knight, but the man is a serious criminal and in essence, a serial killer.'

'That's a little dramatic.'

'Is it? You've covered stories before about people being killed and have been more than willing to label others as killers.' Tom said with a frown. 'So no, in my mind, I'm not being dramatic. Because from where I'm standing, Ruth Ashton isn't the result of hundreds of deaths.'

'You don't think it's a little too convenient that a few days after we get a confession by Michael Hartson all this comes to pass?' Lynsey said, refusing to back down. 'High-ranking political figures linked to a global terrorist network, but that gets kyboshed. And then almost instantly, a new task force comes out to bring Sam Pope in?'

'Yes. It's pretty easy to make the connection. I'll agree with that,' Tom said. 'But we still can't condone a man abducting someone and making them confess under duress. From the eyewitness accounts, Sam Pope assaulted two men who were just doing their jobs at the airport. Is that violence justified?'

'If it gets to the truth.'

Tom took a step back and folded his arms.

'Wow.' He shook his head. 'You genuinely believe that Pope's actions are reasonable?'

'No. Necessary.' Lynsey wasn't backing down. 'Throughout all our tracking of Sam, when have we ever known him to target the police?'

'Never,' Tom agreed. 'However, no one had painted

Sam in quite the light Ashton had. As we've already seen, some of the public are turning against him.'

'And what do you think they're going to do now he's being accused of blowing her fucking head off?'

Both Tom and Lynsey took a step back, realising that their voices, along with their anger, were rising. With perfect timing, the outside office burst into excitement as Morganna Daily walked through the door, like a triumphant hero returning from battle. As always, the immaculately presented reporter seemed more than happy with the attention, as the other journalists flocked towards her like sheep.

'Let's put a pin in this,' Tom said as he headed to the door.

'You can,' Lynsey said coldly. 'But you know me—'

'I do.' Tom sighed. 'And that's what worries me.'

She could see the inner-conflict loud and clear on his face, as his desire to protect them both was clashing with his journalistic integrity. With a dramatic blow of his cheeks and a shake of his head, Tom regarded her with a sigh.

'Fine.'

With that, Tom Alderson marched out into the open plan office and headed towards the hum of excitement that had clustered around Morganna. Lynsey stepped back, leant against the wall and took a few deep breaths.

She was tired of the world, and the way the elite held such control over the truth.

Somebody didn't want something coming to the surface.

She'd heard herself, whether under duress, or not, that Michael Hartson had been involved with a man called Vladimir Balikov. But any evidence of the man even existing had been eradicated.

But she did have one potential lead.

The list that had apparently been recovered and then, rather conveniently, disappeared.

But the one name she did have to go off was the one person who'd been involved in whatever happened with Sam Pope at Gatwick Airport a few months before.

She needed to get in touch with DS Jessica Sutton.

CHAPTER TWELVE

It had been a whirlwind few months for DS Jessica Sutton.

Before the turn of the year, life had fallen into an almost metronomic pattern. She'd wake early, go for a run to shake off any drowsiness from the bottle of wine the night before, and then find herself at her desk in Charing Cross Police Station, looking to get ahead of the day before anyone else from CID had arrived. Usually, after an hour or so, DS Connor Vokes would arrive with a coffee for her, some witty comment about the ease of her life before boring her with a story about parenthood.

The platonic love between the two of them made her feel closer to him than her two older brothers, and when she'd cradled him in the back of the car with her hands pressed to the bullet wound in his stomach, she'd worried she'd lose him forever.

But like her, Vokes was a fighter, and he'd clung to life long enough for the doctors to stabilise him.

It had been a few months since that night, and Sutton had only been to visit once. Laura, his doting wife, seemed to hold Sutton accountable for the incident, and in some ways, she wasn't wrong.

It had been Sutton's refusal to ignore a hunch that had seen her collide with Sam Pope's world, as they both investigated the deaths of two young police officers. From hunting the vigilante herself, Sutton soon found her depending on him to knock down the doors some senior police figures had slammed shut in a vulgar attempt to cover their tracks.

Many people died over the course of those rainy nights in December, and all for a corrupt politician, Graham Henshaw, who had staged a robbery to boost his campaign.

She'd expected it from a politician, in truth. The government she served seemed bereft of integrity and witnessing it first-hand wasn't a shock.

But the corruption within the police service she'd dedicated over a decade of her life to, that was what changed her life.

After ensuring Graham Henshaw was arrested, Sutton had informed Commissioner Sarratt of her intention to transfer to the Office of Professional Standards, where the trustworthy DI Thomas Gayle ran a very tight ship. He had big shoes to fill in the absence of Adrian Pearce, but Gayle was as respected as he was feared.

To him, the law didn't stop at the door of the Met Police, and he was more than willing to kick it down in pursuit of justice. A few months in, and Sutton was still learning the ropes, but had already felt the backlash of investigating the police itself. Former colleagues, people she'd shared drinks with, now sneered when she walked into a room, and what had been a slightly lonely existence now felt completely isolated.

But it felt fulfilling.

But the same brick walls were still in place.

Sam Pope had left her with a list of names that held prominent roles within the UK's economic structure and told her that most of them would be out of her reach. He also implored her not to look at it, knowing full well it would paint an even bigger target on her back. She passed it onto DI Gayle, who himself, ran it higher up the food chain.

Nothing ever came of it.

Crushed under foot by the power of those who deemed themselves untouchable.

It was why she knew the work she and DI Gayle did was so vital, and it was why, on that morning, as she watched the final few moments of Ruth Ashton's life play out on live TV, that she knew Sam Pope wasn't behind it.

For all his misgivings, Sam Pope wasn't a murderer.

He killed people.

He broke the law.

But he wasn't a murderer.

After the news feed was cut off, Sutton had felt herself rock back in her chair in a state of shock. Four years had passed since she'd served on the Sam Pope Task Force, and although her dealings with Ashton were both brief and rather unpleasant, watching the woman executed on TV had shaken her to her core.

'You okay?' Gayle's voice called out from the other side of their small office in Bow Road Metropolitan Police Station in East London. On that morning, Sutton was very grateful that Gayle had insisted on the OPS operating outside of New Scotland Yard.

'Yeah. Just…' Sutton trailed off.

'I know. It's crazy. I never worked with Ruth myself, but we had met a few times.' He shook his head. 'A terrible shame.'

'You think he did it?' Sutton asked, looking up at her boss, who peered over his glasses.

'Who? Pope?' He knew about her history with Sam. In fact, beyond Vokes, and to an extent, Commissioner

Sarratt, he was the only one. He offered her a smile. 'I think there's always more going on than we can see.'

Sutton nodded, and then excused herself for what Gayle called her 'fresh air break'. As she stepped out into the bitter chill, she pulled her coat tight as the wind whipped through her short, brown bob that framed her striking face. She cupped her hand around her cigarette and tried her hardest to summon a flame from the cheap lighter.

No avail.

'Come on,' she muttered, and clicked with increasing rage, knowing full well that her anger wasn't truly directed at the lighter.

'Need a light?'

A soft voice echoed behind her, thick with a Northen Irish accent, and as Sutton turned, she felt an instant recognition. The voice and face were both familiar, but she was unable to place from where. The woman held out a lighter and then offered both hands to help Sutton shield the flame from the wind.

With a few puffs, Sutton began her cigarette and tried her hardest to scan her mind for an identity, as the mysterious yet recognisable woman lit one of her own.

'Thanks,' Sutton said. 'Do I know you? I feel like—'

'Lynsey Beckett.' She extended her free hand. 'I work for the BBC.'

Sutton clicked her fingers and then shook the hand.

'That's it.' The realisation kicked in. 'You're a journalist?'

'One of the best, apparently.' Lynsey smiled. 'I need to talk to you about...'

'Look, any links that your company or any press have tried to make between myself and Sam Pope have already been officially denied and—'

'Oh, let's not do all this shit.' Lynsey waved it off. 'Let's just say we have a mutual friend who, at some point in time, has proven that he wouldn't…I don't know…kill an innocent woman in cold blood?'

Lynsey stared at Sutton, as if admitting that she knew more than most, and Sutton felt an almost instant bond between them. Sam Pope's circle was so small, it was barely a dot, and to meet someone who had been or was inside it was something she didn't expect to happen.

Tentatively, she took a pull on her cigarette and looked at the journalist.

'Say we did have a mutual friend?' Sutton looked around, ensuring they were alone. 'Why reach out now?'

Lynsey finished her cigarette with a long drag and then stubbed it out on the metal ashtray affixed to the brick wall of the station.

'Because I don't believe for one fucking second that Sam pulled that trigger,' she said with such clarity. 'And I think, you know the reason why people might want to say he did.'

Sutton held Lynsey's stare, trying her best to figure out if there was a hidden agenda. As a detective, she'd always regarded the press with the scepticism the majority of them deserved. But if Lynsey was genuine, then there was a chance that the brick wall she'd run in to previously might begin to wobble.

Sutton glanced at her phone.

She'd been gone for five minutes. Any longer, and Gayle would start probing her for reasons when she got back.

'You got a card?' she eventually asked, and Lynsey retrieved one from her coat with the efficiency of a magician.

'We need to be quick on this.'

'I finish at six—'

'Call me at one minute past, then.' Lynsey smiled. She

then turned, stuffed her hands into the pockets of her thick overcoat, and headed back down the road towards the train station.

Sutton watched her leave, looked down at the card once more and then pocketed it. As she headed inside, she felt a small rumble of either apprehension or excitement in the pit of her stomach.

Either way, she was going to try her best to get answers.

Commissioner Sarratt stood in front of the press, a thick Metropolitan Police coat wrapped around her athletic frame, and an unfortunate police constable stood holding an umbrella over her. As the rain lashed down, Sarratt spoke sincerely into the soaked camera and the sodden microphones that had been shoved in front of her face.

'We can only take comfort in the fact that Ruth Ashton would have felt no pain in her death, but there is no comfort to be taken in what has happened. Ruth Ashton was a commendable woman, driven to the safety and protection of not only this city, but of this country. Over thirty years within the police service, she'd even returned from retirement to aid us in our pursuit of Sam Pope. A pursuit, that has now turned into a murder scene.'

As Sarratt spoke about the severity of the situation, Sam Pope had tuned it out.

Considering he'd been sitting in his flat, trying his best to read through *Moby Dick* by Herman Melville when the assassination happened, he knew what was happening.

He was being framed.

When he'd seen Ruth Ashton emerge on his screen a two days ago and address the nation in an attempt to smoke him out, Sam had wondered what was happening. Why has Ashton, who'd resigned in disgrace three years ago, suddenly been thrust back not only into a position of power, but into his life?

Now it was obvious.

Her tirade against him had worked to an extent, and Sam had tossed and turned all night with the guilt of beating down those three men. Although they'd instigated the confrontation, in reality, they were just a group of wannabe tough guys who bit off more than they could chew.

Sam was trained.

Lethal.

And by all accounts, should have just made a break for it. But he'd reacted in a way that would only fuel the flames against him, and how better to pour gasoline on them than kill the woman committed to finding him. Live for the whole country to see.

Already, the news channels were scouring social media, highlighting posts of condemnation of Sam and his 'one-man killing spree'.

The tide was turning.

And as Sarratt carefully and diplomatically read him the riot act, he didn't take it personally. By all accounts, Sarratt was a good woman, and through his discussions with her predecessor, Bruce McEwen, he'd formed a picture of a woman of integrity and morals. She was just doing her job, and doubling down on their efforts to bring him in was the only course of action she could take in light of the events of that morning.

But Sam wasn't paying attention.

His eyes were focussed on the group of people in the background, where he could see a well-dressed man of considerable authority, most likely military. But beside him, with the sling still strapped across his chest, was Piers Bloom.

The man's name had been on the list of associates of

Balikov, and it was thanks to Sam that he was currently strapped up. He'd gatecrashed a covert meeting between Bloom and a few other elite businessmen who were cowering in fear after Balikov's arrest.

Someone had to be funding the operation, and Sam would bet his word, the one thing he held in the same regard as his son's memory, that it was Bloom.

On the screen, a well-built man stood behind the two of them, but the picture wasn't clear enough for Sam to make out who.

It was a long shot, but Sam realised that was all he had.

Whoever had blown Ruth Ashton to Kingdom Come had done it on the express orders to frame him.

To portray Sam Pope as a killer.

The breadcrumbs were falling into place, and it wasn't hard to follow them back to Bloom. Associates like Graham Henshaw and Michael Hartson had both been arrested or interrogated in the past few months, and if Bloom was sensing a pattern, then he would want to get ahead of it.

Want to have Sam stopped.

By any means necessary.

He clicked off the TV and swept up his thick coat and slid it around his muscular body. Then he stuffed his Glock 17 into the back of his jeans and headed to the door.

As he stepped out into the bitter cold and freezing rain, he pulled up his hood, hoping it would hide him from a city that was now baying for his blood.

It wasn't about clearing his name.

It was about exposing who wanted to frame him in the first place.

And with that purpose echoing in his mind, Sam stuffed his hands into his pockets, and headed towards the city and the head offices of Bloom Enterprises.

CHAPTER THIRTEEN

'And you're certain I'll be safe?'

Piers Bloom, despite being one of the most respected and feared businessmen in the UK, was just like everyone else when the chips were down. Murray wasn't surprised by the man's fear. When someone who was used to getting what they wanted was finally challenged in a way that their money or position couldn't stop, they usually had no other response than sheer terror.

'I should think so,' Murray said with a sly grin. 'Although, I can't make any concrete guarantees.'

The immediate eye-widening fear on Bloom's face gave Murray a small rumbling of satisfaction.

'What do you mean?' Bloom stammered, looking to Wainwright, who, as always, remained stoic.

'I mean, I believe Pope will most likely want answers, so he'll need you alive,' Murray said casually. 'But there's always the chance that he'll just storm in and put a bullet through your skull.'

'Then I won't do it,' Bloom insisted, with a startling lack of conviction.

He looked around the room. Both Murray and Wainwright looked at him with apathy. Jensen chortled. Quickly, Bloom realised he was the least powerful of the four men in the room and shrunk into himself.

'Piers, we've been friends for a long time,' Wainwright said, leaning forward in his seat. 'Trust me. We made sure you were on screen when Sarratt spoke earlier today for this very reason.'

'To use me as live fucking bait?' Bloom snarled. Jensen chuckled again. 'Sorry, is this funny to you?'

Jensen locked his eyes on Bloom and pushed himself from the back of the room.

'You're damn right it's fucking funny to me,' Jensen said as he smacked on his chewing gum. 'Nothing like seeing a rich prick squirming like a worm on a hook.'

'Sorry, can we get him out of here?' Bloom asked, looking to Murray and Wainwright. They said nothing, and Jensen walked around the table and sat on the edge, right in front of Bloom who leant back in his chair with alarm.

'Who do you think's going to take Sam down when he comes for you? Huh?' Jensen said, leaning into Bloom's personal space. 'See, the good admiral over there, he's a little too old for combat, and my boss Murray, he's the guy pulling the strings. Me, I'll be the one pulling the fucking trigger. Now, whether I do that before or after Sam pops one through your bald little dome, that's in the balance.'

'Enough, Fabian,' Murray said with a sigh. Now and then, he knew he needed to tighten the leash. 'Mr Bloom is funding this operation, after all.'

Jensen nodded, and then turned back to Bloom and grinned.

'Just let us do our fucking jobs,' Jensen said menacingly, and then pushed himself off the table and headed back to the far end of the room. Bloom, considerably shaken, tried to calm himself as he addressed the others.

'I just don't want things to get messy.'

'And it won't,' Murray promised. 'Just as long as you do as I say. Now, how quickly can you get the email out?'

'It's already being drafted,' Bloom said. 'My PA may be a useless little twit most of the day, but he can at least send an email out.'

'Good. Get it out as soon as possible,' Murray said. 'Ensure that when security closes down the building, we're given the required access to open it back up and to keep all the pathways cleared up to your office.'

'Won't Pope find it suspicious?' Bloom asked. 'The lack of people in the office?'

'Maybe.' Murray shrugged. 'But remember two things. One, Sam Pope is a highly trained soldier who can handle pretty much ninety-nine out a hundred situations. The man is trained to survive. And second, he's going to want to know who framed him for murder. So even if he senses a trap, he'll most likely fancy he can get through it.'

'But he won't?' Bloom asked, looking to Murray and Wainwright. 'Right?'

Murray took his turn to walk around the table, and he plonked his sizable frame in front of Bloom, who was sweating with nerves. Murray cleared his throat and then fixed Bloom with a warm smile.

'Look. I didn't ask Admiral Wainwright why we're so intent on catching Sam Pope. He said it was a matter of national security, and I'll take him at his word. The thing is, without you, I don't get paid.' Murray leant in a few inches from Bloom's face. 'And me and my team, we don't work for free. So, it's in our interests to keep you safe. Is that good enough for you?'

'Y-yes.' Bloom stammered, shooting a quick glance to Jensen who was once again smirking. Bloom straightened, trying to hide his nerves. 'That's good enough for me.'

Murray patronisingly patted Bloom on the cheek.

'Good, lad.' He stood and walked back around the table. 'Jensen and his team will escort you back to your offices. Ensure they're cleared out before you get there. I'll be along shortly to run point from the car park. Jensen, you get your team into position. How many men?'

Jensen blew out his cheeks.

'Six ought to do it.'

'Take ten,' Murray said. 'Bloom can afford it.'

Jensen clapped his hands and headed to the door, and then beckoned for Bloom to follow. The billionaire obliged, shuffling rather meekly towards Jensen like a disobedient dog towards an abusive owner. As Bloom passed Wainwright, the admiral reached out and placed his hand on his friend's arm.

'Don't worry, Piers. This will all be over soon.'

Bloom gave an unconvincing nod and then headed through the doorway. Jensen smirked, shaking his head as he followed, and Murray waited for the door to close before turning back to Wainwright.

'Admiral, a quick word before I go.' Murray showed none of the fear that most men regarded Wainwright with. 'I never ask much for detail when taking a contract. People have things they don't want coming out, or they're doing things that other people might try to stop. That's the way the world works. Just to be clear, the plan is to bring Sam Pope in *alive*. He can be tried and sentenced as a criminal.'

'Correct,' Wainwright said, holding the eye contact. Murray still didn't believe him.

'Well, in that case, I think we need to keep an eye on Commissioner Sarratt.'

'Oh, she's on board.'

'Sir, I think she's looking to do something. I've been in this game a long time and—'

'And I have been in longer, son,' Wainwright cut in; his voice laced with menace. 'Trust me, I'm dangling that woman so far over the edge of the building I barely have a grip on her ankles. Once we've taken care of Sam, I'll make sure her reputation goes away with him. You have nothing to worry about.'

Murray held the eye contact for a few more moments and then smiled. He stood, straightened his jacket, and then headed to the door. Before he left, he turned back to face the admiral once more.

'I'm just doing my job, Sir. I don't think I'm the one who should be worried.'

Murray then headed through the door and back down through the New Scotland Yard building, ready to lay the trap that could potentially cost Sam Pope everything.

Over the years, Guardian had successfully carried out more than three-hundred operations, and for over half of them, Fabian Jensen had been the man on the ground. When James Murray had founded the company, he'd done it as a way to respectfully leave the military and lead a safer life. At first, the jobs were usually just as a security detail for businessmen, but as the money came in and the reputation grew, Murray allowed himself to chase the money at the cost of his morals.

The team grew, and Murray took more of a political role, using his ageless charm and handsome face to be the man in the room with the client.

Jensen's skillset was out in the field.

It was a show of respect from Murray, and Jensen knew he trusted him completely, although they did clash when it came to the severity of Jensen's methods. When they were hired by a ruthless war lord to extract information out of a team of captured rebels, Murray was seemingly offended by the lengths Jensen went to get what was needed. In

Jensen's mind, people could still see if you took out only one of their eyes, and they could still eat if you only took out some of their teeth.

Over the years, Murray had been more particular on the level of client they took on, and Jensen had pinned that to his rise among the elite businessmen in the world. Small-time drug dealers didn't pay as much as billionaire businessmen, and Murray liked dining at the top table in his expensive suits.

Jensen didn't give a shit.

He loved the thrill of the job, and in a way, he missed being down in the gutter with the low-level criminals. There was more chance of him being called into action, and although Murray had questioned his sanity at times, Jensen knew he had a clearer head than most. He was an elite-level soldier no longer in battle, and sometimes, babysitting criminals as they made their deals, or escorting rich people to meetings didn't quite scratch that itch.

But this one, this was everything he could have wanted.

Sam Pope was a name that was whispered as legend during his time in the military, and Jensen had heard many senior officers wax lyrical about the man, long after he'd left Project Hailstorm. Once he'd been enveloped into Blackridge, not a week went by where someone didn't mention Pope, and when Wallace made it clear that Pope was now a threat, Jensen was champing at the bit to be the man to put him down.

It never happened.

Wallace had put unwavering faith in another sniper who apparently had a score to settle with Pope, and Murray made it his personal mission to leave and start on his own. Jensen was his first hire, and since then, the two of them had naturally settled into the roles that had made Guardian such a profitable business. As Jensen would often say:

'You stay behind the desk. I'll stay behind the scope.'

It was inaccurate, as often, Jensen didn't need to shoot, but the meaning was clear.

Murray was the brains. Jensen was the bullet.

The plan seemed pretty easy. Bloom had evacuated his building of civilians, with a companywide email sent to the employees about a potential asbestos problem that needed to be fixed, and all of them were to work from home for the next few days. Jensen found it funny that these stuffed shirts and corporate shills would likely complain about the idea of being "exposed" to such danger.

They didn't know danger.

They'd probably shit their pants if they sent an email to the wrong person.

But with the building empty, Bloom had used his access to reopen the security doors and grant access to Jensen and his ten-strong team of mercenaries. Spread across the building as Jensen had demanded, with all of them strapped with Glock 17s. It was one man, albeit one with a reputation, but Jensen didn't feel it necessary to rampage through the building with assault rifles.

Especially as Murray had given strict orders to take Pope alive. Murray had arrived roughly half an hour ago, taking his place with two of the team in the van in the underground car park. Jensen knew that Murray half-hoped that Pope would arrive and park up nicely next to him, and he'd be able to talk him into surrender.

The easy route.

Jensen was hoping for the hard way.

The chance to go toe-to-toe with the man he'd constantly been compared to was the most tantalising offer he'd had in his career to date, and it was his own ego that told the rest of the team to take the other floors.

Jensen would be waiting for Sam in the meeting room opposite Bloom's private office.

Nowhere to run.

Just Jensen and Sam Pope.

One on one.

Someone in the team had posed that it might just be a waste of time, and that if Sam Pope had any sense, he'd just hightail it. The man clearly had fake identities and the skills to completely disappear. But Murray and Jensen both knew that running away from the fight wasn't something Sam Pope could do.

It wasn't something a true soldier could do.

And Sam Pope had a rigid moral code that Jensen found annoyingly admirable. Pope had killed multiple people but drew the line at being accused of just one.

It was admirable, but ultimately, when Jensen had Pope on his knees and a gun to the back of his head, it would be foolish.

And he knew that in the aftermath, Murray would be seething, and their relationship might never fully recover.

But Admiral Wainwright had reached out to Jensen personally, and demanded that should the opportunity arise he was to blow Sam Pope's brains out the back of his skull.

As the rain spattered against the floor to ceiling windows of the meeting room, Jensen cast his eyes out over the gloomy, grey skyline of London, and wondered how much the news of Sam's death would shake the city?

And what would happen to his reputation and career when he was the man to do it?

A cruel grin spread across his bearded face, and he skilfully checked the ammunition in his gun with heavily tattooed hands.

The earpiece in his ear crackled with Murray's voice.

'Target spotted. Do not engage.'

Jensen frowned and spoke into the mic attached to the collar of his black polo shirt.

'Let's just take him now,' Jensen offered.

'*Not on the street.*' Murray's voice echoed. '*Wait until he makes it to the top floor. Jensen, you're on point.*'

'Roger that,' Jensen said with a smirk.

'*And remember. Contain. Not kill.*'

Jensen turned his mic off and tossed his earpiece.

He wasn't willing to follow that order.

CHAPTER FOURTEEN

It was a trap.

Sam knew that the second he saw Bloom on the TV screen, but still, his feet continued to take him through the rainy streets of London to the HQ of Bloom Enterprises. Up until that moment, Sam had theorised that the rebirth of his own dedicated task force was in response to his list-ticking exercise of whittling out the weeds within the British power structure. Bloom was an influential man who wielded power with senior political figures. Sam had hoped that the bullet he'd put through Bloom's shoulder would have sufficed, but seemingly, Bloom was now happy to get blood on his hands in an effort to lure Sam out into the open.

Powerful men often thought they were untouchable.

Above the law and out of reach.

Ervin Wallace had thought the same, but that hadn't stopped Sam from launching a rocket at his motorcade on the streets of London a few years ago to hijack the man and hold him hostage. But that was a different time, with a very different motive.

That was to save the life of Amara Singh, a woman

who had stolen a piece of his heart and was only in harm's way because of her loyalty to him.

This was different.

This was to clear his own name, and if the country and the media were spinning the narrative that he'd blown out the back of Ruth Ashton's skull to stop the task force, then doing the same thing to one of the most powerful men in government would only stoke those flames.

Sam wasn't fighting for justice.

He was fighting for the truth.

When Sam finally saw the huge Bloom HQ loom large around the corner, he slowed his pace and scanned his surroundings. His lifetime of training kicked in, the muscle memory to visualise and store every outcome becoming as natural as breathing. But there was nothing that stood out.

No police cars.

No obvious covert officers.

No gunmen perched in neighbouring windows.

He had a clear path to the office.

Which is what told him it was a trap.

On the opposite side of the road, Sam ducked into an independent coffee shop, and the warmth and smell of the fresh coffee was a welcome difference to the harsh bitterness of the winter's morning. Beyond a few suspicious glances, nobody said a word to him, and he ordered a coffee and took the table in the corner, his eyes firmly fixed on the office opposite.

Just as he was finishing the expertly made flat white, he noticed a flood of employees exiting the building. Scrambling to get their coats on, the wave of staff coasted off in different directions and within minutes, Sam watched as the security guards emerged through the door and locked it down.

The building was empty.

Something didn't feel right.

As Sam kept his eyes locked on the building, the young waitress in the coffee shop approached his table.

'Can I get you anything else?'

'Err, yeah. I'll have another coffee.' Sam offered her a smile. She nodded and collected his empty mug. But before she left, she paused and turned back to him.

'For what it's worth, I don't think you did it.'

Sam looked up at her, met her eyes, and nodded his thanks. It was re-affirming to know that the whole country hadn't completely turned their back on him, and it just underlined the thought that they needed to know the truth.

That those put in power to protect them were only trying to protect themselves.

A few minutes later, the young lady returned with the coffee, but just as Sam lifted the mug, he saw a man he knew.

Piers Bloom.

Stepping out of the back of a jet-black Range Rover, the business mogul looked completely dishevelled as he waited by the locked door of his office. The passenger door flew open, and another bald man stepped out, his every movement screaming military, and he smiled and stroked his beard with a heavily tattooed hand. Despite his status, Bloom was clearly under orders, and the bald man barked them at Bloom, who opened the doors to his office block. The Range Rover sped off and was replaced on the side of the road by a black van. The back doors burst open, and Sam counted as ten men emerged in pairs, all of them moving with the precision and fluidity of soldiers.

The cavalry.

They filed in through the open glass doors to Bloom Enterprises and disappeared out of view, and Sam watched as Bloom stepped through after them, followed by the man clearly calling the shots. Sam sipped his coffee, making logical conclusions in how the men would be circulating the eight-storey office, the formations they'd use, and the possible orders they had. With Ruth Ashton being used as a symbol of Sam's murderous rage, it was likely the squadron now patrolling Bloom's building would be armed, although Sam saw no evidence of weapons during their swift entrance.

Either way, if Sam was going into the building, he'd need a way out.

He rose from the corner of the coffee shop, his hulking frame looming large over the small, distressed-wood tables, and he slid a fifty-pound note under the mug. As he headed to the door, he nodded to the young waitress and then stepped out into the cold. Pulling the hood of his coat over his head, Sam's eyes fell upon the building that was separated from Bloom's offices by a small, narrow alleyway. Another nondescript office block, only this one was heavily loaded with scaffolding, with the metal poles and treacherous wooden panels cascading all the way up to the top of the six-storied building. Sam hurried across the road, holding a hand up to a car that had to brake, and then disappeared into the alleyway.

The stench of wet rubbish hit him instantly, and he shimmied past the overstuffed metal bins and looked up at the scaffolding above. Tarp sheets blew in the wind, as the windowless building was clearly empty while under construction. The alleyway was wider than he initially thought, and he pressed himself against the wall of Bloom's building and then took seven long strides to the other wall.

Roughly six to seven meters.

A hell of a distance.

'Fuck it,' Sam uttered to himself, and he turned back, and headed back towards the main road, his hand instinctively reaching for the Glock that was pressed to the back of his spine.

He hoped he wouldn't need to use it.

As he stepped out of the alleyway, he lowered his head, stuffed his hands in his pockets, and walked the short distance to the entrance to the Bloom Enterprises HQ. Inside, there were eleven highly trained men, all of them there with the express purpose to put him down.

But Piers Bloom was also inside, and he was a man who knew what was going on.

And Sam wanted answers.

As his foot cleared the sensor, the glass doors to the office slid open and welcomed Sam inside.

'There he is.'

Murray tapped one of the screens that lined the inside wall of the van. Next to him, the young techy, Ranjit, peered through his glasses, and quickly enhanced the image.

'What's he doing?' Ranjit asked, his thick brow furrowing. 'Looking for a way in.'

'No,' Murray said with an appreciative grin. 'He's looking for a way out.'

They watched as Sam disappeared into the alleyway, and the CCTV cameras dotted around the front of the building sent their feed through the concrete to the car park beneath the building. Ranjit wasn't a soldier, but he was a hell of a technician, and their mobile surveillance van was one of Murray's prized possessions. With Jensen keen to get his adrenaline fix running point on the missions, Murray was happy to sit back and direct proceedings from a distance. If push came to shove, he was just as deadly with both a weapon and the hands he'd use to wield it. But Becky was happier with him taking a more supervisory role on the job, and Murray didn't disagree.

But seeing Sam Pope for the first time in years, live, and in the flesh, sent a sudden shiver of guilt through his body.

He owed Sam his life.

'Shall I tell Jensen to fallout?' Ranjit asked, his eyes still locked on the wall of screens before them. As he reached for the radio, Murray lifted his hand.

'No. Not in the open.' Murray shook his head. 'Let's let him enter the building first. Here, pass me the radio.'

Ranjit obliged, and Murray clicked it to life and then spoke.

'Target spotted. Do not engage.'

He released the call button and held up the speaker to his ear. He counted back from three in his head, and sure enough, Jensen's excitement crackled through.

Let's just take him now.

'Not on the street.' Murray replied into the radio. 'Wait until he makes it to the top floor. Jensen, you're on point.'

Another crackle.

Roger that.

'And remember. Contain. Not kill.'

Murray held the radio up, waiting for the confirmation, but it never came. He sighed. There was always an element of risk when he put Jensen on a job, but that was just the man's insatiable yearning for combat.

You could take the soldier out of the war zone, but you couldn't take the war zone out of the soldier.

Murray had stepped away from that mentality and saw himself as a rather successful businessman. Jensen still saw himself as a walking weapon, and Murray had his concerns that Jensen would see Sam as the ultimate test.

But Jensen *was* a soldier, and Murray was confident he'd follow orders.

'He's back,' Ranjit said excitedly, and on the screen, Sam emerged from the alleyway, pulled up his hood, and headed towards the front door above them. Murray felt a frown form across his face.

'What building's next door?' he asked, his eyes locked on the image of his target heading towards the trap they'd set. Ranjit's fingers rattled the keys in front of him and a window popped up.

'Oakes Pharmaceuticals,' Ranjit read from the screen. 'Head office is under renovation for the next few months, with all employees remote working until then. Says so here.'

Ranjit pointed to his screen, but Murray waved him off. He didn't need to see it with his own eyes. Instinctively, he pulled out a Glock from the armoury on the floor behind them and snapped the pyramid cut slide to ensure it was loaded.

'Keep Jensen updated,' Murray said as he tucked the gun into his jeans. 'If they start firing, the police will likely intervene.'

'Where are you going?' Ranjit asked, as Murray pushed open the back door of the van and dropped down onto the concrete.

'Just covering our bases,' Murray said with a grin.

'Should I tell Jensen?'

Murray slammed the door.

He hurried up the exit ramp of the car park, heading towards the gloomy grey light of the world above. He'd known Sam for years during their military days, and he could recall Sergeant Marsden chastising Pope for his recklessness.

That Sam didn't believe in 'no-win situations'.

It meant if Sam Pope was willing to enter a building likely filled with armed men, he was doing it for a reason.

And he also had a way out.

Murray emerged onto the street and looked up at the darkening clouds, allowing the rain to fall on his face. The bitter cold felt like a slap to the skin, and he turned away from Bloom Enterprises and headed towards the locked gates that surrounded the neighbouring building. Using his hefty upper body strength, Murray was able to shift them enough to breach a gap, and then, with considerable effort, he forced himself through.

With one hand locked on the grip of his gun, Murray headed into the desolate building, not sure what he was looking for.

But something in his gut told him that Sam had no intention of leaving Bloom Enterprises via the front door.

CHAPTER FIFTEEN

There was nobody in the reception area.

Sam wasn't expecting a parade, but as his boots echoed off the polished floor, it gave an eerie sense of abandonment as he strode towards the security barriers. He'd had his hand on his gun the entire time, half expecting the team to pop out from behind the desk and unload on him.

But nothing.

Easily, he scaled the security barrier, and he strode purposefully towards the far end of the entrance, where two large, silver lift doors were embedded in the wall. As he headed past the plush leather sofas of the waiting area, he heard the muffled sound of a hand dryer emanating from behind the door to the gentlemen's toilets. Instinctively, Sam darted to the wall beside the door, pressing his impressive frame against the white painted bricks. Moments later, the door was pulled open, and out stepped one of the nondescript, black-clad men who had leapt from the van.

The man was there for Sam.

So, Sam felt it only polite to introduce himself.

As the man shook the last remnants of water from his

hand, he stepped past Sam, oblivious to his presence, and Sam's eyes locked onto the Glock 17 that was secured in the holster around his waist. The mercenary was roughly the same height as Sam, but had a leaner frame, and as the man stepped away, Sam fell in stride behind him. After a few steps, the man sensed Sam's presence, but it was too late.

Sam clasped his left hand around the man's weapon and spun him, driving his right elbow forward as he did. The momentum swung the man to his right, and his cheek collided with the solid, sharp bone of Sam's elbow. The impact shattered the bone, and as the man woozily stumbled, Sam relieved him of his handgun, and then drove the weapon into the man's skull, sending him sprawling across the floor.

It was over in seconds.

Hastily, Sam hauled the man's legs up by the ankles and dragged him across the floor and pushed open the gents with his back. Leaving the unconscious man beside the urinals, Sam tucked the stolen weapon alongside his own in the back of his jeans, and then rushed to the lifts.

The building was empty, clearly under direction, which meant they were likely covering the stairs and lift doors.

This was going to be a fight, and Sam pulled out one of the Glocks as the small screen above the metal door signalled the elevator's arrival.

The doors smoothly slid open, and without thinking, Sam swung the gun up to his expert eye.

It was clear.

Sam stepped in and tapped the button for the top floor

A man like Bloom would sit atop the building. An ego that big would demand that he himself look down upon the rest of the company, as well as the City of London. Considering his company had probably built half of the city or had a say in it, meant he'd want to look out and sneer at what he'd accomplished. The lift shot through the building to the top floor, and with a gentle ping, it stopped on the eighth floor.

The doors slid back, and Sam once again instinctively raised his weapon.

Clear.

Where was everyone?

Sam stepped out, keeping his gun drawn, as he moved down the corridor, clearing each potential hiding spot en route to the large office at the end of the hallway. The shutters to the floor-to-ceiling window were down, but the words *Piers Bloom, CEO* were emblazoned on the door to the office. Sam approached, and with his gun raised, he threw open the door and stepped in.

'Jesus fucking Christ!' Bloom yelled as he stood from behind his desk, his eyes widening as he saw the gun in Sam's hand. 'Look, just put the gun down.'

'You've got until I step around your desk to start telling me what's going on,' Sam ordered, as he marched forward with intent.

'I don't know what you're talking about,' Bloom squealed, but his voice cracked as Sam pressed his gun against his functional shoulder and pushed him back into the seat.

'What the hell happened to Ruth Ashton?' Sam spat through gritted teeth, pressing the gun deeper into Bloom's pressure point, causing him to groan with pain.

But Bloom found a resolve and glared up at Sam.

'You should know.' Bloom grimaced. 'You killed her.'

The gunshot sounded like a clap of thunder, and the following howl of agony from Bloom was just as loud. The man rocked back in his chair, the bullet ripping through his shoulder and embedding into the wall behind, leaving an artistic spray of blood across the carpeted floor. Tears fell down Bloom's world-weary face, and Sam yanked Bloom's other arm from its sling and slammed the hand across the fresh bullet wound.

'You might want to keep pressure on it,' Sam said grimly.

'You piece of fucking...' Bloom tailed off, as Sam pressed the now hot metal of the gun against his sweat covered forehead.

'The next bullet will be through your skull,' Sam promised. 'Now, tell me, what the hell is going on?'

'Okay. Okay.' Bloom breathed through his obvious agony. 'That night at Bakku. When you put a different bullet through me. You rattled cages that you shouldn't have fucking rattled. There are a lot of people who want what you know to stay hidden, Sam.'

'Men like you? Men like Hartson?' Sam asked, already knowing the answer. 'Thing is, Bloom, I've been doing this a long time now. I know what happens when you knock on doors that people keep locked. But the country deserves to know what you were planning.'

'I didn't fucking plan anything,' Bloom spat with venom. 'I just saw what way the wind was blowing.'

'And fuck everyone else, right?' Sam said with a shake of his head. He then readjusted the gun, pressing it firmly against the man's sweaty skull. 'So, who ordered the hit? Sarratt?'

Bloom let out an involuntary laugh.

'Miss Goody-Two-Shoes'?' He sneered. 'Don't make me laugh. She's cut from the same annoying cloth you are. However, she did sign off on everything. All it took was some pressure.'

'Then who?' Sam barked, stepping forward a little further, pressing Bloom further back into the chair. 'Who killed Ashton? And, if Sarratt *isn't* running this thing who's chasing me?'

But Bloom smirked and just closed his eyes.

Was he daring Sam to finish things?

Sam felt the cold steel of a gun press against the back of his own skull and realised he'd been lured in. He knew a trap had been set, but his own anger had blinded him. He'd let his guard down for the split second it took a trained killer to exploit. Bloom looked beyond Sam to whoever it was who had him it gun point and breathed a sigh of relief.

'I need a doctor,' Bloom stammered with desperation.

'Shut the fuck up, old man.' The voice echoed behind Sam. 'Now, Mr Pope. Drop the gun.'

Sam slowly retracted the gun from Bloom's brow and tossed it onto the table.

'There's a good boy. Now let's move.'

With slow steps, Sam moved as the man directed and found himself heading back towards the door of the office, as Bloom called out once more for help.

Sam knew he was a dead man walking.

And worse, the man who had a gun to his head was clearly enjoying it.

Jensen had sat patiently in the meeting room.

He wondered what panic was echoing over the radio, especially as he hadn't responded to Murray's strict order, but that was all part of the rush. Unlike Murray, who derived his pleasure from making money and wasting his time raising a family, Jensen lived and breathed combat.

Putting a bullet through Ruth Ashton's head had been the closest thing he'd come to a gunfight in over a year, and apart from the odd beating he had to administer to fake thugs now and then, the lifestyle had grown boring.

This.

This was a chance to cement himself as a legend.

The man who not only stopped, not only killed, but the man who bested Sam Pope.

It would make Jensen the most valuable commodity in the country, as other powerful men would be falling over themselves for his service. They'd look beyond Murray, and soon, he'd be the one with the seat at the top table. But he'd still have a space for his long-time friend. Murray had been good to him after all. But he'd have to follow Jensen's lead, and he most likely wouldn't agree with what Jensen had in mind.

The world was a lot less fun when you played it safe.

Jensen had crossed his legs as he sat in the middle of the desk, ensuring that any peeps under the frosted glass wouldn't reveal his position, and as he patiently waited for Pope to make his way to Bloom, he took the liberty of carving a devil image into the centre of the oak desk with his Bowie knife.

Bloom was rich enough to afford a new one.

Sure enough, he heard the arrival of the elevator, and as he gazed at the glass that ran along the bottom of the frosted protection, he saw the boots march towards Bloom's office.

Whoever they belonged to moved with purpose.

Without fear.

They didn't belong to his men.

As he heard the raised voices from Bloom's office, Jensen took a breath, and slid himself off the table, making sure he embedded his blade right in the centre of the wood before he left. Then, just as he reached out for the meeting room door, he heard the devastating blast of a gunshot.

Sam wasn't fucking around.

Jensen smoothly pulled open the door, his gun drawn, expecting a blood-soaked Sam to come marching out. But then he heard the pathetic whimpers of Bloom escaping through the open door of the office.

Pope hadn't killed the man.

He may have had the killer instinct, but Sam Pope wasn't a killer.

That was what set him and Pope apart, and Jensen was more than happy to prove it to him.

'Who killed Ashton? And if Sarratt *isn't* running this thing, who's chasing me?'

Jensen realised it was the first time he'd heard Pope speak, but in a strange way, he sounded exactly like Jensen had imagined.

Gruff.

Purposeful.

Full of conviction.

Jensen slipped through the door of the office without a sound, and looked with delight at the quivering, bloodied billionaire who was whimpering in his chair. It was Jensen's job to keep him alive, but seeing someone who had so ruthlessly built his fortune off the backs of others shed a little blood filled him with a morbid satisfaction.

Pope was a larger-than-life presence, an impressive specimen who loomed over Bloom in both physique and stature. Jensen trod carefully, eating up the distance between himself and his target with silent steps.

Bloom saw him.

The foolish man almost gave the game away with a smirk, but Jensen stepped forward and pressed his Glock to the back of Pope's head.

He had him.

'I need a doctor,' Bloom begged pathetically.

Jensen kept his eyes on Pope and his gun pressed firmly to his skull.

'Shut the fuck up, old man. Mr Pope, drop the gun.' Pope did as he was told, pulling the weapon back from the quivering, bloody wreck of Bloom, and then tossed it onto the table. 'There's a good boy. Now, let's move.'

Jensen directed Pope with the gun, turning him round, and then nudged him forward towards the open door. Without a hint of fear or a useless protestation for his life, Pope obliged, walking carefully where he was directed, with his hands up in a display of surrender. As they walked, Jensen noticed the second Glock pressed to the base of Pope's spine, and he snatched it from the waistband and tossed it.

'Sneaky,' Jensen quipped. Pope didn't even move.

They exited the office, and as he pushed Pope down the hall, he guided him towards the meeting room he'd previously used.

'Open it,' Jensen ordered, and Pope did as he was told, and the two men shuffled into the room, and Jensen kicked the door closed behind them. With the gun trained on Pope, Jensen stepped to the side, walking carefully around the table until his eyes met Pope's.

There was no fear.

No acceptance of the situation.

All Jensen saw was fight.

It brought a smile to his bearded face. Admiral Wainwright had given him the personal mission of putting a bullet through Pope's skull, but where was the fun in that? It would be no different from pulling the trigger on Ashton.

No satisfaction.

No sense of accomplishment.

Jensen had every intention of fulfilling Wainwright's wish, but he would do it on his terms. And with his eyes locked on Pope's, Jensen could sense that he was beginning to realise what was going on.

'Messy business, isn't it? Killing people,' Jensen said with a grin, and then, with his heavily tattooed hands, he slid the magazine from the Glock, wrenched back the chrome slide, and popped the live round from the barrel, letting the bullet drop to the floor. Pope raised an eyebrow, and Jensen tossed the empty gun across the room.

'You sure about this?' Pope asked, slowly sliding his meaty arms from his coat.

Jensen grinned. His eyes flicked to the knife still embedded in the centre of the table between them.

'Oh, I'm sure.'

Sam shrugged, tossed his jacket, and the two men burst forward with their fists clenched, knowing there was only one way they'd be leaving the meeting room.

CHAPTER SIXTEEN

Jensen threw the first punch, but Sam lifted his arm, absorbing the impact in his bicep. Jensen drilled his left jab into Sam's ribs, and then thrust a knee forward into his gut. Sam hunched over, but he caught the incoming knee a mere inch from his nose. Using his size advantage, Sam then hoisted Jensen up and dropped him onto the edge of the oak table. The mercenary gave out a grunt of pain but pushed the incoming Sam away with a kick to the chest.

Sam took a few steps back upon absorbing the blow, and Jensen pushed himself off the table with a grin.

'This is going to be fun.'

Like an Olympic sprinter hearing the gun, Jensen shot forward, ducking the right hook from Sam and buried his shoulder into Sam's stomach, and he launched both of them into the thick glass pane that overlooked the city below. The glass rattled, but didn't break, and Sam drove his elbow down into Jensen's spine, and then caught the man with a rising knee that sent him sprawling back across the table. Jensen hit the oak, then turned back to Sam, his grin now stained with blood.

Sam frowned.

The man seemed to be enjoying it.

Jensen stood, rolling his shoulders, and then launched forward again, unleashing a barrage of rights and lefts that Sam managed to deflect with his forearms, before one snuck through, and caught him flush on the jaw. Staggering backwards, Sam tried to steady himself, but Jensen launched forward with a rising knee that caught Sam in the chest, and Sam's back hit the pane of glass so hard it shook in its fixture. Relentless, Jensen arrived with a few more hard shots to Sam's ribs, but as he threw a vicious uppercut, Sam swung his body to the side and the fist skimmed the stubble on his chin. Instantly, Sam grabbed the outstretched arm by the bicep, and swung his elbow inside, catching Jensen flush in the jaw, before wrenching the arm over his shoulder and hurling Jensen up and onto the table. The mercenary let out a growl of anguish, but as Sam reached for the scruff of his black polo shirt, Jensen swung a knee up, sending Sam staggering back into the wall.

Sam dabbed at his eyebrow, which was trickling blood, and Jensen slid off the table with a bloodstained grin, and then leant across, and yanked the Bowie knife from the wood. With a sickening twinkle in his eye, he pointed it at Sam.

'You got guts, Pope. I'll give you that.' He licked the blood from his own teeth. 'I'm going to take them from you.'

Sam pulled his fists up as Jensen marched back around the table and lunged forward, swiping at Sam with the blade. The sharp metal made an audible swish through the air as Sam stepped away, the blade missing his stomach by inches. As Jensen continued on, Sam kept stepping backwards, rounding the table, and he pulled out one of the chairs to block Jensen's path. Jensen stumbled, and Sam drove his elbow into Jensen's forearm, and then turned his body into his attacker, his hands locked around Jensen's wrist, trying to disarm him. As Jensen fought back, he drilled his knee into the back of Sam's legs, and then, with his free hand, yanked Sam back by the hair. The sudden pull loosened Sam's grip, and Jensen lifted the knife and brought it down as hard as he could towards Sam's exposed throat. In the nick of time, Sam lifted his forearm, the blade slicing across the skin and ripping it open. Jensen tried to force his weight down, but Sam lifted his foot to the edge of the table and pushed backwards, sending both men sprawling over the chair and crashing onto the floor.

The knife clattered somewhere under the table.

Both men scrambled to their feet, and as they did, Jensen tried to reattach his comms device to call for back-up. But Sam burst forward, driving his shoulder into Jensen's midsection and sending the air flying from the man's lungs. He carried him a few steps before both men hit the edge of the wooden desk and fell onto the meeting table. Pressed against the wood by Sam's frame, Jensen tried to cover his face with his arms, but Sam rocked him once again with a hard right.

Then a second that sent two teeth spinning across the wood with a trail of fresh blood.

Then a third that shattered his nose.

As Sam lifted for a fourth, Jensen unlocked the adrenaline needed for survival and swung his hips to the side, knocking Sam a little off balance, and he managed to drill Sam in the jaw with a hard right that sent him crashing off the table to the floor. As Sam crumpled to the carpet, Jensen spat out some blood and began to chuckle.

'Fuck me, Pope.' He gurgled the blood as he sat up and spat it against the glass window. 'You really don't know when to quit, do you?'

Sam gingerly began to push himself to his feet as he responded.

'Yeah, it's a defect of mine,' he grunted as he stood, clenching his fists. Jensen tongued the gap of his missing tooth as he pushed himself off the table, and then spat blood onto the carpet.

The meeting room resembled a war zone.

Just as Sam was readying himself for another onslaught, Jensen drove his foot into the back of the chair they'd fallen over, sending it crashing into Sam's legs, and then he turned and scarpered down the meeting room. Sam grunted as the chair slammed into his thigh, but he understood Jensen's intentions.

He was going for the gun.

Having cockily disarmed and disposed of it, Jensen was now showing his desperation as he bounded down the meeting room and swiftly dropped to his knees. He scooped up the empty weapon, and the loaded magazine, and he slammed them together with ruthless efficiency. He intended to turn and shoot, but as his body began its turn, he heard the thudding sound of boots as they rattled the table, and he turned just in time to see Sam launch himself off the table and the two men went sprawling across the floor once more.

A gunshot rang out.

The bullet blasted one of the panes of glass to smithereens, sending a hailstorm of jagged, broken glass down to the road below. Instantly, the wind and rain swept into the room, and as both men got to their feet, Jensen drew the gun. In one swift movement, Sam snatched the man's wrist, arched his back, pushed his hips into Jensen's stomach, and flipped him clean over. Jensen's spine hit the edge of the table hard, and Sam wrenched the gun from his hand and turned it on him.

'Don't fucking move,' Sam yelled, looking down at the hired gun who was already getting to his feet and doing his best to mask the agony he was in.

'You going to kill me?' Jensen said with a smile.

'If I have to,' Sam said, the rain washing away some of the blood that was trickling down his face. 'Who killed Ashton?'

Jensen shrugged and smirked.

'Guilty, your honour.'

'Why?' Sam spat angrily. The woman may have tried her best to deny him his freedom, but she was ultimately innocent. 'Why bring her in just to kill her?'

'I couldn't give a fuck.' Jensen spat blood once again. 'You know how it is, Sam. You get given a target and you pull the trigger. Wainwright said if—'

'Wainwright?' Sam frowned. Jensen saw his opportunity, as Sam's moment of confusion was all he needed. He launched forward, wrapping both hands around Sam's wrist and pushing the gun upwards, and Sam embedded two bullets in the ceiling panel. Debris fell on top of them, and the two men wrestled for control of the gun, their feet edging precariously near to the eight-storey drop. As they wrenched the weapon back and forth, Jensen spat blood into Sam's face, and then swung his boot up, kicking Sam right between the legs.

As the pain echoed through his body, Sam relinquished the weapon, and dropped to one knee, as the conniving Jensen took a step back and adjusted his grip on the gun.

He lifted it in line with Sam's skull.

Then let out a scream of agony as Sam drove a shard of glass into his thigh muscle. As the jagged glass ripped through the flesh into the muscle, Sam rolled to the side, evading any gunshot as he twisted the make-shift blade. He could feel it shredding the muscle inside Jensen's leg, and ignoring the lacerations across his fingers, he let go and stood. Jensen crumpled back against the table, the colour already draining from his rain-soaked face, and as Sam approached, he feebly lifted the gun, and Sam easily disarmed him.

Beaten, Jensen smirked and immediately grimaced.

'What now, then?' he managed, acknowledging his defeat. Sam lifted the gun. Jensen scoffed. 'See. You're a killer just like me.'

Then Jensen's world went black, as he crumpled to the floor, the blow delivered by the butt of the gun to the temple shutting his lights out. Sam stood over the unconscious man, the wind whipping between them, and the blood still trickling from his brow and down his cheek.

'No. Not like you.'

With the pain echoing throughout his body, from his bloodied forearm to his battered testicles, Sam shuffled towards the door of the meeting room. As he yanked it open, he heard the *ping* of the lift down the hallway, and his head snapped in its direction. The door opened, and two more black-clad mercenaries emerged, concerned expressions across their face. Clearly, they'd been sent to check on the man Sam had just put down, or from a distress call from Bloom, but their eyes lit up as they saw Sam.

They reached for their weapons.

Sam dropped to his knee and drew up the handgun.

With pinpoint accuracy, he sent one bullet careening through one of the men's shin bones, before swinging it to the left and embedding another bullet through the other's knee cap. Red mist burst out of both bullet wounds, and the men hit the ground, screaming in pain, as Sam gingerly got back to his feet. He peered into Bloom's office, and the man had passed out, laid back in his chair as the blood loss from the wound in his shoulder had sapped his strength.

They'd sent help.

Sam shrugged.

A man as powerful and as treacherous as Bloom had no place in his small archive of compassion.

Sam hurried back down the hallway, towards the two men. Having counted eleven of them entering the building, he wondered how many more were making their way to the top floor. The gunshots and the sprinkling of glass on the street below would be enough to tell them that it wasn't going smoothly, and whatever trap they'd set was now in flames. As he approached, one of the men reached out to him, and Sam shut him down with a hard kick to the face. The other was too busy clutching the hole in his shin to do anything else.

But the cavalry was coming.

The other lift was making its way up through the building, and Sam turned and barged open the door to the stairwell, and came face-to-face with another man who was stepping off the first step.

Behind him, two steps behind, was his partner, and their eyes widened with rage at the emergence of their bloodied target. One of them went for his weapon, but Sam instinctively pulled his gun up slightly and pulled the trigger, blowing a hole right through the top of the man's foot. As he arched over with pain, Sam thrust his foot over him, connecting with the chest of the man behind, and sending him sprawling backwards down the stairs. As the man flopped down onto the landing beneath the window, Sam had no idea if he was alive or dead.

And no time to check.

A few storeys below, he could hear the pounding of more footsteps, and the gunshot had clearly put them on high alert. As he peered over the bannister, a bullet clattered into the stone ceiling above, followed by a few more as he pulled away. Beyond the doorway, he could hear the elevator arrive, and surely, once the men had swept the floor, they'd come hunting in the stairwell.

He was blocked in.

More gunshots echoed up the stairs, and Sam leant over and returned fire, but after the first bullet, the gun clicked ominously.

He was out of ammo.

'Fuck'. He uttered, and then with a deep breath, he smashed the window above the motionless body with the butt of the gun. The glass shattered on impact, littering the body with falling shards, and Sam used the gun to rub out any fragments in the frame. The footsteps below were getting louder, maybe a floor away from getting a clear shot, and Sam shook his head, wondered how the hell he got himself into these situations, and then grabbed hold of the window frame.

He hauled himself up, his feet balancing ominously eight stories above the cold, wet concrete that would surely welcome him to the afterlife.

Another gunshot rang out, and a bullet drilled into the brick wall beside him.

Behind him, the door to the stairwell flew open.

With his eyes firmly fixed on the scaffolding two stories below, Sam had previously worked out that he needed to clear six to seven meters.

Another bullet hit the brickwork, and Sam pushed himself off the sill with all his might.

As he flew through the air, the rain and wind rushed against him, and the drop was almost instant. Gravity clawed at him as flashes of Jamie raced through his mind, and with outstretched arms, he reached for the thick, metal poles that ran along the outside of the sixth floor of the building.

They were too far away.

Sam continued falling and slammed into the metal railings that had been constructed around the fifth floor, the impact rattling his ribs as he clung on for dear life. The rain had made them slick, and he fumbled slightly before he managed to haul himself up and over the metal, and collapsed onto the thick wooden boards that comprised the makeshift balcony. The air had left his body.

His soul had almost gone with it.

As he gasped for air, he heard the vague sound of raised voices from the building above, and sure enough, another gunshot rang out, and a bullet slammed into the wooden board a few feet from his head. Sam scrambled up, pulled open the tarp sheet covering the exposed window, and dropped into the dilapidated building.

He needed to move.

And quickly.

CHAPTER SEVENTEEN

Murray had heard the gunshots.

As he was walking carefully through the fifth floor of the desolate building, he heard the echoes of gunfire through the tarp that was straining against the elements. He barked into the radio to cease fire, but once again, he heard nothing from Jensen.

'Bastard,' Murray uttered to himself.

Murray had made it clear that Sam Pope was to be taken alive, and now, as he turned on his heel and headed back to the stairwell, he wondered if stepping back and allowing Jensen to take point had been the right call.

Was Sam Pope dead?

Was Jensen?

Just as he placed his foot on the first step to descend through the building, he heard the sickening impact of something colliding with the scaffolding on the other side of the building, followed swiftly by two more gunshots. Any distress calls going through to the police would be intercepted, with Wainwright making it clear to Sarratt that they needed the immunity to carry out their operation.

There was no backup coming.

No sirens wailing through the bitter winter air signifying the arrival of the law.

Guardian was the law. And Murray turned back off the top step, drew his weapon, and carefully headed back through the gutted floor of the building. As he cleared another one of the large, empty rooms, he could hear the heavy breathing beyond the concrete doorway that led to another barren part of the building. The bitter chill whipped through the building, and as he approached the threshold, he could hear the shuffling of someone.

Sam?

Stepping carefully, Murray approached the wall, pressed himself against it, and raised his weapon.

He spun around the edge of the doorway but was instantly knocked off balance. A hand shot out and latched onto his wrist like a snake's bite, the fingers embedding into the pressure points of his wrist and eliminating his grip. Smoothly, the expert hands dispossessed him, spun the weapon round, and Murray held his hands up as he was looking down the barrel of his own gun.

Behind it, he looked into the eyes of Sam Pope.

'Hello, Sam,' Murray said with a grin, seemingly unphased by the predicament.

Sam, breathing heavily, and wincing as he did so, took a few moments, scanning through his memories to put a name to the face he clearly recognised. The greying hair and the beard made it difficult, but the confusion soon melted into recognition.

'Murray?' Sam said in disbelief.

'Been a while, huh?'

'What the hell are you doing here?'

'Believe it or not, I'm not thinking about buying the building.' Murray chuckled, but cut it off when Sam didn't join in. 'I'm here for you.'

Sam reaffirmed his grip on the gun.

'What the hell are you talking about?'

'It's been a long time,' Murray said, blowing out his cheeks. 'You've been pretty busy.'

'Yeah, well, things seem to keep propping up.' Sam shrugged, still holding him at gunpoint. 'How's Becky?'

'Good.' Murray started to reach into his pocket. 'We've got two boys—'

'I don't need to see pictures,' Sam said firmly. Murray held up his hands in acceptance.

'I'm sorry as all hell for what happened to your boy,' Murray said sincerely. 'I can't imagine—'

'Don't,' Sam said with a shake of his head. 'Because you can't—'

'You know, I tried to reach out to you when you took that hit all those years ago. Wallace told us you were on life support, and I asked him to put me in touch.' Murray sighed. 'He said you were off limits.'

'I appreciate that.'

'Is that what all this is about?' Murray asked, still unperturbed by the gun being pointed at him. 'This whole thing you've been doing. Your way of dealing with it?'

'It was,' Sam answered coldly. 'But somewhere along the way, I made peace with it. With what happened. But it's about so much more than that now.'

'You're telling me. They're paying me an obscene amount of money to stop you.' Murray smiled. 'I told them I owed you my life, and wasn't planning on putting you in the dirt. So how about we lower that weapon, eh?'

'I can't do that.' Sam shook his head. 'I need to get going.'

'Where are you going to go to, Sam?' Murray held out his arms. 'My guys are already on their way. You're a crazy bastard, I'll give you that. But they've got express orders to bring you in and trust me, my guys get the job done.'

'Really? Then why the hell did one of your guys try to kill me up there?'

'Bald guy?' Murray asked. Sam nodded. 'Yeah, Jensen has the propensity to act out a little…is he dead?'

'No,' Sam replied curtly. 'But he'll be out of action for a while. Now step aside.'

'And then what, Sam? Huh?' Murray refused to move. 'God damn it, we're just going to keep coming for you. The government. The Met. They're all behind us. The only way you walk out of this alive is if you walk out with me. That's what I told them.' The echoes of footsteps began to thunder up the stairwell of the deserted building. 'I owed you that much.'

Sam stepped forward and shoved the gun under Murray's bearded jaw, pressing him back against the wall.

'Wainwright?' Sam asked, his brow furrowed with fury.

'The Chief of Defence Staff,' Murray countered.

'Did he tell you why he wants me taken out?'

'I don't ask questions. They pay the money, they give us the name—'

'And you point and shoot, right?' Sam said with a sneer. 'You're no better than Wallace and Blackridge. I'll tell you what, James, when you wake up, and you pick up the pieces of your team, you go ask Wainwright why he wants me dead. Because your boy wasn't trying to bring me in alive.'

Murray frowned. Sam's words were gnawing at a thought burrowing through the back of his mind. Then a couple resonated with him.

'Wait…wake up?' Murray asked.

Sam clobbered him with the butt of the gun, and he then caught the body of his old comrade before he hit the floor. As he laid Murray down carefully on the damp, cold stone, Sam then hurried towards the stairwell, pressing himself against the brickwork as the footsteps grew louder and louder. The first of the men burst through, gun drawn, completely bypassing Sam, who then swung his elbow into the doorway. His elbow collided with the second man's jaw, taking him clean off his feet, and alerting his comrade who spun instantly. Sam lunged forward, locked his arm over the man's outstretched arm, and he wrenched it backward before he launched a ferocious right hook that instantly sent the man to sleep. Sam let the man drop to the ground, not showing the same courtesy he did for Murray, then lifted the man's gun from the ground and took to the stairwell, a Glock in each hand, as he heard more footsteps slam against the stone. As soon as he got to the fourth floor, Sam stepped out of the stairwell and hid behind the open doorway, waiting as the two men raced past, heading to the fifth floor. Sam spun out, unloaded two bullets, and then headed down the stairs, with the cries of both men echoing throughout the building as they clutched the bullet wounds in the backs of their legs. Sam took the next three floors without incident, but just as he passed the doorway of the first floor, two hands reached out and wrapped around his throat, dragging him back off the steps and down onto the ground. Whoever was attacking him had a grip like a vice, and Sam struggled for air as the man locked his arm under Sam's jaw and began to crush down on his throat. Gasping and clawing for air, Sam drove his elbow back a few times, hitting the man in his solid torso, but the grip was unwavering.

Fatal.

As Sam spluttered on the last few traces of oxygen, he lifted one of the guns up, tilted it over his own shoulder, and pulled the trigger. The bullet ripped through his attacker's shoulder and buried into the concrete beneath them in a bloody puddle, and the man roared with agony as he relinquished his grip. As soon as the air flowed back into Sam's lungs, he drove a few more elbows into his assailant, before spinning onto a knee and then driving a ferocious forearm into the man's jaw.

Seven down by his count.

As Sam stood, a gunshot rang out, followed by the instant burning sensation as the bullet skimmed the back of his arm, ripping through the skin, and first layer of his triceps. Sam instinctively turned, his left arm now limp, but he dropped to one knee and lifted his right.

He put the shooter firmly in his eyesight, as another bullet whizzed a few feet above him and clattered into the stone.

Sam pulled the trigger.

The bullet erupted from his gun, the noise elevated by the confines of the stairwell, and as it connected with the shooter's collarbone, it lifted him off his feet in a tremendous cloud of red mist and sent him spiralling down the remainder of the staircase.

Eight down.

Sam grunted as he pushed himself back to his feet, his left triceps screaming in agony as he felt the warm blood pouring down his arm. It was the epitome of a flesh wound, and he knew he'd live.

It just hurt like hell.

Taking the final two steps two at a time, Sam emerged onto the ground floor, the Glock still gripped in his expert right hand, and he scanned the rooms as he passed through them. He made his way to the entrance to the building, the skeletal frame of the automatic glass doors had been replaced with mud-smeared tarp sheets. He pulled one open and stepped out into the rain. The metal gating around the building had created a narrow corridor, with the view to the street blocked by thick wooden boards to keep the public out. Sam shuffled down the walkway towards the gate, but as he approached, he saw two more men yanking it open, desperate to get through and join the rest of their squadron in the firefight. Sam ducked down behind the large barrel of a cement mixer. The gate finally wrenched open, and the two men barged in, and Sam waited as they rushed through the walkway, their focus locked on the entrance to the building ahead of him.

Beside him was a stack of scrap metal, sheets and beams ripped out from within the building, and he carefully tucked his gun into his jeans, and then wrapped his finger around a metal pole.

The last thing he wanted to do was open fire in the street.

As the two men bounded towards him, Sam kept himself as low as possible, and then, as the first man's boot crunched on the wet, sludgy cement next to the mixer, Sam stuck out his leg. The man's feet clipped it at full speed, and he clattered over, crashing face first onto the concrete, and causing the man behind him to yell out in shock, and pull his weapon.

Sam swung out from behind the mixer, pole in hand, and as the man drew his gun up, Sam swung the metal weapon as hard as he could.

As it collided with the man's wrist, Sam could feel the bones shatter, and the man dropped the gun and stumbled back, before the red mist ascended over his eyes and he charged forward. Sam ducked the wild right hook, and then drove the pole into the man's ribs, drilling the air from his lungs, before he struck the man across the jaw with a pinpoint elbow. The man hit the ground motionless, and Sam wasted little time, throwing the pole down and running towards the gate. The thick, rusty chain had pulled it shut again, and with only his right arm, Sam yanked the gate towards him and pressed his body weight against the fence to force an opening.

A gunshot echoed.

A bullet clattered against the metal gate a few inches

from his head, and Sam turned in time to see the man he'd tripped staring murderous daggers at him from behind the gun.

He was taking aim again, but just as he pulled the trigger, Sam fell through the gap of the gate and tumbled out into the street. Unsurprisingly, with the symphony of gunshots, the street had been abandoned, and he clambered to his feet, clutched his left triceps with his right arm, and began to run.

The rain was lashing down, and as he raced across the street, the gunman approached the gate and pulled the gun up, putting Sam firmly in his sights.

But he didn't fire.

A hand fell on his shoulder, and the man turned, and looked up at his boss, who was scowling with a blood-soaked brow.

Murray shook his head, told the man to come with him, and he got on the radio and demanded that Ranjit bring the van up now.

'He won't get far,' Murray assured the man, as they watched Sam hurry as fast as he could down the street.

This wasn't over.

Not by a long shot.

CHAPTER EIGHTEEN

As Sam ran as fast as his battered body could manage, he looked up to the sky as the rain lashed down from the darkening clouds. Hidden behind them, the sun was already beginning its descent, turning the grey afternoon into a dark and morose early evening. The streetlights began to flick on, almost in time with his passing, and he noticed the pre rush-hour traffic being lit up by headlights.

He was half expecting to see hordes of blue flashing lights swarming on his location.

But this was off the books.

Somehow, James Murray, a man he'd served with and had considered a brother in arms, had been brought into an investigation to bring him down and had the Metropolitan Police at his command.

Well, not quite his.

Wainwright.

Sam's mind was racing, trying its best to pinpoint the exact moment he'd crossed paths with Wallace's successor. As he rounded a corner, he saw the instantly recognisable sign for an Underground station and picked up the pace, his eyes locked on the stairwell that burrowed into the walkway. Heads turned as he passed, the blood trickling down his face and the obvious limp made him a beacon for attention, and just as he approached the stairwell, two young police officers rounded the corner, and one of them instantly sparked into action.

'Excuse me, Sir…' he called out, taking a few brisk steps towards Sam, his hand instinctively reaching for his ASP.

Sam sighed, not wanting to confront the officer, but from behind them both, the screeching of tires announced the arrival of the black van hurtling around the corner.

They were coming for Sam.

Without hesitation, Sam went to step past the young officer, who threw his arm out and wrapped it across Sam's chest. As he did, Sam shuffled his weight to his back foot, twisted the man's arm in his right hand, and flipped him over his shoulder onto his back. The officer gasped as the collision winded him, and as the other officer rushed to his defence, Sam flashed a glance back to the van, which had dangerously climbed up onto the curb, and the back door flew open. Sam recognised the man who stepped out. He'd tripped him minutes earlier as he'd run past him, and now, with his horrible, grazed face twisted in a snarl, Sam could see he was back for round two.

As the man locked eyes on Sam, the other officer rushed to his colleague's aid, not noticing the gun that was being drawn in Sam's direction. Panic spread among the nearby civilians, and their screams did their level best to drown out the gunshot.

The bullet hit the other officer, ripping through his Met-vest, and exploding out of his shoulder, sending him spinning to the floor in agony.

Sam wanted to help.

He couldn't.

The next bullet was coming straight for him.

Taking the steps two at a time, Sam hurtled down into the Underground Station, pushing past terrified commuters who were frozen in fear from the gunshots above. A few voices called out at him, decrying him for pushing past, but he burrowed through, ignoring the searing pain in his blood-soaked left arm. As he burst through the crowd and out onto the station concourse, he heard a voice bellow out behind him.

'Get out of the fucking way!'

A gunshot echoed, a bullet blasted into the roof, and screams of panic turned the narrow stairwell into a tunnel of chaos. The people parted like the Red Sea as Sam's pursuer charged down the steps, and as Sam approached the security barricades, he pushed one hand on the gate and scaled it in one leap.

As he landed, he stumbled, his ribs roaring with pain and threatening to ground him, but he pushed on, found his footing, and raced towards the escalator. Behind him, he heard the station staff call after him, but they quickly ran for cover as another gunshot rang out, and the electronic advertising board near Sam's head exploded as the bullet just missed. Sam raced down the escalator, bounding down the steps as fast as his balance could manage, and as he approached the bottom step and got ready to move, another bullet ripped past him and shattered the tiles on the floor a few feet ahead of him.

He shot a glance up the stairs, seeing the gunman charging down the escalator as the civilians ducked and clung to the sides of the electronic stairwell in terror, and the gun was once again pointed in his direction. Sam rushed forward, dodging another bullet, as he heard the terrifying sound of the train on the platform shutting its doors.

'Fuck,' Sam uttered as he darted under the archway onto the platform, just in time for the train to make its swift departure from the station. A few of the people who had disembarked the train looked at his bloody and beaten state with concern, and Sam glanced up at the screen that clung to the low roof.

Two minutes until the next train.

There was nowhere for him to go.

Sam grimaced as he held his right hand to his left arm, the pain now a deep and thorough numbing. He could hear the commotion echoing from the archway as the gunman raced towards the platform, and Sam took a step to the side and pressed his back to the wall beside the arch. The few commuters on the platform were worriedly stepping further down the platform, and Sam took a few moments to draw in deep breaths.

Calm his heart rate.

Ignore the pain.

Focus.

Fight.

The gunman marched through the archway, gun drawn, but Sam snatched forward with his right hand, twisting the man's wrist and obliterating his grip. The gun hit the concrete floor, and as the man scrambled under Sam's grip to reach for it, Sam swung his boot forward and kicked the weapon. It slid across the stone, over the yellow line, and dropped onto the tracks. The gunman spun violently, and then swung a hammer-like right hook right into Sam's left arm. The pain was an explosion that rocked Sam to his core, and he stumbled back, allowing his attacker to launch forward and shoulder tackle Sam to the ground. Sam hit the concrete hard, his busted ribs sending another wave of agony jack-knifing through his body, and Sam raised his arm over his head as the man rained down with hard punches. With his left arm out of use, Sam's defence was brittle, and a few fists broke through, crashing into his jaw.

Then the man was gone. Sam looked up to see a noble commuter hauling the man back, trying his best to be a good civilian and break-up the fight.

All he got was a vicious right hook to the stomach, and a brutal knee strike to the face.

Sam pushed himself up, sliding his coat from his body to reveal his blood-soaked left arm, and then clenched his right fist. The gunman turned back to him, a cruel smile across his face as he tossed the battered commuter to the wall.

'You're done, Sam,' the man said as he approached.

'No.' Sam stepped forward, too. 'Not yet.'

The man was the first to throw a punch, swinging a hard left that Sam weaved under, and then followed it with a brutal right uppercut to the man's stomach. Sam swivelled, hopped onto his back foot, and lifted the man off the ground with a savage knee strike that shattered the man's nose on impact. The man hit ground, rolled onto his front, and pushed himself up, his bloodied face twisted with hatred as the adrenaline kicked in. Beyond the man, the tunnel burst into a bright white light as the intercom above announced its arrival. With fury spewing from his jaws, the man darted forward again, throwing wild punches that Sam absorbed in his arm blockade, or with gritted teeth as they thundered into his ribs. The man caught Sam with a jab that sent him a few steps back, just as the train burst through the tunnel, the high-pitched shrill of the brakes echoing all around them. The train thundered past, the passengers glued to the window at the fight breaking out on the platform, and the man lunged forward with a right hook. Sam ducked under it, looped his right arm over the wayward punch, and locked it in. Then he swung his body-weight into his attacker, spinning him by the shoulder, and slammed his face against the still moving train. The impact was gut-wrenching, and as the man's face bounced off the carriage, Sam pressed against the back of his head with his elbow, holding it in place.

The passing carriages ripped the man's face to shreds, with the lips of the windows, and the gaps between the carriages, chipping away at the layers of skin and muscle, leaving a long, bloody smear that began to trickle down the train. Sam stepped back as the train stopped, allowing the man's body to slump against the train and slide down, motionless, to the floor. A few commuters who had braved the far end of the platform vomited at the violent act, while those who'd witnessed the brutality from inside the train were too scared to leave.

The emergency alarm had been rung, probably countless times, and Sam looked up the platform as the driver stepped out of the control room and froze in shock.

Another train hurtled into the station on the opposite platform, and Sam turned, leaving his jacket, and began to hobble back through the archway towards his only ticket out of there. As he ran past the escalators once more, another cry of tangible panic erupted, and another gunshot echoed out. The bullet shattered the window of a staff doorway a few feet behind Sam. He turned and looked up at the escalator, where Murray, and another man were bounding down the steps. Sam pushed through the pain as he raced into the archway, as the high-pitched beeps began, signifying that the train was ready to depart.

Sam threw his body forward, launching himself through the closing doors and landing on the floor of the train with a thud, startling those sitting peacefully, oblivious to the carnage that had erupted on the opposite platform. They gasped in shock at the bloodied man as he pushed himself up with one arm, and he turned to back to the door as the train began to move. Murray and his minion arrived, and they made a pointless attempt to run along the platform as the train picked up speed, but quickly, they were gone, and the view of the station was replaced with the complete darkness of a tunnel.

Sam blew out his cheeks and dropped onto his back, staring up at the ceiling as the train zipped through the darkness. A hand reached out, and Sam turned to see an elderly gentleman offering him a kind smile.

'You okay, son?' the man said. He was dressed smartly, something that Sam always found endearing about the older generation. 'You look like you're having a bad day.'

'I've had worse.'

Despite the agonising pain coursing through his body, Sam felt his bloodied face crack into a smile. He reached up with his right hand and took the offer, and with a little help from the kind stranger, he got to his feet. The other passengers looked on with a mixture of fear and interest, and understandably, a parent was shuffling her young kids further down the carriage. Sam held up an apologetic hand to her, but then dropped into the nearest seat he could.

He turned back, and the elderly man offered Sam a packet of tissues, which he gratefully accepted. He managed to pull one out, and then began to wipe the blood from his face and his hands, unsure how much of it was his own.

The only thing he was sure of, was that Wainwright wanted him dead.

The ruse of the task force was to hide their real intentions. Murray had told him as much. The only way he got out of it alive, was if he went with Murray.

But Sam knew there was another way.

A path he'd trodden too many times over the past few years.

A road that was becoming his usual route home.

As he glanced at himself in the reflection of the window, he saw a man who'd been through hell. A man, splattered with blood, who'd been beaten, and chased to the very edge of existence.

But Sam Pope was built to survive.

He glanced up at the Tube line map that was posted above every door of the train, trying his best to collect his bearings and find anywhere safe where he could regroup.

He spotted a station, five from his current stop, and hoped that she'd be home.

But until then, he rocked back in his chair and tried to ignore the pain that had a stranglehold over him.

He needed to be ready if he was going to go down that road again.

He needed to be ready to go to war.

CHAPTER NINETEEN

Murray wasn't used to failure.

Over the years, under his assured leadership, Guardian had become a slick and effective operation, that always delivered. Whether a security detail, an assassination, or even a raid, Murray had always put the right people in the right place to ensure the result. The time where he had to rely on himself to pull the trigger had long since passed, and now, as he stood in the doorway of Jensen's hospital room, he wondered whether, or not his grip over the situation was slipping.

Jensen was his usual volatile self. Murray had found him unconscious, beaten, and battered, and lying dangerously close to an eight-storey plummet. Whatever had transpired between Sam and Jensen in that room, Murray was sure Jensen would embellish, but there was one overriding sense that Murray felt a twinge of guilt about.

Jensen felt a blind fury.

Sam Pope had shown Jensen mercy.

The deep stab wound that had butchered Jensen's thigh was enough to inhibit most men, but Jensen was as tough as they came, and he was already barking at the poor nurses assigned to patch him up and get him out the door. The agony of the injury didn't seem to even register with the man.

No, it was his ego that was truly hurting.

As Jensen snapped once more at a doctor, who was trying to explain the damage done to his quadricep, Murray sighed, and stepped in.

'For fuck's sake, Fabian. Just listen to the man.'

'Oh, here he is,' Jensen said with an eye roll. 'Our great leader. What a fucking shit show.'

'I'll leave you to it,' the doctor said wisely, and Murray smiled as he and the nurse vacated the plush room of the private hospital. As soon as the door closed, Murray's smile dropped, replaced by an ice-cold stare of fury, and he lurched forward, his face a mere inch or two away from Jensen's.

'If you ever try to undermine my operation again, I will feed you your own fucking liver. Do you understand me?' Murray's words came through gritted teeth. 'I don't care how long I've known you. Don't fuck with my operation.'

Jensen smirked, turning his face so the tip of his nose touched Murray's.

'I was just doing what I was fucking told.'

'I told you to contain. Not kill,' Murray snapped. His hand shot out, and he squeezed the butchered thigh and Jensen grunted with pain. 'You went off plan.'

'No, he didn't.'

The calming voice of Admiral Wainwright filled the room, and he followed it in, pushing through the door and letting it slam closed behind him. Murray relinquished his grip, and Jensen breathed through the pain.

He was as tough as they came.

Murray turned, his face twisted in a mix of anger and confusion, and he stormed towards the admiral, towering over the old man. Yet Wainwright showed little fear.

'Spare me the tough guy act,' Wainwright said dryly. 'Today was a monumental disaster, and I want to know what the next move is.'

'I'm sorry, I don't know on account that you seem to know more of what's going on than I do.' Murray folded his meaty arms across his chest, pulling his jacket tight against him. Wainwright, as always, was a picture of calm, and he lowered himself onto one of the leather seats of the private room.

'I trust my friend, Piers, is also receiving medical attention.'

'Who? Bloom?' Jensen said with a snarl. 'You should have heard him beg. The man's a coward.'

'Maybe.' Wainwright said, nonchalantly polishing the lenses of his glasses. 'But he is footing the bill not only for your hospital treatment, young man, but also for the damage you have done today. So maybe, show a little respect.'

Jensen grunted and rocked back on the hospital bed like a petulant child. Murray ignored him, his eyes still locked on the powerful puppet master before him.

'So, you want to tell me why the plans changed?'

'Because I changed them.' Wainwright was as blunt as could be. He put his glasses back on and then looked up at Murray. 'Just remember who is in charge here, young man.'

'We had a deal,' Murray said forcefully. 'Sam to be taken alive and—'

'And that was the best-case scenario.' Wainwright cut him off. 'Yes, we pitched to Sarratt that her bringing in Sam would help her career, but let's be honest, she's dead-weight. Her career doesn't outweigh the situation—'

'Which is?'

Wainwright shifted uncomfortably. Just for a moment, but Murray clocked it.

'There are things, young man, that a man of my position needs to do in the interest of national safety. While you walk in here in your expensive designer suits, and run a very successful operation, you are still just the help.' Wainwright's unblinking stare bore through him. 'I operate on a level that's so far beyond your paygrade, you couldn't reach it with a fifty-foot ladder. So, when I say the plans change, and when I say that Sam Pope needs to be taken out, that's all the justification that's needed. Is that understood?'

The tone made the threat very clear. It wasn't so much a question as it was a declaration of power, and Murray refused to break the stare. Wainwright smiled, gingerly got to his feet, and adjusted his suit jacket. He then stepped towards Murray, who physically towered over him. But in that room, when it came to the balance of power, Murray could feel himself shrinking. The pain medication was starting to wear off, and he could feel his skull throbbing.

Wainwright approached him, lowering both the volume and bass in his voice.

'I said, is that understood?'

Murray drew his lips into a thin line, the frustration pressing against his skin, threatening to burst out.

'Understood, sir.'

'Good lad,' Wainwright said patronisingly. 'Remember, you're being paid handsomely for what should be a straightforward job.'

Wainwright stepped past Murray, who bit his tongue. He could feel his fists clenching as Wainwright approached Jensen, who looked more bored than anything.

'And how are you, young man?' Wainwright said with a warm smile.

'Fucking pissed off and ready for another round,'

Jensen said back. Wainwright looked down at the injured leg and shook his head. He spoke to both of them without looking up.

'He comes with me.' Wainwright turned and started heading towards the door. 'After today's incident, I feel it is time to take myself out of the firing line. I have a few loose ends to tie up and will then be heading to a safehouse. As you can understand, the location will be held on a need-to-know basis. And seeing as how young Jensen here is incapacitated, having him close by as personal protection would be appreciated.'

Murray looked to Jensen, who shrugged.

'Is that okay with you, Fab?' Murray asked, sounding like he was out of ideas.

'It doesn't matter if he is,' Wainwright said, his voice firm. 'Don't forget who is in charge here.'

Murray went to respond, but the door to the private room opened and Commissioner Sarratt barged in, pushing one of Murray's men out of the way as she did. Murray gestured for the man to stand down and leave, before standing silently as the Commissioner of the Met scanned a furious eye over the room. She folded her arms and shook her head.

'When I agreed to the rebirth of the Sam Pope Task Force, I had assurances that it would be done tactfully and professionally. That the results would be swift, and that plans were in place to ensure minimal panic in my city.' Sarratt looked at all three men. 'Now, I don't want to sound unprofessional myself, but what the fuck happened today?'

Murray stepped forward to explain the situation, but Wainwright held up a dismissive hand.

Another show of power.

Murray felt his knuckles whiten as the admiral stepped

in front of the commissioner and fixed her with his forced smile.

'It's all in hand, Commissioner.'

'Is it?' Sarratt spat back. 'Do you know how many calls we had regarding gunshots in my city? We had over ten men hospitalised, as well as one man in a coma, after he went face first into a moving train. All of it playing out in front of a terrified public, who we promised would be kept sa—'

'*You* promised,' Wainwright interrupted.

'Excuse me?' Sarratt's eyes bulged.

'*You* promised.' Wainwright grinned victoriously. 'If I recall, Henrietta, *you* were the one on the television, promising a safe and swift resolution. *You* were the one who handed the reins over to Ashton, and *you* were the one who put her in the firing line. Well, that's what the operation shows.'

Wainwright took a menacing step towards her.

'Now, I have some business to attend to, and then I think it is best I remain out of sight until Sam Pope is put down. You all have your orders. Jensen, I will send a car for you.'

'Yes, sir,' Jensen called from his bed.

Wainwright turned back to Sarratt, who looked like she was holding back a hate-filled fist. Wainwright leant in a little closer to the commissioner and spoke in a sinister whisper.

'Let's not lose sight on who is *really* in charge here.'

It was the same ominous warning he'd fed her before, and with that, Wainwright pulled open the door and exited the room. The doctor once again appeared in the doorway, and Murray beckoned him in now that the tension had deflated. As the doctor strode in with the nurse, a revitalised Jensen was more accommodating to them.

He still had a role to play.

Still had a shot at Sam.

Sarratt stood silent, her mind clearly racing, as she, like Murray, had been made aware that they were nothing more than pawns in a game of chess that somebody else was playing. Murray approached the commissioner, who looked up at him with indifference.

'There's more to this,' Murray insisted. 'Something personal.'

'You're right.' Sarratt nodded.

'This doesn't end with Sam in cuffs. You know that, right?' Murray asked rhetorically. 'That wasn't what I agreed to.'

Sarratt looked up at Murray, slightly confused.

'So what are you going to do?' she finally asked.

'I'm going to find out why the hell Wainwright wants Sam dead. And then I'm going to try to get to him first,' Murray said with a firm nod. 'It's the only chance Sam has of making it out alive.'

'Bloom's in the private room at the end of the corridor,' Sarratt said quietly. 'He's awake.'

Murray got the message and nodded. Just as he went to leave, he turned back to the commissioner, realising they were both heading down blind alleys. Wainwright had put them both front and centre of an operation to kill the most wanted man in UK, while he slunk in the shadows.

Hidden, along with whatever reason had put him on Sam's hit list.

'I'll let you know what I find,' Murray said as he reached for the door handle.

'Same.'

'Same?' Murray raised an eyebrow.

Sarratt motioned for him to open the door for her, which he did, and as she passed through, she looked up at him.

'I might know someone who knows what the hell is going on.'

As she strode down the corridor, she stopped at the elevator, watching as Murray continued his powerful stride towards Bloom's room. The elevator announced its arrival with a ding, and Sarratt entered, hit the ground floor, and willed it to move faster.

She needed to find out what the hell was going on.

She needed to speak to DS Jessica Sutton.

CHAPTER TWENTY

It was hard not to get caught up in the chaos.

DS Sutton had tried to keep her mind clear all day, but Ruth Ashton's assassination, live on television, had shaken her to her core. Gayle had been understanding, but had made a few well-worded comments about how she had a job to do, and so she'd tried to bury herself in the work at hand.

Then the reports began to filter through of the gunfight at Bloom Enterprises.

Then the gunshots on the Underground.

Details flickered through, but rapid response was held back and the official line was that the Sam Pope Task Force was dealing with the situation.

Sutton doubted it.

Someone was trying to frame Sam Pope for the murder of Ruth Ashton, and although her time spent with Sam had been brief, she had enough of a measure on the man to know what was happening.

Sam Pope wasn't taking it lying down.

The press and even the officers within the Met itself had painted a mythical picture of what Sam Pope represented. There were those who leant heavily on the side of the law, convinced he was a violent man who needed to be stopped. There were just as many who understood his motives and even championed the idea of a rogue vigilante cleaning up the streets without mercy. To all of them, Sam Pope was a walking weapon, capable of anything.

But Sutton knew firsthand the type of man Sam was.

When she'd been abducted by the treacherous Chief Inspector Dummett, and handed over to Dominik Silva, Sam had laid siege to their hideout and pulled her out alive.

Her captors had not been so lucky.

To her, Sam Pope was more than just a symbol of justice or a beacon of violence.

He was a hero.

By mid-afternoon, Sutton had fished out Lynsey Beckett's card and sent her a message with her address in it. They needed to speak somewhere secluded, and Sutton would rather be on home turf until she knew she could trust the woman.

So when she turned out onto her street, a ten-minute walk from Finsbury Park station, she wasn't surprised to see the brash reporter leaning against the wall that surrounded her block of flats, braving the elements as she smoked her cigarette. As Sutton approached, her white plastic bag swinging in her hand, Beckett saw her, stubbed out the cigarette, and then pushed herself off the wall.

'Detective,' Lynsey said with a warm smile, her face soaked by the rain.

'Please.' Sutton held up her free hand. 'Jess. You must be soaked.'

'Meh. English weather, eh? Just the same as back home.'

Sutton felt a smile creep across her face. She motioned for the reporter to follow her, and they headed into the building, shaking off the rain as they made their way up the stairs to her flat. Sutton unlocked the three locks she had on her door, drawing a raised eyebrow from Lynsey.

'I have my reasons.'

That was all Sutton was willing to divulge. It wasn't Lynsey Beckett's business to know that people working within the Met had sent armed men to silence her a few months ago.

Or that it was Sam who stopped them.

Once they were in the apartment, Sutton flicked on the lights, and then headed to the island in her kitchen, plonking the carrier bag down on the worktop. It made a familiar clonk.

'I'll have a glass if there's one going,' Lynsey said with a grin, and a few moments later, Sutton handed her a glass of wine and then took a sip of her own.

'So…what do you want to talk about?' Sutton said dryly.

'Oh, come on now,' Lynsey replied with a chuckle. 'We both know all the bullshit today wasn't Sam. Well, the killing of Ashton certainly wasn't. The rest…it sort of has his fingerprints all over it.'

'But why are you here?' Sutton fixed her with a stare. Lynsey had a hell of a poker face.

'Because despite the *official line* from your organisation, something tells me a hell of a lot went on at the back end of last year. Dead police officers. Missing gold. Burning warehouses. Gatwick shut down. Ring any bells?' The question was rhetorical, and Sutton treated it as such. 'You rattled a cage, Jess. I know, because a few years ago, I rattled one, too.'

Sutton pushed open the small window in the kitchen and lit herself a cigarette. She offered one to Lynsey, who gratefully accepted.

'What happened?' Sutton asked, trying her best to push the smoke through the gap.

'I dug too deep into a company who set some people on me. They beat the holy shit out of my fiancé. He's still recovering to this day.' Lynsey shook her head as she recalled the memory. 'Turns out, he's a friend of Sam's, who, let's just say, wasn't happy with what they did. That's the thing, right? If something needs to be set right, then Sam will do his best to do it. So what actually happened?'

Sutton had heard enough. Her new role in the DPS had elevated her ability to read people.

To detect sincerity.

Lynsey wasn't here for an ulterior motive.

She was trying to help Sam.

For the next few minutes, as the two women finished both their cigarettes and glasses of wine, which were swiftly topped up, Sutton relayed the events of the past December. Lynsey listened intently, and Sutton found herself shaking as she spoke of her abduction and how close she came to death.

The two women could relate to each other.

As she brought her story to a close, she made reference to the list that Sam had given her.

'I heard about that,' Lynsey said before taking a sip. 'Apparently, it was sent up the flagpole and—'

'And that was it. My boss was the one who took it to them. He wasn't thrilled about it, but we never heard anything back.'

'Shocking,' Lynsey said dryly.

'Sam said it would bring down a lot of people who weren't used to being challenged.'

'Why didn't he just use the list himself, then?'

Sutton smirked.

'Because he said it would mean more to the country if

the police were the ones who brought these people down. It would inspire belief in the system again.'

The two of them smiled.

'Fucking boy scout.' Lynsey joked. 'You think that's what this is about?'

'Maybe.' Sutton nodded. 'At least, it would make sense. Powerful people have a lot of sway, and just a few days ago…what's his name?'

'Hartson,' Lynsey said firmly. 'I covered that story. Guess what happened?'

The two women sighed. Seemingly, they were colliding with the same brick wall, just from different angles. Sutton flicked open her phone and navigated to the food app. Just as she was about to recommend a wonderful Thai delivery, there was a knock at the door. Instantly, her guard went up, and her head snapped towards Lynsey.

'Who did you tell about this?' Sutton said accusingly as she stepped towards the door.

'Nobody. I swear.'

Tentatively, Sutton peered through the peephole and then frowned. She pulled open the door.

'Ma'am.'

'Please. Not off duty,' Commissioner Sarratt said with a smile.

'Please, come in.'

Sutton stepped aside, and the rain-soaked commissioner stepped into the flat, taken aback at Lynsey's presence.

'Sorry, I didn't realise you had company.' Sarratt then turned back to Lynsey, a confused look across her face. 'You're from the BBC, aren't you? Beckett, isn't it?'

'Lynsey, Ma'am.'

'Please. Henrietta will do.'

'Yeah, I'm not calling you that,' Sutton said as she closed the door. She walked past the senior officer and joined Lynsey, and for a few tense moments, it felt like they were two naughty schoolgirls in front of the headteacher. Sarratt, realising her intrusion, offered a smile.

'Well, this is fun.' She nodded to the bottle of wine. 'Why don't you pour me a glass and get me up to speed?'

'Excuse me, Ma'am?' Sutton asked, surprised.

'Well, I assume we're all trying to connect the same dots, right?' Sarratt smiled. Lynsey joined her. 'Trust me, you don't get to my position by failing to read a room.'

Sutton obliged, poured out another glass, and then she and Lynsey ran Sarratt through everything. Lynsey recounted her issues with Bowker from a few years back, and how she'd aided Sam on a few occasions since. Sutton finally relayed what actually happened before Christmas, and how Sam had saved her life. The issue of the list came up, and Sarratt finally contributed.

'I never saw that,' she said firmly. 'Who did Gayle pass it on to?'

'I don't know. I can try to find out for you—'

'Was Wainwright on it?' Sarratt asked curtly.

'Wainwright? Admiral Wainwright?' Lynsey asked, her finely shaped eyebrows raised.

Sarratt then took her turn to explain the situation from her side, and how Admiral Wainwright had made it a personal mission to bring down Sam. How Bloom was funding the entire operation. How they were willing to tear a hole through her city to bring him down.

None of them had conclusive evidence.

But all three of them silently acknowledged that there was a damn good chance that Wainwright's name was on the list.

As Sutton opened another bottle and returned to the sofa, she poured out another three glasses. Sarratt, sitting opposite, thanked her as she took hers. Lynsey was deep in thought.

'So, just speculating here, if Wainwright's name is on the list, then we need to know what the hell the list was about.' She turned to Sutton. 'You didn't look at it?'

'Nope. Sam said it would be safer.'

'And he was clearly right,' Sarratt said with a sigh. She noticed Sutton look at her cigarettes and then waved her approval. 'It's your house, my dear.'

'We need to know what that list was about,' Lynsey said, her journalistic brain racing ahead. 'If we think Bloom was on the list, maybe he's worth speaking to?'

'No chance,' Sarratt said with a shake of the head. 'He's got people watching him.'

'What about the other gentlemen who were at Bakku that night?' Lynsey turned to Sutton. 'You said you were investigating that incident? Who was it? Simon Grant, right?'

'He's fled the country,' Sutton said. 'Hutchins, too.'

'Shockingly, rich people don't like having a gun shoved in their face and being forced to admit their crimes,' Sarratt said drily, taking a sip from her glass. 'The only person who knows what that list was about, and why Wainwright wants it buried, is Sam Pope. Now, I don't want to know how or why, but if you have had dealings with him, Lynsey then—'

'He contacts me.' Lynsey shrugged. 'Usually just walks up to the front fucking door of the BBC.'

All three of them laughed.

'Well, unless Sam Pope drops into our lap and tells us what the hell is going on, we need to start doing some real detective work,' Sarratt said with a smile. 'Let's order some food and get to work.'

Sutton nodded and whipped her phone off the table to place the order. Sarratt had kindly offered to pay, and the decision for pizza had been made already. She placed the order while Lynsey went to the kitchen for a cigarette, and Sarratt called her husband to inform him of her lateness.

Knock. Knock.

All three of them looked to the door.

'Blimey. That was quick,' Lynsey said, her hand hanging out of the kitchen window.

Sutton looked to Sarratt, who nodded for her to answer it. The commissioner followed, her stance indicating she was prepared for a potential fight, and Sutton put her eye up to the peephole.

She gasped.

She threw open the door, and Sam Pope stumbled in, almost collapsing onto her. She steadied him under his immense frame, and Sarratt quickly jumped in to assist. He was soaked through; his face was stained with blood. As Sarratt lodged herself under one of his arms, he groaned with pain, his ribs battered from the death-defying leap from Bloom's building.

His entire left arm was limp, soaked with blood.

They helped him to the sofa, and he dropped down, clinging to the final strands of his consciousness.

Sarratt rushed to the kitchen for a glass of water, while Sutton rummaged for her medical kit.

The three of them shared exasperated looks with each other.

They'd said they'd needed Sam's help.

Yet here he was, collapsed on Sutton's sofa, very much in need of theirs.

CHAPTER TWENTY-ONE

FIFTEEN YEARS AGO...

'I'm telling you right now. Marriage is the best thing that ever happened to me.'

The claim drew jeers from the rest of the tent, and Corporal James Murray just shrugged them off and looked down at his hand of cards. Despite the searing heat that had engulfed the Afghanistan landscape, the small air conditioning unit they were using as a makeshift table was offering a little respite. Beside him, Theo Walker shook his head, the young medic still loving his life as a handsome bachelor and clearly in disagreement with the previous statement. Opposite him, sitting behind a pile of cash that he'd already won, Corporal Paul Etheridge snickered, offering a few dry comments about his second marriage being just as shit as his first. Private Lawrence Griffin looked on oblivious, seemingly too inexperience, or disinterested for a discussion about marriage. But to his right, Sam Pope sat, cards held in his powerful arms, and he smiled bashfully.

'Well, we'll see,' Sam finally offered, and Theo threw a bottle cap at him.

'Don't do it, Sam.' He jokingly pleaded. 'I need my wing man.'

'Oh come on,' Etheridge pitched in. 'You don't need a wing man, Theo. You've got more game than all of us combined.'

'And no strings, baby!' Theo said with a pearly white grin.

Murray waved Theo off and then folded his hand.

'Look, all I'm saying, mate, is that marrying Becky was the best thing to happen to me. Not because of all the lovey dovey bullshit, but because now I have a reason to fight. To make sure I get my arse back on that plane and get home to her.'

'Like Sam needs a reason to fight.' Theo chuckled.

'I can speak for myself, Theo,' Sam said with a grin. 'I don't know. This just feels different. Theo, you've met Lucy. She's incredible, right?'

'Oh, way out of your league, mate,' Theo said, and then sipped his lukewarm bottle of beer. One of many they'd all enjoyed.

'Exactly,' Sam agreed. 'Wait…hang on…'

All five of the men broke out into laughter, and none of them noticed Sergeant Carl Marsden emerge through the flap of the tent. The wise leader of the platoon had a frown on his face, and stood with his hands on his hips.

'Something funny, chaps?'

All five of them spun to their commanding officer, and the laughter quietened.

'No, sir,' Murray said with a smile. 'We're just giving Sam some sage relationship advice.'

Marsden nodded and looked at Sam.

'I see. Well, don't take any from Etheridge. What wife are you on now, Corporal?'

'Very funny, sir,' Etheridge said, as he placed some more money into the middle of the game. 'It's just that our Sam here is head over heels in love and doesn't know whether or not to pop the question.'

'Is that so?' Marsden raised his eyebrows. 'Well, take it from someone a little longer in the tooth. This world is a shitty place, son. If you find something good in it, hold onto it with both hands like your life depended on it. Otherwise, what the hell are we fighting for?'

The five men all took a moment, absorbing their leader's words.

'Very romantic, sir,' Theo finally said. 'You should have your own line of Valentine's Day cards.'

The group laughed again, sipping their beers, and Marsden walked over, and pulled up a crate and sat down beside them, helping himself to a beer.

'I'll have a special line for you, Theo. Happy Valentine's Day – here's your STD.'

The others laughed, and Theo shook his head in defeat, taking the light-hearted barb on the chin like a champ. Despite the constant danger they called their job, the six men had become a tight-knit unit, and although Sam and Theo's friendship preceded Project Hailstorm, Sam considered all the men around the table his friend.

As did Murray, who with his large frame and bullish manner, had taken on the role as second in command.

'I'll tell you what, mate. You put a ring on Lucy's finger, and she puts one on yours, every time you pull that scope up to your eye, you'll see it. And it'll remind you what you need to get back for.'

Murray's words hit Sam hard, and he knew, despite the inevitable banter, that his mates supported him. He was going to get back to the UK, and he was going to propose to Lucy. Build a home and a life that he'd always thought was out of reach. As a military kid, he was shifted from place to place, country to country, station to station. His mother had left them when he was young, seemingly burnt out from the chop and change that his father's job dictated.

His father had passed away when he was seventeen.

Sam had always felt alone, but now, in this tent, surrounded by good men who shared his bravery and his values, he finally had a family.

'Here, deal me in this time, Murray,' Marsden said, swigging his beer. 'And be nice to Sam. He needs to be in a good mood to write all that lovely poetry in his journal.'

The whole crew cracked up again, and Sam mockingly gestured for them all to bring it on. He took a sip of his own beer, grimaced at its temperature, and then looked at the mocking group.

'Well, considering without me you'd all be dead, you should be begging to hear my poetry.'

'Touché,' Murray responded.

It was true.

Somewhere along the way, Sam had kept them all alive. When the job had put them in a position of no return, Sam had found them a way.

Death from above.

That was what the terrifying General Wallace had labelled him, and Murray knew that there wasn't a man alive more ruthlessly dangerous than Sam Pope. Hearing that his friend might have found a path to a happier life meant he was going to try to guide him down it.

Otherwise, what was Sam truly fighting for anymore?

Just as Murray finished shuffling the deck of cards, and Etheridge scooped up more winnings, the flap of the tent flew open, and the detestable Trevor Sims poked his head through and summoned Marsden. Their sergeant sighed, finished his drink, and excused himself, and Murray went back to dealing.

'Just for the record…' Theo said. 'You haven't had to save my life, Sam.'

'That's because you're a medic, Theo,' Sam said with a grin. 'You never put yourself in harm's way.'

Merriment echoed from the tent once more, and Murray knew, as he dealt out the hand, that despite the bloodshed, and the inescapable dangers of the war they were fighting, he was smack-dab in the middle of the good old days.

Fighting the good fight, with the best of people.

It had been a long time since Murray had thought about *the good old days*. Ever since he'd left the military to launch Guardian, Becky had rightfully made him push that part of his life to the back of his mind. He was a family man now. A husband. A father. A successful businessman. The adrenaline of running into battle, weapon drawn, not knowing if he'd be walking back out, was no longer needed to fulfil him.

He had everything he wanted.

Everything he needed.

But now, as he sat in the Sam Pope Task Force office in New Scotland Yard, he couldn't help but let his mind wander.

It had been years since he'd seen Sam and although he knew the moment was inevitable, seeing a man he'd fought alongside had brought up memories of what felt like a different life entirely.

Camo replaced with expensive suits.

Weapons replaced with money.

Maybe it was the thumping headache Sam had given him, or maybe it was the fact he was now taking orders from Wainwright, but Murray felt like his brain had been scrambled. Control was the one thing he exuded, and running the operations had seen him turn Guardian into an extremely profitable and well-regarded business.

Now, they were just hired guns for Wainwright.

As he blew out his cheeks, Murray scanned through the CCTV footage from Bloom's offices, watching as the man he once called a friend systematically took his team apart. The difference in competence between Sam and Murray's team was stark, and watching the fight unfold made Murray shift uncomfortably in his seat. Years ago, Sam had a reason to fight.

His family.

With that a distant memory, Murray watched as Sam fought ferociously to get away.

What was he fighting for now?

Something sat uncomfortably in his gut, and Murray knew that Wainwright's reasons were bullshit.

Sam knew something.

Wainwright wanted him dead.

As if the man could read Murray's thoughts, the door to the office burst open, and in walked Wainwright, who waved off Murray's limp attempts to stand out of respect. Wainwright walked past the desk and to the floor to ceiling window of the room, gazing out into the gloomy night sky that hung over the city. The city skyline was illuminated against the rain, and the glass pane was blurred from the droplets cascading down it.

'Forgive me, sir, but I thought you were going dark,' Murray said. Wainwright didn't turn to respond.

'Like I said, I had a few things to attend to. My car is downstairs.' Wainwright sighed as he looked out over the gloomy view. 'I trust my taking Jensen as security is agreeable?'

'Whatever you say,' Murray said dryly. 'A one-legged Jensen is still more dangerous than most men in this building.'

Wainwright kept his eyes forward, a clear show of power, and Murray rolled his own and returned to the laptop before him.

'You feel betrayed, don't you, James?' Wainwright finally said. He wasn't inviting a conversation. 'I can appreciate that, but I don't think you quite understand how much is at stake here.'

'Well, why don't you enlighten me?' Murray said, sitting back in his chair. Wainwright turned, his arms clasped to the base of his spine, and his immaculate suit displaying his medals.

'Do you know what true responsibility is, James? I know you believe the men who work for you are your responsibility. I know you are a father. How are Jasper and Oliver by the way?' Wainwright sneered, and he saw Murray's fist clench in response to the thinly veiled threat. 'See, there is responsibility on a human level, and then there is responsibility on a global level. I make decisions and plans that affect not just the safety of this nation, but the delicate balance that exists between others. *That* is a responsibility I take very seriously. Now, along the way, there are decisions that are… let's say, not what one would deem honourable. Legal, if you will. But those are the decisions that I have to make, and if they get pulled apart, then this country, the place that you can provide a safe home for your boys, it all falls down.'

Murray held Wainwright's stare. Whatever respect that existed between the two men had all but diminished.

'What the fuck does that have to do with Sam?'

'Sam is a threat. Plain and simple. He may have access to information that would undermine my position, and if my position becomes untenable, then so does that of hundreds of good men and women across this planet.' Wainwright took a step towards Murray. 'You know how it works, James. We have a multitude of covert cells across the world, and if I get compromised, it won't take long for them to be found out. Soldiers, James. Just like you. Just like me.'

'And like Sam,' Murray said firmly. Wainwright's lip twitched in a sneer.

'Sam gave up his position as a soldier when he fought against his country. And that's what he is doing.' Wainwright straightened his tie. 'By going against me, he has turned his back on his flag, and I will not let a rogue such as Sam, a man with a saviour complex, breakdown the hard work I've done, and threaten the lives of so many under my wing. Now, whatever hang-up you have. Whatever connection you think you still have to the man, I need you to get over it. Do you understand? You work for *me* now?'

Murray slowly stood, his eyes locked on Wainwright,

and as he walked towards the admiral, he made himself as big as possible.

'I was hired by the Metropolitan Police.'

'And they *also* work for me,' Wainwright said with a cruel grin. 'Sarratt is so far in my pocket, I've set her up a sleeping bag and pillow in there. If it's money, then consider it doubled. All I ask is that you bring this to an end swiftly and completely. Do the right thing, son.'

Wainwright stepped aside, heading back towards the door and to hide away in his cowardice. Murray felt sick to his stomach and wanted nothing more than to put the admiral down himself.

Just as Wainwright pulled open the door, Murray called out to him, determined to have the last word.

'And if I don't?' he asked defiantly. Wainwright stopped, turned, and smiled.

A cold, calculated smile of a man who had won.

'If you do the wrong thing, James. Then you will go the same way as Sam Pope.' Wainwright's smile dropped. His eyes seemed to darken. 'And so will your children.'

The threat hit Murray like a hammer, and Wainwright disappeared through the doorway to be whisked off to an unknown location. Left alone in the office, Murray dropped back into his seat and ran an anxious hand through his greying hair.

The stakes had been raised.

He now *needed* to put Sam Pope in the ground.

The lives of his children depended on it.

CHAPTER TWENTY-TWO

Sam took a deep breath, as he questioned for the first time in years his decision to quit drinking. Lynsey didn't have the stomach to watch, and she'd retreated to the kitchen, the powerful stench of her cigarette wafted through the flat. Sutton sat opposite Sam, her face twitching with concern.

'You sure you don't want a drink?' she asked hopefully.

'No, thanks.'

'This is going to hurt like hell,' Sutton said, turning to Sarratt, who was sitting next to Sam. In her hands, she was threading the needle.

'You're a big boy,' Sarratt said as she drew the needle up. Sam chuckled. 'You ready?'

'Nope,' Sam said, and then gritted his teeth.

Thankfully for Sam, the bullet hadn't penetrated his arm, but it had ripped through the skin when it grazed him. The tear was pretty severe, and the blood loss had caused him to collapse for a few moments and Sarratt had taken control of the situation. They'd bandaged up the wound, pumped him with a sugary drink and paracetamol, and now, an hour after he'd arrived, Sam was sitting beside her, his T-shirt removed, and his muscular body covered in blood. His ribs were already heavily bruised, and all three women had shared shocked expressions when they laid their eyes on his naked torso. The patchwork of scars that covered him was a testament to how much Sam had been through, and as Sarratt lifted the needle to Sam's decimated triceps, she knew this would be just another one for the collection.

'Here we go,' she said, and then plunged the needle into the torn skin of the wound. Sam jolted, grunted, and gripped the sofa cushion with his other hand, but he didn't move away. Sarratt breathed slowly, keeping her eyes on the task at hand, and moved swiftly as she did her best to pull the wound together. Four minutes of excruciating pain later, Sam pulled away from Sarratt as she snipped the end of the thread.

'Thank you,' he said gingerly, slowly rolling his left shoulder to try to push some life back into his arm.

'Hold on,' Sutton said, and scampered off to her bedroom, before returning with a fresh, black T-shirt. 'Connor lent me this shirt a few months back. It should fit.'

'Thanks,' Sam said, peeling the rest of the blood-soaked T-shirt off his battered body. The fresh shirt was a tight fight, but it would have to do. 'How's he doing, anyway?'

'He's getting there.' Sutton smiled warmly. She was instantly transported back to that frenzied drive to the hospital, with her hands pressed down on the blood that was pumping from his stomach. It then shifted to the attempt on her life by Silva, and once again, it was Sam who had come to her rescue. 'He's a fighter.'

'Good to hear. Send him my best.' Sam grimaced slightly in pain and then turned to Sarratt. 'So what now? Are you going to arrest me?'

The commissioner looked up at Sam. Despite

attending to his wounds, the thought of calling for back-up when he'd first collapsed had crossed her mind. Her city was being torn apart in a quest to bring that man in, a mission she'd pinned her name and reputation on to. She would have been a made woman had she delivered Sam Pope, gift wrapped and unconscious, to Wainwright and Guardian.

But something had stopped her.

Something she hoped that Sam would be able to provide.

The truth.

As Sutton and Beckett turned and awaited her answer, Sarratt stood, and clasped her hands together.

'Probably not. Not right now at least.' She fixed Sam with one of her unwavering glares. 'But I will give you five minutes to explain to me why the Chief of Defence Staff is tearing up my city to find you. Or a five-minute head start. Your choice.'

The tension in the room rose instantly, and Sutton gave a worried glance to Sam, who drew his lips together as he contemplated his options. After a few moments, he turned and walked through to the open-plan kitchen, around the island, and clicked on the kettle. Lynsey raised an eyebrow and turned back to the two police officers, who seemed just as confused by his calm behaviour. Sam turned back to Sarratt and smiled.

'I need a cup of tea. Then, you might want to get yourself a drink. Because you won't believe what's going on.'

With their interests piqued, Sarratt and Sutton poured out another glass of wine each. Lynsey had made a shift to bottles of beer, and she popped open a fresh one as Sam ambled around the kitchen, making himself a cup of tea before he joined them once again in the living room. Sutton couldn't help but savour the surrealness of the evening.

She was sitting in her living room with the Commissioner of the Met, one of the country's leading political reporters, and the most wanted man in the country's history.

Connor would never believe her when she told him.

Sam took a long, thoughtful sip of his tea and then set the cup down and then carefully rested his damaged arm on a cushion.

'We need to go back a few years…'

And he did. Sam went back all the way to the first iteration of the Sam Pope Task Force, and he was surprised to hear that Sutton had been part of it. He ran through the catalogue of events that had led him to the office of Michael Stout, where he and Singh were presented with the opportunity to join a shady government outfit.

Singh jumped at the chance.

Sam declined.

'Ah. So that's where she went?' Sarratt said with surprise.

'I couldn't possibly comment.' Sam joked. He then spoke about the events surrounding Sean Wiseman, Lynsey's fiancé, and how he'd tried with all his might not to return to a life of violence. But he saw how necessary he was. As he recounted the steps that led him to Olivier Chavet, and a collision course with Pierre Ducard, which ultimately cost Sarratt's predecessor his job. Sam reintroduced Singh to the story. She'd accosted him, along with her boss, in the home of his friend Renée Corbin and presented him with an impossible task.

To infiltrate an underground fighting tournament in Hungary.

Boytsovskaya Yama.

Despite Sarratt pushing for details on Singh and the outfit she'd joined, there were none forthcoming, and Sam continued with his journey through Sremska Mitrovica

Prison in Serbia and the horrors that awaited him upon arrival. All of it to get to the tournament.

To *Boytsovskaya Yama*.

To Vladimir Balikov.

Poslednyaya Nadezhda, or as was explained to Sam, *The Final Hope*, was the single biggest terrorist act ever to be attempted. Through a series of different channels, many from the UK themselves, Balikov was planning on obliterating Europe and rebuilding it in his image. The Russian oligarch, who held considerable sway and an unfathomable wealth, had promised those in power seats at his table. The very fabric of modern society was on the chopping block, and the only way to Balikov was through the tournament.

Sarratt couldn't believe it, but as Sam continued and spoke of their successful mission, her ears pricked up when he spoke about the list.

'The list you gave to Sutton?' Sarratt interrupted, and all eyes fell on the young DS.

'Yes,' Sam said with a calm nod. 'There were names on there, like Bloom and Hartson, who I knew had too much sway for you to ever put them in cuffs. But the majority of them...I figured it would restore more faith if the boys in blue brought them to justice.'

'Very noble,' Sarratt said, slightly irked. 'And you think we need that, do you?'

Sam could sense that Sarratt was offended, and he held up his right hand in surrender.

'I wish I didn't,' Sam said with sincerity. 'Trust me, I wish I wasn't a necessity. But the fact of the matter is, these people, these power hungry, untouchable people, will never see a day in court. You and I both know that.'

'He's right,' Lynsey said, and shrugged. 'Look at Jasper Munroe.'

The reminder of Sam's altercation with the powerful Munroes seemed to draw a further scowl from Sarratt, who had spent her first few months in her dream job trying to clean up that mess. Eventually, Sarratt downed the last of her wine and then shocked both Sutton and Lynsey by reaching for a cigarette and lighting it. She let out an audible groan of exhaustion as she took her first pull and rocked back in her chair with her eyes closed.

'You okay, Ma'am?' Sutton eventually asked.

'No,' Sarratt snapped. 'I'm tired. I'm pissed off. I've got Admiral Wainwright draping a noose around my neck and I'm sitting here with the one person who could get it removed.'

'Then arrest me,' Sam said. Sarratt sat up and looked at Sam with confusion. The other two women did, too. 'If you honestly believe, the best thing to do is to put me in cuffs and march me to his doorstep, then do it. I won't fight you.'

'Sam…' Lynsey began, her despair clear.

'I mean it. This isn't your mess, Commissioner. I know that. And if it makes it easier, and it gets things moving the way you want them to, then do what you have to do.'

Sam held Sarratt's stare, unwavering in the conviction of his words. Sarratt took a long, thoughtful pull on her cigarette and then stubbed it out on the inside of Lynsey's empty beer bottle and dropped it inside.

'Is Wainwright on the list?' she eventually spoke.

'I didn't see his name, Sam admitted. 'But he did order the hit on Ashton. That woman was sacrificed to put more heat on me, and I'd say the reason for doing that was to get to me before I got to him.'

'And if you did get to him?' Sarratt asked cautiously. 'What then?'

'Then I end it,' Sam said bluntly. 'He either goes to jail or he goes in the ground.'

A chill spread through the room, and Lynsey shuffled

uncomfortably at the response. Sarratt ran her tongue against the inside of her bottom lip.

Her husband's words echoed through her head.

'Sometimes, you need to do what is sensible as opposed to what is right.'

Not this time, Jordan.

Sarratt rubbed her temples and then stood.

'If we do this, we need to act fast.' Sarratt spoke with the authority that her role demanded. 'I can do my level best to push back what happened today, but there's only so much I can do. You put a lot of people in the hospital, Sam. Whether they deserved it or not, I can't really make exceptions right now. Wainwright would smell it a mile off—'

'Understood.'

'And also, Wainwright has now gone into hiding.'

'I guess you really shit him up, huh?' Lynsey joked, drawing a smile from Sam. Sarratt continued.

'Ideally, we need this to be resolved with minimal damage.'

Sam looked up at Sarratt, admiring the authority she commanded and the integrity in her position.

McEwen was right about her.

'Best-case scenario, we get Wainwright to confess,' Sam said. 'Like I said before, it would mean more to the people if they saw you bringing someone like him down. Give them a reason to believe in the badge again.'

Sam's words seemed to invoke pride in both Sarratt and Sutton, who shared a glance. Sarratt took one last deep breath, knowing she'd long since passed the point of no return.

The only question now was which direction of the abyss was she running into.

'I can probably give you a day. Tops,' she said firmly.

Sam stood, grunting with agony as his body, once again, screamed out for him to stop.

He wouldn't listen.

'I have an idea,' Sam said with a calm sense of dread. 'I need some guns, I need a location, and then I need you to stay out of my way.'

Sarratt stepped closer, a little annoyed by the challenge, and she stared at Sam, trying her level best to find something about him that she could call a criminal.

'And what if you can't get it done?' she asked.

All eyes fell on Sam, who nodded with acceptance.

'Then I'm as a good as dead.'

CHAPTER TWENTY-THREE

The view from the safe house balcony was a welcome one, and Admiral Wainwright shuffled through the bifold doors and out onto the tiles. The awning above shielded him from the rain, and ensured he wouldn't slip, and he stepped out into the bitter chill of the morning and took a deep breath.

The air felt fresher this far from London.

He had been widowed for over eight years now, losing his wife in a battle with breast cancer after thirty years of marriage. It was why he'd rejected the notion of retirement and was more than willing to step into Ervin Wallace's shoes when he met his untimely demise.

The stunning safe house was a six-bedroom mansion, with high walls, electronic gates, and enough CCTV to fill the Pentagon. It was furnished with the latest mod-cons, and Wainwright felt a sense of self-satisfaction knowing that it was all paid for by the taxpayers of the country he protected.

Just a little *thank you* gift for all his hard work.

Beyond the walls were miles of woodlands, and beyond those, the stunning village of Tilgate.

With its expansive woodlands, stunning lake, and tourist attractions, the little village was a tourist magnet and was less than a mile away from the West Sussex town of Crawley. While Murray was back in London working on delivering his end of the contract, Wainwright was cursing the thought of not being able to experience the beautiful village and its splendour.

He was on lockdown until it was over.

As he gazed out across the trees, he could see the downpour clattering across the Tilgate Lake, and he wondered how long it would be until he received the word of Sam Pope's death. Of course, there would be mayhem in the aftermath, as they would need to build the narrative around why Sam wasn't brought into custody and given a fair trial. Ashton, who was now but a footnote in Wainwright's clean up act, had tried that once before.

But Pope had shown that not even the most secure prison could hold him.

And until Murray called with the news that he'd personally put a bullet through Sam Pope's skull, Wainwright was on high alert.

Fifteen men had been drafted in, eight from Guardian and the rest from assorted private security groups the government called upon to clean things up covertly.

Men who were trained to kill.

All of them armed and positioned strategically throughout the grounds, switching every few hours to take their fair share of the elements. Roughly a half a kilometre away among the trees was an outpost, which connected to the mansion itself through a dimly lit underground tunnel. There, Jensen was posted up, with enough supplies to last him a week, and a sniper rifle he had locked on the premises.

Wainwright wasn't taking any precautions.

He lit his cigar and took a victorious puff, and sipped

the freshly made coffee from his mug. After a few puffs, he dropped the cigar into a puddle on the balcony for the housekeepers to clear away, and then returned to the study. His laptop was open on his calendar, and he sneered at the sheer number of calls he was expected to join.

The only one he cared about was his meeting with the Deputy Commissioner of the Metropolitan Police and the Minister of State. Although the minister was supposed to be in charge of police, crime, and fire, Wainwright knew that the feeble little pissant would roll over and agree to anything.

Especially his request to remove Henrietta Sarratt from her position as commissioner.

They would agree, then the ball would roll, but Wainwright had already discussed with Jensen about making Sarratt's removal from the equation a little more permanent. Without even a flicker of doubt, Jensen agreed, and joked about adding her name to his list.

That's what Wainwright wanted.

Obedience.

Clean, clinical obedience.

The jingle of an incoming call erupted from his laptop, and Wainwright's thick, grey brow furrowed as he lowered himself into his seat, his body creaking with age. He put on his glasses, saw Murray's name on the screen, and accepted the call.

'I trust you're calling to inform me of Sam's death,' Wainwright said curtly. Murray sighed. He looked like hell, and Wainwright could see the visible dark bags under the man's eyes. He'd clearly been working through the night, and it just made his own comfortable night's sleep feel even more satisfying.

'Not exactly…' Murray began. Wainwright peered over his glasses like a disciplinarian father.

'Then I see no point in continuing this call.' Wainwright leant forward to hit the exit button.

'We retrieved Sam's coat from the Underground station, and it had his wallet in it.' Murray spoke with as little emotion as possible. 'His assumed identity, Ben Carter, is now being run through the necessary systems by my tech guy. We'll have access to his banks, his payments, his movements. We're also cross checking his account with any other accounts to see of any rental payments. Hopefully, we get a hit and can trace his home address.'

'You really think he ran home?' Wainwright scoffed. 'Sam Pope is a violent, psychotic criminal, son. But he's not an idiot.'

'We're just covering our bases, sir,' Murray spat. 'For all we know, judging from the blood we found on his jacket, he could have bled out in a ditch somewhere. Or maybe he's had enough and just fled.'

'Well, we both know that's not likely. That man's sense of justice won't allow him to.'

'Justice for what, sir?' Murray asked. Wainwright glared into the camera.

'This is no longer about justice, Murray. Are we clear?' Wainwright leant forward; his wrinkled face contorted into a vile sneer. 'I want Sam Pope dead. Understood?'

He could see Murray take a long, calming breath. Eventually, Murray slowly nodded, and then hung up the call. Wainwright slammed the laptop shut and then scolded Murray's name for ruining his morning.

The man had one last chance to prove himself of any use to him.

Otherwise, as previously discussed, Wainwright would hand Guardian over to Jensen.

And Murray, along with his family, would go the same way as Henrietta Sarratt.

The same way as Sam Pope.

Six feet under, at his request.

Somehow, Sam had managed to sleep.

Despite Sutton's protests that he should have her bed for the night, he'd defiantly stayed on the sofa. It was comfortable enough, and once Sarratt and Lynsey had left, she'd fetched him a spare blanket and pillow, but it was the numbing ache through his body that should have kept him awake all night. But the exhaustion of his race through London had caught up with him, and for a few hours, Sam had been dead to the world. Now, as he blinked himself awake, he could hear the sound of roadworks in the distance, fighting to be heard against the relentless downpour that shook the windows of Sutton's apartment.

With a grunt, he pushed himself up, allowing the blanket to fall from his naked torso, and he glanced down at his ribcage. The entire left side of his body was painted a nasty purple colour, and along with the lack of movement in his left arm, it meant he was effectively operating at half capacity.

But he had to keep going.

The night before, as Sam began to formulate his plan, he remembered leaving his coat behind, thus compromising his assumed identity.

Murray was a smart man, and no doubt had people watching his rented flat.

There was no way back from this now.

The only way Sam could walk away from this was by taking Wainwright down.

And those odds were stacked so highly against him, he wouldn't be able to see past them with a ladder.

'Coffee?'

Sutton's voice echoed behind Sam, and he turned

gingerly to face her. She was dressed for work already, her short, dark hair still wet from her shower, and she was shuffling around her kitchen. She turned to face him, and he could see her wince at the state of his body.

'Thanks,' Sam said with a smile, as he pulled the loaned T-shirt over his body with some difficulty. Sutton watched, saw him struggle to manoeuvre his limp arm, and hurried over to help. As she helped him pull it down across his solid stomach, the two of them locked eyes for just a moment.

There was a spark.

But that was all. Despite the attraction that existed between them, both of them knew it was moot. There was no possible future for them, and although certain needs would often steer people into rash and passionate situations, both of them exercised their restraint.

As Sutton hurried back to the kitchen, her cheeks blushing, Sam felt an ache in his body.

But it wasn't from his myriad of injuries.

It was for Mel.

Somewhere, up in Glasgow, the woman Sam loved was going about her day, most likely with her daughter Cassie pushing her buttons with her relentless wit, and Sam wished for nothing more than to return to her.

To walk through the doors of the Carnival Bar and wrap his arms around her.

But he couldn't.

His fight had threatened both of their lives, and if he had to keep his distance to keep them safe, then it was a pain he would gladly withstand.

'Here,' Sutton said, handing Sam the coffee. The tension in the room was teetering on awkward, Sutton sighed. 'Look, I didn't mean to—'

'It's okay.' Sam smiled. 'In another life, perhaps.'

Sutton smiled warmly and then went back to the

kitchen. All the windows in the flat were open, despite the bitter cold of the winter's day, in a lame attempt to remove the house of the stale smell of smoke. It didn't help that Sutton herself lit a cigarette and made a lame attempt to blow the smoke out of the window.

Sam approached her and smiled.

'You shouldn't smoke,' he said dryly. 'They'll kill you.'

Sutton took another drag, blew out the smoke, and then smirked.

'I think you're probably the last man in the world to give advice on doing things that might kill you.'

'Touché.'

Knock. Knock.

Sutton frowned, stubbed the cigarette on the window frame and tossed it into the elements as she strode towards the front door. Sam sipped his coffee and readied himself for the inevitable but was pleasantly surprised to see Commissioner Sarratt when the door was pulled open.

'Ma'am,' he said respectfully as she marched in, a heavy-looking sports bag in her hand.

'You don't work for me, Sam,' she said curtly, and then placed the bag on the coffee table between them. 'Are you ready? Because I don't have much time before people start asking where I am.'

'You're not coming with me,' Sam said firmly, finishing his coffee, and then putting the mug down beside the bag. 'This isn't your fight.'

'Yes, it is,' Sarratt replied. 'This is *my* city. And I'm tired of people trying to tell me how to keep it safe. Now, are you going to look in the bag or what?'

Sam shot a confused glance to Sutton, who shrugged, and then unzipped the bag. His eyebrows raised with surprise, and then he looked up to Sutton who nodded.

He reached into the bag and pulled out a Heckler & Koch G36 Assault Rifle. The weapon was used throughout the country, with many police constabularies issuing to their armed response and counter terrorism units. It was a light rifle, weighing roughly eight pounds, and Sam hauled it up and looked through the dual optical sight. Luckily, his arm was functioning enough to steady the gun as he drew it up, causing a mild panic in Sutton. Sam checked to ensure it wasn't loaded, before noticing a few of the proprietary 30-round magazines to turn the shell of a gun into a lethal instrument.

'There's enough ammunition in there to get you through a small army,' Sarratt explained, a little conflicted. 'There's also a tactical vest and a Glock 17.'

Sam looked up at Sarratt who took a deep breath as if accepting what she'd done.

'How did you—'

'Commissioner privileges.' Sarratt waved her hand dismissively. 'But unfortunately, the location of Wainwright's safe house isn't something I'm privy to.'

Sam lifted the Glock, admiring the weapon as he responded.

'That's okay. I have ways of getting information people don't want to divulge.'

'So do I,' Sarratt continued, making it clear who was in charge. 'And mine don't involve using that weapon right there. The safe house is run by MI5, and while I don't have access to their systems, I did manage to get the name of the person who organised the safe house for Wainwright. And I've made contact with them to meet me at midday to discuss an urgent police matter.'

'And they won't be suspicious?' Sam asked, his split eyebrow raised.

'Well, we'll just have to find out won't we?'

'Like I said, you're not coming with me,' Sam said, snapping the Glock open by the slide and peering into the barrel.

'You need me.' Sarratt maintained her authority. 'Besides, what else are you going to do?'

Sam snapped a magazine into the gun and looked at her.

'What I do best.'

CHAPTER TWENTY-FOUR

'Sometimes, you need to do what is sensible as opposed to what is right.'

When Jordan had said those words to Sarratt, it had come from a place of love and understanding. Their marriage had always been one of honesty, and although they'd never built upon their family, the two of them had supported each other vehemently when it came to their careers. Watching Jordan thrive as one of the most talented chefs in the country, and build his own Michelin Star restaurant, filled Sarratt with the same sense of pride as her own ascent through the Met had.

She knew Jordan felt the same.

He had told her, time and again, that a woman of colour breaking down barriers and scaling such an institution would have an impact that went beyond just what she did behind the desk. For all the policies she would introduce, and for all the high-profile meetings she would attend, it would be the sense of pride that so many young Black women would feel when they saw her.

Knowing she was a role model to so many, Sarratt had always ensured she did things by the book. That she'd never let her integrity or her sense of right and wrong be compromised.

But life had a way of throwing curveballs and as she sat in her car, her hands glued to the wheel, she wondered how she'd let things get this far.

Beside her, Sam Pope, the most wanted man in the country and a person she herself had spoken about in front of the national media, was sitting, armed and ready to go to war.

With her permission.

Perhaps she should have been stronger.

Sarratt had constantly championed for people to speak up against corruption and had for those with a voice to use it to push back against those who abused their power. Yet she'd found herself backed into a corner by Wainwright and had latched onto the hand he'd offered to protect her career. Now she knew that those words were empty, and the likelihood of her recovering her status was slim to none.

Even if Sam's plan worked, the backlash would soon begin the more people looked into the series of events, how they played out, and who had authorised it.

But she needed to do the right thing.

The sensible thing to do would have been to turn the car around and head back towards New Scotland Yard with Sam in cuffs. He wouldn't fight her. He had already made it clear that if she wanted to resolve the issue by handing him over to Wainwright and then effectively be his puppet, then she was well within her rights to do so.

Instead, she'd handed Sam Pope a bag of firearms and her permission to do what he needed to do.

The same thing she knew he'd been doing ever since he took down Frank Jackson and Inspector Michael Howell all those years ago in the High Rise.

The right thing.

The traffic lights turned green, and the hum of the London traffic picked up, and Sarratt moved through it slowly. The two of them had hardly spoken since leaving Sutton's apartment, although Sarratt did read Sam the riot act for bringing Sutton unwillingly into the state of play. Despite his apologies, she knew that Sam kept few people in his circle, and the fact that Sutton was one of them just confirmed to her what she already knew.

DS Jessica Sutton was an asset to the Met. Someone that trustworthy was worth keeping around, and Sarratt made a mental note to try to prise her away from DPS and into somewhere where she could make a real difference.

That was something Bruce McEwen had always told her.

Surround yourself with people you can trust, and those you know can exceed you. It was what he told her throughout every performance review, that he saw her as the future head of the Metropolitan Police and that she could take things further than he ever could. Back then, Sarratt didn't believe him, and even loathed the idea that a man as influential as McEwen could have tentative links to a vigilante like Sam Pope.

But now she understood why.

Despite her brain feeling like it had spent the past twenty-four hours in a blender, she'd latched onto one train of thought that cut through her mind like a hot knife. That despite dedicating her life to making the city, and the country, a better place, the lines of justice had become blurred. People of power and influence only wanted a legal system that maintained the status quo while simultaneously protecting their own positions.

Only Sam seemed to have a clarity of vision.

Existing primarily in the grey area between hero and criminal, Sam Pope was the only one not afraid to do what was right.

No matter what it cost him.

It was why she hadn't slapped him in cuffs, and it was why, as they pulled into the car park where she'd arranged to meet their unsuspecting informant, she was willing to let him off the leash. She guided the car up the narrow, curved rampways that spiralled up to the roof, and emerged onto the rain-soaked concrete. Unsurprisingly, not many people had opted to park under the thunderous downpour, and Sarratt pulled into a parking spot opposite the entrance ramp.

'I can take it from here,' Sam told her as she killed the engine. He was wearing a black hooded sweatshirt that Sarratt had taken from her husband's wardrobe. It wasn't much, but it was at least another layer against the wet, miserable weather.

'The hell you will,' Sarratt replied, her eyes fixed on the rampway. 'I'm still the Commissioner of the Met.'

'Yes, Ma'am,' Sam said with a smile.

Sarratt tried her best to hide hers. Despite being painted as a cold-hearted killer, being hunted by every law enforcement in the country, and despite being beaten and shot at just twenty-four hours before, Sam still respected the chain of command.

Was still a soldier.

Sarratt sighed and looked out of the window. Sam had said he didn't mind if she smoked, but her manners dictated that she wouldn't trap him in the car as she choked him with second-hand smoke. As she watched the rain dance across her windscreen, she muttered under her breath.

'A myriad of shit.'

'Excuse me?' Sam asked. Sarratt turned to him, only then realising that she'd spoken out loud. She rolled her eyes and shook her head.

'Sorry. It was just something McEwen had passed on to me when I was sworn in.'

'A myriad of shit?' Sam chuckled. 'Sounds about right.'

'Apparently, it was the same thing Commissioner Stout had said to him.' She drummed her fingers on the steering wheel. 'I guess, it doesn't really matter who sits in the seat or what they have to face. It's just an endless stream of problems, and countless people wanting to get what they can from it.'

'The way of the world,' Sam said glumly.

'Is that why you do what you do?' Sarratt turned to him. 'A lot of people who want your head on a stick say it's because you went loopy when you lost your son.'

Sam shuffled uncomfortably in his seat as Sarratt continued.

'I can't imagine what that was like, Sam. And I'm truly sorry if you never got justice for it. But is that the reason?'

'It was,' Sam said quickly. 'At first, I wanted to hurt every person who broke the law and got away with it. Not for any sense of justice, but just to try to feel something again. Just to try to feel like I had a purpose. But the more layers I peeled back, the worse it became. All I found was a world where everyone is trained from a young age to fall in line and accept the world for what it is. A place where those who had climbed to the top could push people, keep them down. If they broke the law, they had enough money, or power, to keep the wolves from the door. Someone had to fight back.'

'Is that why you do it? Because you think you should?'

'Maybe.' Sam turned to her, shrugging. 'Or maybe it's because I can.'

Sarratt held Sam's gaze for a few more moments, understanding what both Stout and McEwen saw in Sam. Their bonding was interrupted by the sound of an engine roaring through the car park, and moments later, a plush looking sports car emerged onto the top tier of the car park, its sparkling black paint job twinkling in the rain. It swung into the spot opposite, and then flashed its lights, as if signalling to begin the deal. Sam went to open his door, but Sarratt placed her hand on his forearm.

'Let me handle this. Please,' Sarratt said firmly, and then stepped out into the rain. Sam watched as she strode purposefully across the car park to the car, and the driver's door opened. A small, rotund man stepped out, his thinning hair instantly flattened by the rain, and he looked nervous. Sam watched as Sarratt calmly spoke, but the man's gesticulation and body language told Sam it wasn't a friendly interaction. As Sam threw open his door, he could see the man waving Sarratt away and pulling open the door to his car again.

Sam pulled the Glock 17 from his jeans as he stormed towards the car, hearing the tail end of Sarratt's protests as he approached.

'Listen, Ricky, this *is* a matter of national security and…'

Sam stepped past Sarratt, and with one swift swing of his arm, he drove the grip of the pistol into the corner of the driver's window. The glass shattered on impact, covering the terrified office worker in hundreds of tiny shards who squealed in terror.

'Sam. Stop right now,' Sarratt yelled, but Sam ignored her. With his right hand, Sam grabbed the man by the scruff of his shirt and tie, and hauled him out of his seat, roughly dragging him through the window and standing him straight. Then, with considerable force, he pushed the man back against the car door, forced the barrel of the Glock under his chin and pressed his head back against the roof of the car.

'You have exactly five seconds to give us Wainwright's location.'

'Sam!' Sarratt yelled.

'Five.'

'Please. Please.' The man was panicking.

'Four.'

'I can't, I'll lose me job.'

'Three.'

The man began to wet himself, and warm urine flooded the front of his suit trousers and trickled out from the bottom. Sarratt felt the guilt rise through her body and she stepped forward.

'Sam, put the gun down,' she ordered.

'Two.'

'Okay. Okay!' the man finally yelled, as tears of terror rolled down his cheek for the rain to wash away. 'He's at the Everly Estate in Crawley.'

'Crawley?' Sam repeated.

'Well, just outside,' the man stammered. 'Please, that's all I know.'

Sam held the gun to the flab beneath the man's chin a moment longer, and then finally stepped back. The man hurried into his car, shaking with fear and embarrassment, and within seconds, he was speeding back down the ramp and as far away as he could get. Sam watched the car leave, tucked the gun away, and turned back to Sarratt who fixed him with a hard stare.

'That wasn't what we agreed.'

'We needed the location,' Sam reasoned. 'And we got it.'

Sam turned to head back to the car, but Sarratt stepped in his way, pushing her hand to his chest to stop him.

'You want me to trust you, Sam? Then don't pull shit like that.' She shook her head. 'This plan only works if we trust each other.'

'I trust you,' Sam said without hesitation. 'Do you trust me?'

He held out his hand.

With the rain falling around them, Sarratt glanced out over her rain-soaked city. When she'd sworn to protect it, she didn't realise it would be from the very man in charge of the country's safety. Least of all, with the help of the most dangerous vigilante the country had ever known.

A myriad of shit.

That was what her career had become.

With a little reluctance, Sarratt reached out, grasped Sam's drenched hand, and shook it. Sam nodded respectfully and then headed back to the car, retrieving the sports bag with the rest of his weaponry.

'He'll tell Wainwright he's compromised. You know that, right?' Sarratt asked, and Sam nodded. 'He'll either up sticks or double down his security.'

Sam swung the bag containing the rifle and the body armour over his good shoulder and smiled.

'I'm counting on it.' Sam reached out and rested his hand on Sarratt's shoulder, thanking her, but indicating the end of their exchange. The next part of the plan was for him and him alone. 'Just be ready when we need to go.'

Sam grimaced slightly as he adjusted the bag, but began to head back across the car park towards the stairwell. Sarratt stood in the rain, watching the most wanted man in the country walk away from her.

The line in the sand had been drawn.

Once he was about ten paces from her, the commissioner called out over the crashing rain.

'Are you sure about this, Sam?'

'No.' He stopped and called back. Without turning, and with the call to war burning within him, he spoke again. 'But I don't have any other choice.'

CHAPTER TWENTY-FIVE

The day had gone by without incident.

Wainwright was sitting in the dining room of the expansive mansion, the remnants of his dinner smeared across the plate before him. He reached out for his glass of port, and took a long, satisfying sip before turning to Jensen who was finishing off his food.

'Is everyone in position?' Wainwright asked calmly. Jensen didn't wait to finish the food in his mouth before responding.

'Yup,' he said through his chewing. 'As soon as we got word your location was compromised, I made a few calls. There's more than twenty men guarding this place. Basically, you've got more guns than the streets of Harlem.'

'Quite.'

Wainwright offered a polite smile at the insensitive joke. Jensen was a bullish man, lacking in tact, and manners, but Wainwright appreciated the man's finer qualities. He seemed to be completely without empathy. The idea of killing someone was what drove him on, and once Pope, Sarratt, and unfortunately, Murray were taken care of, Jensen would make a handy ally going forward.

Aligning himself with such a man, and using Guardian as his own personal army drew parallels with his predecessor and Blackridge, and Wainwright was more than aware of them.

But Wallace had been sloppier than he ever would be. The man craved power and attention, whereas Wainwright craved only the former. His status as a noble and respected leader and the weight of his word in the House of Commons was something Wainwright cherished. Rumours were rife that he was due a knighthood for his service, and that was a title he would wear with pride.

No matter how much blood, innocent or otherwise, needed to be shed for him to get it.

Wainwright took another sip of his drink and watched Jensen finish his food greedily.

'Do they not feed you at Guardian?' Wainwright joked.

'Oh, I love my grub.' Jensen smiled back. 'Plus, nobody likes blowing someone's head off on an empty stomach.'

'Well, if you had done as you were asked the first-time round, we wouldn't be in this situation, would we?' Wainwright's tone shifted. 'And you'd still be able to walk.'

'Look. I saw an opportunity and I—'

'You let ego get in your way. I appreciate that being the man to bring down Sam Pope has a morbid sense of prestige, but you had a loaded gun to the man's head, yet you didn't pull the trigger.' Wainwright shook his head. 'Ego is one of the greatest weaknesses within us. How can I be assured it won't happen again?'

'Well, for one thing, I can't fucking walk properly,' Jensen snapped back. 'And second, there's only one man more dangerous than me behind the scope of a rifle, and he'll be the one in my crosshairs.'

'Well, you won't do any good sitting here, will you?' Wainwright looked out of the tall, wide window of the room at the torrential storm laying siege to the mansion.

'If he's coming as you suspect, he'll want the cover of darkness. I suggest you move.'

'Yes, sir.' Jensen pushed himself to his feet. 'This ends tonight.'

Wainwright kept his gaze on the dark, thundering sky beyond the window. He didn't turn back to face Jensen.

'Let's hope so.' He finally turned and smiled. 'And once all this mess has been cleared up, Jensen, you will be richly rewarded.'

Jensen offered a respectful, half-hearted salute, and then hobbled to the door, ready to make his way through the icy rain to his outpost, where he would have the whole of the mansion within his deadly sight. As soon as Sam Pope stepped into it, he would blow him to hell. As for the reward, the control of Guardian, and being the Chief of Defence Staff's personal clean-up crew, Jensen was champing at the bit to get started. The moral compass that Murray had used to dictate some of their contracts would be buried six feet deep, along with Murray, and whoever else Wainwright directed him towards.

Whatever the admiral had done, Jensen didn't care. In fairness, he'd probably done worse, and combining both their disdain for the modern world and their ruthless efficiency in eliminating those before them, he was interested to see what changes he and Wainwright could make.

For better or worse.

As Jensen pulled open the door to the dining room, a loud, shrill siren began to wail, and he turned back to Wainwright, who didn't so much as blink. The alarm had been tripped, meaning somewhere across the acres of property that surrounded the gorgeous home, there was an intruder.

Sam Pope.

Wainwright calmly lifted his glass and finished the rest of his drink, before reaching for his box of cigars that sat neatly beside his cutter. He took one out, cut and lit it, and then turned back to Jensen.

'Well, don't just stand there. Go and kill him.'

Jensen nodded, and as fast as his hobbled leg could manage, he headed for the outpost.

The storm that had laid siege to the capital city offered Sam a blanket of cover as, for the most part, the streets were clear. Those, who like him, were braving the elements, did so under the cover of umbrellas and walked at such a pace that they paid no heed to who went by them. With his face still beaten from the day before, he was likely to draw attention, something the current situation didn't call for, so for once, Sam was thankful for the reliability of the British weather.

Having left Sarratt to continue her part of the plan, Sam had walked gingerly through the city, stopping only once at a dodgy looking off-licence based on the sign they'd failed to take down in the window.

Thankfully, they had what he needed, and he stuffed them into his bag along with the weapons Sarratt had provided. Then, he'd walked the six miles needed to get to Victoria Station, and as he stepped onto the massive concourse, he kept his hood up and his head down.

The last thing he needed was someone identifying him and raising a panic.

He was still a wanted man, and after the events of the past twenty-four hours, he was certain the actual police would waste little time in bringing him down. Then it would be over. Sarratt would do her best, but with Wainwright still in command, Sam's life would be over.

He wasn't ready for that.

Not yet.

Sam bought a ticket for the next train to Crawley, and then a sandwich and coffee from one of the stands, and then hobbled through the barriers to the train platform. The Southern service to Crawley took a surprisingly short amount of time, stopping at just five stops on its way to West Sussex. The mid-afternoon service wasn't too busy, as the majority of the commuters were those heading to Gatwick Airport and were too consumed by their own travels to pay any attention to the man who slumped at the back of the carriage with his hood up and his head down.

As the train departed and began picking up speed as it headed through Croydon, Sam connected his phone to the feeble Wi-Fi that was advertised on the small poster above his head, and tried his best to do some recon. There wasn't much information about the estate online, which made sense given its priority, but by trawling through the maps available, he could see that the back end of the premises connected with the Tilgate Lake and Park. It was his best point of entry, as walking up to the front gate would be suicide.

Undoubtedly, the man Sam had threatened that morning would have already notified Wainwright on what happened. The admiral may have been a despicable man, but Sam was willing to bet he wasn't a coward. Instead, drawing Sam to a remote location and welcoming him with a private army would make the most sense.

Sam was expecting resistance.

And he was ready to meet it head on.

Not a day went by that Sam didn't look in the mirror and see a killer looking back at him. Over a hundred people had died by his hand, whether by pulling a trigger or by his own, beaten fists. There was always a voice in the back of his head, telling him to stop, and begging him to turn himself in. He often thought it was an echo of Jamie's memory. His young son, pleading with his father to be a better man.

But Sam was being the best man he could.

There wasn't a family life for him to return home to. No wife to devote his heart to, nor a son to raise with the indescribable pride that comes with parenthood.

That life had been ripped from him.

Had sent him on this path of redemption that had stopped him from self-destructing.

His old sergeant, Carl Marsden, had arrived at a time in his life when Sam had given up. When he was willing to end it all, and allow his pain and his grief to swallow him completely.

Marsden had told him to fight.

And Sam sipped his coffee, looked out of the window as the morose beauty of the drenched countryside flew past his window, and knew that was what he would do.

If this was his last fight, then so be it.

But he couldn't walk away. It wasn't in him to do so.

Wainwright had tried to lay waste to the country and align with Balikov, and now was willing to kill an innocent woman in Ruth Ashton to try to cover his tracks.

Wainwright would push as hard as he could.

And Sam was coming to push back.

By the time the train had arrived in Crawley station, the sun had already set, submerging the quaint town in darkness. The street lights illuminated the downpour, and Sam hailed a taxi from the rank just to the side of the car park. After trying, and failing, three times to start a conversation with Sam, the driver turned on the radio and joined the rush hour traffic through the town centre.

Sam didn't mind.

There was no rush.

The longer he had to form a plan of attack in his head,

the better. Plus, the longer Wainwright had to wait for Sam to come for him.

Eventually, the car pulled up to the front gate of the Tilgate Park, and Sam duly paid the man and gave him a generous tip. He stepped out into the rain and then headed into the park. The vast woodland spread over two-thousand acres, and Sam kept to the concrete paths that wormed through the park like veins. With the torch on his phone illuminating the path ahead, he saw not a soul as he pushed on, passing the Go Ape and the adventure playground. Unsurprisingly, the pop-up eateries within the park were all shut, and Sam soon found himself looking out over the lake. The torch only illuminated so far, but Sam carefully began his march around the edge of the water. Each step was carefully placed, and after a solid half hour of walking, Sam's torch soon fell upon the mighty trunks of the woodland trees. Thankfully, he hadn't fallen into the water, but the sports bag was beginning to dig into his bruised ribs and his hands were numb from the cold.

Sam carefully navigated his way between the trees, holding the phone with his aching left arm as he used his right to clear any errant branches or twigs from his line of sight.

He carried on for what felt like a mile.

Soon, he came across a high, stone wall that stretched from one edge of the darkness to the other, and Sam hoped it was the wall to the Everly Estate. The reception on his phone had long since evaporated, meaning he couldn't use the navigation function to confirm.

He dropped to one knee and thankfully unhooked the sports bag with a grunt. He unzipped it, and then tentatively wrapped the tactical vest around his broken body and fastened it. Then he checked his Glock 17, sliding out the magazine before snapping it shut again and stuffing it into the back of his sodden jeans. He pulled out a few more magazines from the bag, putting the pistol rounds in the left pouch of the vest, and the rifle rounds on the right. Then he lifted the Heckler & Koch G36 and hoisted the strap over his shoulder. He pulled out the fireworks he'd purchased on his journey and a lighter, and stuffed them into the front of his vest, lodging them against his chest to keep them dry.

Lastly, he scooped up two handfuls of mud beneath his feet and then smeared it across his cheeks and his forehead, and then rubbed it down his forearms too.

It was an extra layer of camouflage, and Sam needed every marginal gain he could get.

He was the walking wounded.

His body was battered, and the pain in his ribs kept threatening to topple him completely.

He could barely lift his left arm.

His head was pounding, likely dealing with an untreated concussion.

But there was a war to be won.

And armed and ready, Sam shunted that pain to the back of his mind and began to scale the nearby tree that hung over the wall.

Minutes later, he dropped down on the other side, pulled up his rifle, and with careful steps, waded through the woods to lay siege to the Everly Estate.

Ready to end things once and for all.

CHAPTER TWENTY-SIX

Murray hadn't seen his kids in nearly two days, and as the afternoon bled into another cold, dark evening, he looked up from his laptop screen and rubbed his eyes with his fists. He was tired, and in need of a shower, but the threat from Wainwright was still echoing in the back of his mind.

The man had made a clear threat to his family.

One of the promises he'd made Becky, when he'd decided to run with the idea of Guardian, was he wouldn't bring any of the mess to their front door. She hardly approved of her husband dealing in guns and blood, but she understood that was where he was from. He was forged in the army and had been able to transfer the violent skills into a multi-million business. While a designer handbag at Christmas was usually enough for her to not judge him so harshly, the idea that his work could put his boys in harm's way would be the end of their marriage.

Despite wanting to put a bullet through Wainwright's skull for even uttering his son's names, there was only one way out of it for Murray now.

He had to find the man who'd saved his life all those years ago.

He needed to kill Sam Pope.

Murray had handed Sam's forged driver's license over to Ranjit and told him to scan through every database he could to try to locate him. It didn't take too long to find the address, and Murray sent two of the last contacts at his disposal to search the place.

It was empty.

The photos they sent through to Murray showed that Sam lived with the bare minimum, the polar opposite to himself. There were no designer clothes or plush furnishings.

None of that mattered to Sam.

It was beginning to matter less to himself.

Beyond that, Ranjit had little else to work on, so Murray ordered him to hold off handing any intel over to the Met. If Ranjit couldn't locate him, there was no hope of the Met succeeding, and the more cooks in his kitchen, the messier it would become.

The grainy CCTV boxes on his laptop screen were beginning to merge into one, and Murray pushed the screen away and stood, stretching out his back, and then he reached for his coat. He pulled the door to his operation room closed, locked it with the only key, and then marched through the hallways of New Scotland Yard. He drew a few glances, either through intimidation or unfamiliarity, but he couldn't be bothered to respond. He took the stairs two at a time and felt himself sigh with relief as he stepped out into the freezing downpour. The instant impact of the cold sent a rush through his body that jolted him awake, and he held his head up to the rain that fell relentlessly.

The fresh air felt good as it filtered into his lungs, and as he basked in the downpour, he thought about just heading to his car, packing up his family, and using his extensive resources to just move them to safety.

But he knew he couldn't.

Wainwright had made it clear that Sarratt was a loose end and had already laid bare how he intended to deal with her. If Murray was to run, he'd be looking over his shoulder for the rest of his life.

And when the time came that he turned and came face to face with a gun, the shooter would no doubt have orders to fire at least three more bullets.

Murray marched past the famous spinning sign outside the modern glass office and headed towards the Starbucks on the other side of the parade. Few cars ventured down these busy streets, although the rain had made it much more accommodating. As Murray opened the door, he noticed the disappointment on the young barista's face, who was already packing up the shop.

'We're closing in like two minutes, mate,' he called out.

'I just want a coffee.' Murray smiled. As he approached the till, he made a show of folding up a twenty-pound note and tucking it into the tip jar. 'Americano. Black.'

The barista offered him a thankful nod and went to work, and as Murray waited patiently, he paid no attention to the door opening once more. As the footsteps drew closer, he turned, and his eyes widened slightly.

'Murray.'

Commissioner Sarratt approached him, her thick, rainproof jacket covering her always immaculate uniform. Despite their early quarrels, Murray had come to respect the woman for how resilient she was.

'Ma'am.' He nodded to the menu above the counter. 'Can I get you anything?'

'Funnily enough, I didn't come in here for a coffee.' She spoke with haste. 'It would seem we both have an issue we may need to resolve.'

'What, find Sam?' Murray scoffed. 'How many haystacks have you been reaching into?'

'Actually, I wasn't talking about Sam.' Sarratt turned

and looked him dead in the eye. 'And if you must know, he's fine by the way. I was with him this morning.'

Murray spun to face her, his eyes wide with desperation.

'Where is he?'

'Right now?' Sarratt elaborately looked at her watch. 'I'd say, getting ready to lay siege to Wainwright's safe house. I take it he made the same threats to you and your family that he's made to mine?'

Her question caught Murray cold, and before he could lie to her, he realised his reaction confirmed it. The barista placed the coffee in front of Murray, turned to take Sarratt's order, but then swiftly read the situation and made himself scarce.

'What the hell are you talking about?'

'Earlier today, Sam and I found the location for Wainwright's safe house, and I loaded Sam up with some weapons and sent him on his way.' Sarratt spoke calmly.

'Why the hell would you do that?'

'Because for the past week, Murray, I've been doing every single thing to upset my conscience, and I haven't eaten, or really slept since I first walked into the room with you.' Sarratt shook her head. 'It's not your fault. You were just doing your job. But we both know that whatever is going on here, it's much bigger than Sam Pope.'

Murray blew out his cheeks. If what Sarratt said was true, then there was a good chance that Wainwright was dead already. On the other hand, there was an even bigger chance that Sam was heading to his slaughter.

The fact that he hadn't thought once about notifying Wainwright and warning him told him everything he needed to know.

Sarratt had clearly realised it as well, and she pulled out a folded sheet of paper and placed it on the counter next to his coffee.

'If it helps, Murray, for the past week, I've been battling the idea of doing what is sensible as opposed to doing what is right.'

Murray stared down at the paper and then looked back up at the commissioner.

'And where did that get you?' he finally asked.

'Here. Next to you. Wondering if you'll do the same thing.'

Sarratt turned and headed back to the door of the shop. Murray watched her leave, before he threw back the coffee in one long gulp, thanked the barista, and strode to the door. With the paper tucked into his jacket pocket, he burst out of the coffee shop into the rain, turned on his heel, and headed in the opposite direction of his office.

Weaving through the trees in the darkness, Sam had to tread carefully. There was no option of a torch, so as not to giveaway his position, and each step was carefully placed into the squelching mud. As he made his way through the woods, the vast building that housed Wainwright soon came into view, illuminated by the bright spotlights that covered the expansive lawn surrounding the mansion. A high-pitched alarm had been triggered, no doubt by Sam moving past a sensor hidden somewhere within the darkness of the woods.

There was no playing it safe now.

They knew he was coming.

As Sam approached the edge of the woods, he could see a concrete path that ran across the perimeter of the garden itself, which was segregated into sections by flowerbeds that had been devastated by the winter months.

Sam pressed himself against one of the trees, submerged in the shadows, and he tried to peer through the rain that burst into his line of sight when it hit the light.

He counted four men by the front of the house, all of them wandering aimlessly as they tried to keep warm in the cold. He couldn't see any weapons, but there was no way that those assigned to protect Wainwright weren't armed to the teeth.

This was going to get messy.

Sam dropped down to one knee, put his rifle down, and then reached into the front of his tactical vest. He pulled out the fireworks he'd purchased on his way into the town, and he pushed their wooden stands into the accommodating mud. The wind picked up, playing havoc with his attempts to spark the lighter to life, and with a groan of pain, he shifted his left arm and cupped the lighter with his hand.

A flame flickered.

He brought it to the wick of the firework, tossed the lighter, lifted his gun, and started running. He kept within the treeline, and as he got thirty paces away, he heard the ear-piercing shriek of a firework as it rocketed up into the sky, leaving a trail of sparks to filter down into the rain. It exploded above the building in a blaze of colour, and instantly, the four men erupted into panic.

Another firework shot up, this time alerting the men to its location, and Sam watched as the four men rushed across the floodlit garden towards it.

Sam pulled up his rifle. The Heckler & Kock G36 was a lightweight rifle, and he drew the scope to his eye, his left arm just about managing the weight as he steadied it in his grip. He nestled the stock into his right shoulder, slid his finger around the trigger and took a breath.

No going back now.

As the four men covered the grass at speed, two gunshots rang out, and two of the men spun to the ground, howling in agony as they clutched their blown out kneecaps. The other two spun expertly, clearly military trained, and drew their weapons within seconds.

That was all Sam needed.

He stepped out from the shadows, gun still locked expertly in his grip, and two more pulls of the trigger took down both men, the bullets shattering their collar bones as he shot to disarm. As quick as he could, Sam raced forward towards the building, holding his rifle as he covered the distance. Just as he was about to reach the pathway that ran along the side of the house, a burst of gunfire exploded and a barrage of bullets tore up the wet mud a few feet behind him. Sam swivelled on his foot, pushing his heel down into the mud to steady himself, and dropped to one knee. He whipped the scope to his eye and drew the crosshair onto the man who was lifting his rifle as well.

Sam pulled first.

The trio of bullets ripped through the man's chest, lifting him off the ground as the blood splatter was whisked away by the rain. The man hit the mud, and Sam scanned the surroundings before continuing on down the pathway. As he approached the corner of the mansion, he pushed himself against the wall, hidden by the shadows, and peered around the edge of the brickwork. Three more men were racing across the gravel covered entranceway, two of whom were loading their weapons as another barked orders. Their feet crunched on the stones below, and one of the men was yelling that he couldn't see a damn thing because of the rain.

That was Sam's saving grace.

He slid out the empty magazine and slammed in a replacement, before he drew up his rifle and stepped out from the corner, already with his weapon drawn.

One shot.

Two shot.

Two men hit the ground, writhing in agony on the sharp stones, clutching the bullet hole that had shattered their shins. The third man unloaded a round in Sam's direction, shooting recklessly into the downpour. Sam dived forward, absorbing the hard fall onto the gravel on his damage ribs, and the pain instinctively loosened his grip. The rifle swung from his hands on its strap, and Sam desperately tried to reassert his grip.

'Don't fucking try it.'

The voice was laced with murderous intent, and Sam held his left hand up and slowly began to push himself to his knees with his right. The man approached, soaked through, with his rifle drawn, and he sneered down the scope towards Sam.

'The admiral is going to give me a big, fat bonus for putting you down, mate.'

As Sam began to draw his right hand up, he slid the Glock 17 from the back of his jeans and swung it out into the rain. The man's eyes widened. He tried to lift his rifle up in that split second, but to no avail.

The bullet blasted from the barrel of the Glock, sliced through the raindrops, and drilled a hole through the man's forehead and out the back of his skull. A puff of red burst out into the rain, and the man collapsed to the floor, the contents of his skull leaking out onto the stones. Sam took a breath, returned the gun, and then pushed himself up. He jogged past the front of the house, reasserting his grip on his rifle, until he rounded the garish statues that sat on either side of the front door. About ten feet away, in the centre of the gravel, there was a stone fountain, with the feature in the middle still pumping out an impressive stream of water despite the rain.

Gunshots echoed, and bullets began to rip into the statues ahead of Sam. He pulled the Heckler & Koch up once more, emptied the rest of the clip and dispatched two more gunmen who were racing across the gravel.

Sam released the magazine, letting it drop onto the stones beneath, and as he pulled another from his pocket, the front door burst open. Instinctively, Sam turned the rifle, slammed in the magazine, but before he could make the shot, a thunderous shoulder barge sent him hurling backwards and he collapsed onto the hard stones. The man thundered after him, and as Sam collected himself, he once again tried to lift his weapon.

Only his left arm failed him.

His attacker was a brute, standing easily over six feet three, and had the build of a heavyweight boxer who had spent a few years in retirement. Although the man had a slight paunch, and seemed more meat than muscle, the man moved with the fluidity of a trained fighter, and he booted the rifle from Sam's grip, pulled him to his feet, and rocked him with a brutal right hook to the stomach. Sam doubled over, and the man clasped the hood that overhung his tactical vest, spun Sam to the right and then let him go.

The momentum sent Sam hurtling shoulder first into the concrete fountain, and the impact sent a shudder through his body. His attacker wasted little time, marching across the stones with thunderous strides, and he hauled Sam up, pushed away his feeble attempt to protect himself, and he hammered Sam in the jaw with a left haymaker that sent Sam tumbling over the edge of the wall and into the water. The ice-cold water hit like a shock to the system, and Sam shot straight back out, catching the attacker by surprise as he tried to amble over the wall and into the water. Sam landed a hard right, ducked the returning left, and then nailed another that sent the man stumbling backwards. Dabbing a hand to his lip, the man saw his own blood and then let out a terrifying roar as he launched forward. But the shin-deep water stifled his movement, and

Sam ducked the sledgehammer of a right fist, drove his own elbow into the back of the man's head, and then planted his foot in front of the man's left leg. The blow sent the man wobbling to the side, and he clipped Sam's leg and collapsed into the actual water feature of the fountain. The blow was sickening, as the man collided face first into the stone. The impact ripped open a gash across the man's cheek, and had clearly rattled his brain, as he laid helpless against the concrete statue.

Sam lifted his boot out of the water and drove it down as hard as he could.

He heard the man's neck break.

He heard the sickening sound of a skull cracking.

Sam took a few steps back and then spat a mouthful of blood into the water that surrounded him. His attacker slid down the stone, leaving a trail of blood across the statue, and then disappeared into the water.

The rain had washed away most of the mud from Sam's skin, and he looked upwards, and welcomed the refreshing cold against the searing pain that was emanating from his jaw. Then, with a deep breath, Sam clambered out of the fountain and retrieved his rifle.

With a trail of bodies left in his wake, Sam slammed the magazine into the weapon, re-established his grip, and headed to the front door.

CHAPTER TWENTY-SEVEN

The walk to the outpost was more laborious than Jensen had anticipated, but it was the stubborn male pride that had stopped him from asking for assistance. Wainwright had handpicked him to eliminate Pope, and he'd even overlooked his failure the day before. With every limp through the squelching terrain, a shot of pain ricocheted from his butchered leg, up his spine, and let off a roar of agony in his brain.

But Jensen gritted his teeth and continued to march.

Halfway to the outpost, Jensen heard the shriek of a firework go whizzing up into the sky, and he turned to watch as it exploded into a beautiful, glittery burst of colour.

Sam was here.

It was clever, Jensen had to admit, as he thundered on. With such a vast and expansive grounds to try to wade through, Sam had done what any experienced fighter would do.

Lure the enemy out.

Another firework exploded into the sky above the trees, but Jensen didn't turn to observe. The outpost was submerged in the darkness, reaching up out of the woodlands and into the night sky. Behind him, Jensen could hear the crackle of gunfire, followed by a few dimmed screams of pain.

He needed to get up the ladder, and quickly.

He pulled out a pair of leather gloves from his coat pocket, pulled them over his hands, and secured his grip on the metal ladder. Every rung was slick with rainwater, but Jensen clasped on confidently and began to pull himself up. Every time he lifted his savaged thigh, he groaned but persevered, and slowly but surely, rung by rung, he pulled himself to the top of the outpost.

As he ambled to his feet, he was welcomed by the darkness of the night sky, but half a mile away, he could see the Everly Estate in all its majesty.

More gunfire.

More screams.

Sam was ripping through the small army Wainwright had pulled together at short notice, and somewhere deep inside, Jensen felt a small pinch of jealousy. He didn't want to dedicate his life to some egotistical quest for justice like Sam did.

But the thought of laying siege to a building on his own, putting trained adversaries down as he went? That was certainly something he'd have enjoyed.

Instead, he'd have to settle for being the man to pull the trigger when Sam Pope was finally put to rest, and as he approached the open window of the outpost, he glanced down at the sniper rifle that Wainwright had promised would be there.

The Accuracy International Arctic Warfare rifle was standard issue throughout the UK military, and the British-made weapon was one that Jensen had been more than familiar with when he served. With genuine discomfort, he lowered himself down towards the weapon, and began to adjust the Bi-Pod beneath, setting it perfectly as he brought his eye up to the scope. As he peered through the lens, the Everly Estate loomed large, and Jensen blinked a few times to get his bearings. He was looking at the back of the huge house, and slowly, as he lowered himself onto his belly, he held the rifle as still as a statue. The years of training and warfare had turned Jensen into a walking weapon himself, and there was only one man he knew of who was more deadly behind the scope of a sniper rifle.

And Jensen was about to put a bullet through his skull.

Slowly, he moved the rifle on the Bi-Pod, scanning slowly across the illuminated grounds of the estate. He saw a number of guards writhing in agony on the grass, clutching either their legs or their shoulders.

Jensen scoffed.

Even when it came down to life and death, Sam was still conscientious enough to make sure he didn't kill if he didn't have to.

'Fucking boy scout,' Jensen muttered, and then continued to scan the grounds. A smile came across his face when he landed on a dead body. The man's chest ripped apart by a small burst of gunfire. 'That's more like it.'

As he amused himself, Jensen then guided the scope up towards the entrance of the house, where he found two more men on the ground, their hands clutching bullet wounds and he had to resist his own impulse to put them down for good.

But his bullets weren't for them.

Instinctively, he ran a hand over the magazine that had been snapped underneath the rifle, and he pulled back the bolt-action chamber. The thick, .300 Winchester Magnum bullet sat, ready to be launched towards his target. Jensen snapped shut the chamber and readjusted himself to the scope.

His phone buzzed.

It was Murray.

Whatever the message said, Jensen didn't care.

Once Sam was in the ground, he'd soon send Murray to join him. It wasn't personal.

But Guardian would be his by morning.

As he pulled it back up, he saw a large man hurl Sam into the fountain before rocking him with a thunderous fist that sent Jensen's target into the water. Jensen readied his finger on the trigger, but then waited. His thigh was throbbing with pain, and the idea of Sam being slowly beaten to death had its appeal.

If the man failed, Jensen would shatter Sam's skull from half a kilometre away.

Through the scope, and the torrential rain, he saw the man lunge for Sam, who ducked, drilled an elbow into the back of his head and sent him tumbling into the water feature. Then, in an act that didn't surprise him in the slightest, Sam drove his boot into the man's skull, sending his body limp, and undoubtedly ending his life.

It was brutal.

It was also impressive.

As Sam stumbled back away from his handiwork, Jensen cursed under his breath as he stepped just far enough to be shielded by the edge of the mansion. There was no clear shot, and Jensen swiftly adjusted the scope, pulling it back slightly to allow a clearer view of the entire estate.

Through one of the windows, he could see Wainwright yelling into a phone.

Through the ones that gave him visibility of the staircase, he saw armed men locking and loading.

Then he saw flashes of gunfire.

Sam was storming the building.

And Jensen smirked, as he reaffirmed his grip on the

weapon, and waited patiently for Sam to walk into his sights.

Sam stepped through the front door of the Everly Estate and drew up his rifle, scanning it expertly around the vast reception area. The white tiles shimmered under the spotlights that were peppered throughout the ceiling, and the large stairwell curved across the back wall and up to a hallway that looked over the entrance. An open doorway led to a dining room, which Sam tentatively stepped into and cleared, but as he turned to step back into the reception, the wooden frame of the door shattered as two bullets ripped through the wood.

Instinctively, Sam swung back into the dining room and slammed himself against the wall, grimacing as his ribs rattled. He could hear the sound of boots slapping against the tiles, as a few armed men raced towards his location. Sam spun out, dropped to one knee to catch them off guard, and lit both men up with three round bursts. The bullets thundered into both men, sending them sprawling across the tiles, and smearing blood as they went. More bullets rained down on Sam's location, obliterating the expensive ornaments on the table beside the doorway, and Sam returned fire before whipping back into the dining room for cover.

As he did, two hands reached out and clasped onto his shoulders, and Sam turned just in time to see the headbutt swinging towards him. The impact sent him stumbling back into the wall, his vision blurring as he felt the warm flow of blood trickle from his reopened eyebrow. He tried helplessly to regather himself, but as his hands gripped onto his rifle, his attacker threw a stinging punch that connected with his left arm. The pain was instant. His muscles relaxed, and Sam felt the rifle swing loosely to his side as the attacker followed up with a clubbing blow to Sam's gut that caused him to hunch over, gasping for air. Relentless, the man grabbed the back of Sam's hood and hurled him across the dinner table, and Sam clattered into the high-back, wooden chairs on the other side and crashed onto the floor.

His rifle spun out somewhere into the room.

Sam tried to push himself up, but his left arm gave out, and as he fell, rib first, onto the ground once more, his attacker slammed his boot into Sam's stomach, and then again. As the boot drove in for a third time, Sam hooked his right arm around the ankle and rolled to the side, sweeping the man off his feet and causing him to slam his head on the side of the oak table. Blood gushed out from the wound, and the man wearily tried to rise to his feet. But Sam pulled himself up via the table and then slammed the man skull first back into the tiles with his boot.

The man twitched, as his brain scrambled, and then slowly began to shut down.

Sam coughed, hacking up a mouthful of blood, and he spat it onto the floor as two more feet thundered towards the doorway. Expertly, Sam dropped to one knee, pulled his Glock from his spine, and rested his right arm on the table.

The man appeared in the doorway, gun in hand, and adrenaline pumping through his veins.

A bullet snapped between his eyes, and he dropped down dead.

Sam stood, wincing with pain as he tried to head back towards the hallway. As he approached the door, he gingerly leant down and scooped up the dead man's gun, and then stepped out into the reception area once more.

Gunfire above.

Two bullets shattered the window to Sam's left, and

Sam lifted his right arm, and unloaded the rest of his magazine at the man who was knelt between the pillars of the balcony that ran overhead.

One bullet hit the stone pillar.

The other two hit the target, the second ripping through the man's neck and sending him sprawling backward, gurgling for air as he drowned on his own blood. To the left of the stairwell, the door flew open, and a man holding a machete looked around at the bloodstained tiles, the dead bodies of his comrades, and then his eyes fell on the battered and weary killer.

Sam saw the anger explode behind the man's eyes, and as the man came hurtling across the tiles towards him, Sam lifted the gun and pulled the trigger.

Click.

Empty.

Sam tossed his gun and shifted the retrieved weapon to his right hand, but the man was too close, and he swung the machete wildly, slashing at Sam's throat. Sam managed to lean back, the blade nicking the edge of his hoody, and the man wasted little time in swiping again. Sam evaded the blade, and then surged forward, driving himself into the man's gut. With his left arm useless, Sam scooped up the man's left leg with his right arm and then toppled them both over the circular, marble table that took pride and place in the centre of the foyer. They obliterated the vase and the flowers within as they slammed to the ground on the other side, and both the gun, and the machete rattled against the tiles as they bounced away from them.

The man rolled over on top of Sam, wildly drilling down with right hands that Sam was able to half block with his right arm. The man then clasped his left hand onto Sam's face, trying his hardest to dig his thumb into Sam's eye socket.

Sam gritted his teeth, straining his neck muscles to turn

his head away, but the man's grip was beginning to take hold.

Just as he felt the man's thumbnail start piercing the flesh of his eyelid, Sam channelled everything he could into his left arm.

All the anger he felt towards the people who had agreed to destroy the country.

All the guilt he had for losing good men like Carl Marsden and Theo Walker.

All the grief he still clung to about the death of his boy.

All of rushed through his body, eliminating the pain of his ripped triceps, and he threw out his left hand and felt his fingers wrap around the handle of the machete.

He swung it.

The blade cut through the man's shoulder muscles, and Sam felt it collide with the collarbone, bringing it to a sickening halt. The man screamed, his voice cracking in agony, as he stumbled off Sam, his hands clasping towards the blade that was embedded in his shoulder. Sam reached up to the marble table, grabbed the lip, and pulled himself up, as the man squirmed as the pain rushed through every nerve in his body.

He turned to Sam, his eyes watering, and snarled.

The adrenaline was kicking in, and he pulled out a knife and charged at Sam. But the damage was already done, and he stumbled as he approached. Sam caught the knife wielding hand by the wrist, twisted it, and loosened the grip. As the knife fell, Sam caught it with his right hand, and swung round, and drove the blade into the man's forehead. Then, without hesitation, he grabbed the back of the man's skull and slammed him headfirst into the marble.

As the man flopped to the ground, all Sam could see was the handle protruding from the man's forehead, as blood tickled over his open, lifeless eyes.

Sam stepped over the body, picked up the gun that had been thrown from his grasp, and then felt a new wave of pain shoot from his left air. Blood was trickling down his forearm as the wound had reopened, and with considerable difficulty, he headed towards the stairwell. As he approached the landing halfway up, the window opposite shattered, and a hole the size of a bowling ball erupted in the wall less than a foot in front of him.

A sniper.

The wind and rain swirled through the shattered window, and Sam knew he had approximately five seconds for the shooter to discharge the round and re-aim.

There was no chance Sam could return fire.

Instead, Sam lifted the gun to the ceiling and blew out the two spotlights overlooking the stairwell. It plunged his location into darkness, and he threw himself forward onto the next staircase, shielding him from the open window.

He was penned in, and he snapped out the magazine.

He had three bullets left.

He took out three more of the spotlights in the ceiling, bathing the upstairs balcony in darkness.

It would at least give him a chance.

Keeping his body pressed to the stairs, he clambered up, and a few steps from the top, one of the windows on the top floor blew open, and another hole was blasted into the wall behind him.

The sniper was shooting blind.

Using the reloading window once more, Sam scarpered up the final few steps, and threw open the nearest door.

Wainwright was sitting behind his desk, his hands on his lap, looking resigned to defeat. Sam locked eyes with the man who had ordered him dead and felt his fists clench.

He'd done it.

He'd made it this far.

He reached into his vest for what was to come next, but he caught Wainwright shooting a small glance to the window.

Sam held his place.

Taking another step across the brightly lit room would be suicide.

Wainwright smiled.

'You're a clever man, Sam Pope. And very impressive. More's the pity, really.'

Wainwright's hand whipped out from under the desk, brandishing a handgun, and without hesitation, he fired, sending Sam sprawling to the ground.

CHAPTER TWENTY-EIGHT

The bullet embedded into the tactical vest like a pneumatic drill, burrowing through the fibre which fought valiantly to hold the bullet back. It did for the most part, but the tip did rip through vest and burrowed a few centimetres into Sam's chest.

The impact alone took him off his feet.

As he spiralled and hit the ground, Sam wheezed, trying to catch his breath, before staggering back to his feet towards the door. Just as he stumbled through the doorway, he heard the explosion of another gunshot from behind him, and the impact of the bullet that clattered into his spine sent him shunting forward into the dark hallway. As he flew past the shattered window, the wind slapped him in the face with a wet hand, and he tried to find his footing.

He stepped onto nothing.

Missing the top step, Sam felt gravity reach out and claim him, and he tried to turn his body as he fell. He hit the step third from the top, absorbing the impact in his right arm, before the momentum sent him tumbling down to the landing.

Left arm.
Ribs.
Left arm.
Ribs.

It was one of the most agonising falls of his life, and as he crumpled onto the landing, he cursed under his breath as he tried to stretch out his back. Thankfully, the vest had caught the bullet, saving him from serious and potentially fatal injury. But it still felt like someone had swung a sledgehammer into the base of his spine, and he felt it lock as he tried to move. As he rolled onto his front and began to push himself up, he heard footsteps crunch on the glass above him as Wainwright ventured out into the darkness.

'There's no use in running, Sam,' Wainwright spoke calmly. 'There's nowhere for you to go.'

Sam carried on down the stairs, gripping the bannister with his left hand, that was now soaked with blood. His triceps had been ripped open once more, and the blood loss was picking up pace. As he got to the bottom step, he felt his legs weaken, and he stumbled into the wall, clattering into a piece of modern art that fell from its hook.

Wainwright turned and opened fire, the bullet ricochetted off the tiles a few feet from Sam.

'I know you're wounded, Sam,' Wainwright called from the steps as he began his descent. 'I also know you're a man who won't go down without a fight. As commendable as that is, I should inform you that the police are on their way, and if I was to hand you over to them in cuffs, they will stick you in the deepest, darkest hole on the planet.'

Sam clutched at his wounded arm. He'd already been through two of the worst prisons in Europe and survived. But something told him that Wainwright would ensure that those seemed like a two-week stay in the Bahamas. Sam tried to make a break for the door, but then remembered it was under the murderous gaze of a sniper and turned back. Wainwright saw the movement in the shadows and fired, then another, and both bullets missed Sam by a matter of inches. Pinned in, Sam dropped down behind the marble table he'd previously soared over and pressed his back against it.

Beside him was the motionless body of the man he'd brutally killed, the machete still embedded in his shoulder.

'I could end it all for you, Sam,' Wainwright called as he made it to the landing. He looked out over the balcony, the darkness now softening to show him the array of dead bodies spread across his safe house. 'Think, Sam. All of this fighting. All of this pain you put yourself through. Just stand up, and I'll make it clean and quick. Right through your forehead. Send you off to be with your Jamie.'

Sam felt his fist clench.

Hearing the man responsible for so much death and destruction utter his son's name made his blood boil, and instinctively, he hauled the machete from the corpse beside him.

'Unless, of course, you want another path.' Wainwright's tone shifted. 'I watched on the CCTV, Sam. I watched it all. You tore through my private security like they didn't even matter. You are, without a shadow of a doubt, the most remarkable soldier I've ever seen. But what's a soldier without a rank? Huh? What's a soldier without a purpose?'

'I have a purpose,' Sam called out into the dark.

Wainwright smirked. He had him. He was behind the marble table. Wainwright navigated the final few steps and then finally stepped off onto the cold, blood smeared tiles.

'Ah yes,' Wainwright said mockingly. 'Your great quest for justice. What has that brought you, Sam? A body full of scars? More dead friends than you would care to count? This is the last chance, Sam. Either a bullet or a place by my side. Either one will be better than the living hell I'll put you through if they carry you out in cuffs.'

There was no response. The open front door was straining against its hinges as it flapped in the volatile wind, which had infiltrated the mansion through the obliterated windows. What was once a chamber of calm and safety had been turned into a war zone, and despite his advancing years, Wainwright was the last soldier standing.

He approached the marble table, peering into the dark that his eyes had become accustomed to, and he could see Sam's legs pointing away as he rested against the marble. Despite his noble attempt, Sam had failed, and now, as he sat dying slowly in the dark, Wainwright would offer him one final mercy.

'Fine. Have it your way.'

Wainwright's voice was laced with venom, and he stepped round the table and blasted a bullet through Sam's skull.

A mass of bone, blood, and brain matter sprayed across the tiles, and Sam slumped to his side. Wainwright pulled the gun back and looked down at his fallen foe.

There was no blood on his left hand.

A huge chunk of his shoulder was missing, sliced viciously by a missing blade.

What remained of his skull had a knife handle protruding between the eyes that were wide and long since dead.

Eyes that didn't belong to Sam.

Wainwright staggered back, the confidence drained as the panic began to swirl through his body. He raised the gun up and spun wildly, only to turn right into a ferocious right hook that rocketed into his jaw. Wainwright yelped as he spun, clattering across the marble table. The gun flew from his hand, and he stretched out his fingers in a lame attempt to pull it back from the darkness.

'Now, Sam…listen…' He began feebly.

But there was no negotiating.

The pain that suddenly erupted through his body took a few seconds to register. First, there was the ear-splitting clang of metal on marble. But then the burning sensation ran up through his arm and to his brain, and Wainwright stumbled back, clutching his right hand.

His fingers were still on the marble.

'Sam…please.' Wainwright begged as he stumbled back, clutching his fingerless hand, only for Sam to once again catch him with a hard right that sent him sprawling across the tiles. Wainwright rolled onto his front, weeping as his blood pooled alongside the rest that Sam had shed, and pathetically, he shuffled towards the open door like a slug.

He just needed to bring Sam into the open.

It was the only way he could survive.

As he reached the doorway, he felt the cold metal of his own gun press against the back of his head.

'Sit up,' Sam ordered.

Wainwright obeyed. He pushed himself onto his knees, still clutching his blood-soaked hand.

'If you kill me, Sam, there's no coming back from this,' Wainwright said through his tears. 'Listen.'

In the distance, there was the very faint wail of a siren, trying its best to be heard against the harsh weather. Sam was beaten and battered, but he was still standing. Whatever was coming his way, he would face on his feet.

'Take the shot,' Wainwright ordered.

'Confess,' Sam said coldly.

'What?'

'Confess?'

'To what?' Wainwright yelled, confused. 'Just take the shot.'

'Confess to it,' Sam demanded. 'To all of it.'

'Fine. Fine.' Wainwright snapped. 'I, Admiral Nicholas Wainwright, ordered the murder of Ruth Ashton.'

'And Balikov?'

'Balikov? He was a smart man. He saw which way the wind was blowing and what needed to be done. Had you not stopped him, then we would have burnt this country to the ground and rebuilt it without the feckless, weak youth of today dictating what and how we did things. It would have been a better country for it.'

'And how many would have died?'

'As many as needed,' Wainwright said coldly. 'Whatever it would have taken. But you, you Sam, you stopped it. You ruined everything, and once you kill me, you will rot in a prison for the rest of your life. Now…take the fucking shot.'

Sam took a deep breath and felt his knees begin to wobble. This vision of the admiral below him began to blur, and he felt his energy seeping through the wound in his arm.

'I'm not going to kill you,' Sam finally mumbled, taking a wobbly step backward.

'I wasn't talking to you,' Wainwright sneered, but his eyes looked out helplessly into the outside world. He'd led Sam right into Jensen's firing line, but he hadn't taken his shot.

Hadn't done what he promised he'd do.

Sam tried to keep himself stable, but felt his knees buckle, and he stumbled back onto the tiles.

As he tried to breathe through the blood loss, he could hear the sound of footsteps crunching up the gravel towards the door, and Wainwright let out a relieved sigh.

'Well. You aren't completely useless after all, are you?'

'Fuck.'

Jensen scolded himself as he watched the spotlights blow out one by one. He'd missed his shot at Sam, and now, the boy scout was proving his wits by eliminating Jensen's line of sight. The rain was lashing down with fury, scuppering his vision, but Jensen had prided himself on his accuracy.

But he'd missed.

But he still held the advantage, as Sam was on the staircase, with nowhere to go. It may have been dark, but Jensen still had the rifle locked on the top of the stairs, a few feet from Wainwright's study. As he waited, he felt his anger grow, and Jensen fired another reckless shot, obliterating the window at the top of the staircase.

He had no idea if he'd made the shot or not. But he shuffled his sight to Wainwright's office, drawing the admiral into his crosshairs. If he stayed locked on Wainwright, he'd be able to gauge from his movements if he was successful or not. The admiral was sitting at his desk, a gun in his lap, as he sipped a glass of the expensive port.

The man was a picture of calm.

The idea of a man raging a one-man war against him seemed to have little effect.

Wainwright suddenly sat upright, and Jensen drew his scope across the room. He could see that the door had opened, but he had no clear shot of Sam.

One step and Jensen would send him to the afterlife.

There was no movement, but suddenly, he saw the flash of a gunshot, and Sam spun into view and collapsed onto the floor.

Jensen pulled the rifle in tight, drew the crosshair over Sam's body, and brought his finger to the trigger.

Then Jensen felt the presence above him.

Taking his eye from the scope, he arched his neck to the right and looked up, his eyes widening at the sight of the Glock pointed directly at his head. As his eyes traced back further, he looked up the gun and arm, before he locked eyes with a furious-looking James Murray.

His friend for many years.

The man he'd betrayed and agreed to kill.

'Look…' Jensen began.

Murray pulled the trigger.

Having blown half of Jensen's face across the concrete, Murray stepped back and holstered his weapon. It had been a little while since a man had died by his hands. Although he dealt in the darkness that spread through the world, Murray had always maintained some level of dignity.

He wouldn't abide traitors.

Least not a man who wouldn't think twice about coming for Murray's family.

After Sarratt had provided Murray with the address, he'd headed to his car and rocketed down the motorway towards Crawley. On the way, he called Ranjit and asked him to send a Trojan message to Jensen. Ranjit, as always, worked quickly, and sure enough, a message was sent from Murray's phone to Jensen's. Upon its arrival, it copied Jensen's mobile signal, and sent it through to an app on Murray's phone, pinpointing his location.

Several speed cameras flashed.

Murray didn't care.

He roared through the village of Tilbit until he came to the park gate and then parked on the curb. Towed or clamped, he could sort it out in the morning. Jensen was located half a kilometre or so from the estate, which meant he was either hiding, or more likely, watching. Murray pulled himself over the park gate and then ran like hell through the woods that looped around the lake. His torch illuminated the path ahead, and soon, he found the wall that surrounded the grounds, and with some difficulty, he scaled it and dropped down into enemy lines. Swiftly, he headed towards the signal, and when the outpost emerged through the trees, Murray killed the torch and began to climb the ladder as carefully as he could. One slip and he'd alert Jensen, and Murray knew that his right-hand man wouldn't look a gift horse in the mouth. Once he climbed to the top, he saw Jensen prone on the ground, sniper rifle pulled up to his deadly eye.

So he executed him.

Things had gone too far, and if he made it out alive, Murray knew that Guardian's days were numbered. They were too entrenched in whatever mess Wainwright had made, and Murray knew he was running out of chances to do something good for once.

To do the right thing.

He scrambled back down the ladder, losing his footing a few rungs from the bottom, but the fall wasn't too bad. He then headed through the woods to the estate and stopped still when he emerged through the trees.

The Everly gardens were littered with bodies, most of them groaning in pain. He marched through the battlefield, ignoring the pleas of Wainwright's men for help, and then stepped out onto the gravel.

More bodies were dotted across the stones, and the water in the fountain was a dark shade of red, as a body floated on the water.

'Fucking hell, Sam,' Murray said under his breath, before he could hear the angered voices from the house. As Murray stepped towards the door, he saw the admiral on his knees, clutching a hand that was soaked with blood. Behind him, Sam staggered backwards and collapsed onto the floor.

Murray picked up the pace.

Behind him, the wailing sirens grew louder, and the

trees that lined the long road to the estate were flashing blue.

Murray approached the steps to the house, and Wainwright smiled at him from the doorway.

'Well. You aren't completely useless after all, are you?'

Wainwright's tone was as smug as his smile.

Murray rocked him with a right hook, sending the admiral sprawling to the side.

'Fuck you, old man,' Murray spat, and then stepped past his employer. He hurried towards Sam, who was barely conscious, and Murray squatted down and pulled Sam up, and looped him over his shoulder. Then, in an impressive display of strength, Murray pushed himself up again, roaring through the tension that ripped at his leg muscles, until he finally stood straight. Murray then lowered Sam onto his feet, hooked his shoulder around his neck, and began to carefully walk him towards the door.

'Thank you,' Sam managed.

'This makes us even.' Murray smiled, and the two former comrades stepped past the pathetic Wainwright, who began to laugh maniacally, as the police cars burst onto the gravel, welcoming Murray and Sam into their lawful arms. Murray stopped and steadied Sam, and the two men waited patiently as the armed police fanned out around them. Other officers were tentatively approaching, their cuffs ready.

'Did you get what you needed?' Murray asked through the corner of his mouth.

'Yep,' Sam said with a pained smile.

'Then let's hope this fucking works, mate.'

And with that, two officers wrenched Sam away, as the armed response held him at gunpoint, and Murray was cuffed, and led to one of the cars. While Sam was roughly guided towards the armoured police van, paramedics flooded from the ambulance and rushed towards Wainwright, who was crying for help.

Despite the war that had been waged, it was Wainwright who was still standing, figuratively, and he watched as Sam and Murray were driven from the premises, ready to face the might of the justice system.

The battle was over.

And Wainwright had won the war.

CHAPTER TWENTY-NINE

Lynsey imagined that every newsroom in the country was the same.

Anarchy.

The reports came through thick and fast about the attempt made upon Admiral Wainwright's life, and as soon as the story gained traction, she, along with the rest of the team of journalists, were summoned to the BBC offices by Tom Alderson. He wanted them to be ahead of the curve on the story, with reports coming in that both Commissioner Sarratt and the brave admiral himself would be giving a press conference at ten o'clock that morning.

The headline itself was sensational.

Sam Pope tries to assassinate the Chief of Defence Staff.

The head of the same armed forces that Sam had served with such distinction. Many of her colleagues in the room were throwing out wild narratives that Sam had finally snapped and was now targeting a government that had let him run loose for so long. Others were pitching that now the net was closing in on him, Sam was determined to go out in a blaze of glory.

Lynsey knew the truth.

But giving it would most likely lead to her being investigated and would scupper the entire plan.

All she needed to do was make sure she was assigned to the press conference.

It was nailed on that Morganna Daily, who was a popular figure both internally and with the public, would once again be the voice of the BBC when the press conference was over. Lynsey could accept that.

She just needed to be there with her.

That was the plan.

As Tom yelled over his enthusiastic team and then confirmed Morganna as the one who needed to get to New Scotland Yard pronto, Lynsey asked if she could have a quiet word. With a resigned sigh, Tom agreed, and ushered her to his office. She stepped through, and as he closed the door, he immediately held up a hand to cut her off.

'Look, Lynsey. The decision is made.'

'I know, but I really think I should—'

'Replace Morganna?' He chuckled. 'That's not your call to make.'

'No, I understand that. But send me with her.'

'I don't need two of you on the scene.' Tom shook his head as he marched across to his desk and took his seat. He gestured for Lynsey to take one, but she didn't even acknowledge it. 'There are plenty of other avenues to go down. More shit that will probably come to light. And I want us to be the first to break it.'

'Jesus fucking Christ,' Lynsey snapped. 'Is that what this has become? Fuck the actual news, just make sure we're the first ones to come up with a new angle. When did that become more important than the truth?'

'Spare me the righteous bullshit, Lynsey,' Tom replied. 'You're in here trying to cut the legs out of a colleague and—'

'No, I'm not.' Lynsey sat down and sighed. 'Do you trust me, Tom?'

It was a loaded question. Her editor was a smart man, and he pressed his fingers together in contemplation as he mulled it over.

'Despite the constant stream of headaches, I do.'

'Then you have to send me,' Lynsey said sternly. 'I can't tell you why, not right now, but there is *way* more at play here than just Sam Pope trying to attack the government.'

'You have to do better than that, mate.'

'I can get you a one-on-one interview with the commissioner,' Lynsey offered.

'Sarratt?' He rubbed his chin with intrigue.

'Yes. And when all this is over, every single news network will want to speak with her about what happens next.' Lynsey leant forward in her chair. 'And if getting there first, and getting the truth, really matters to you, then I can make that happen.'

Tom sat back in his chair and regarded her with scepticism. For years now, Lynsey had been a pain in his arse and the cause of more than a hundred headaches.

But she was a damn fine journalist, and despite the constant stream of irritation, she had more integrity than most.

'Fine.' He sighed. 'Go with her, but I want Morganna on camera, okay? You can support her with everything, but this is *her* story. Understood?'

'Absolutely.' Lynsey shot out of her seat and headed to the door. 'Thanks, Tom.'

Before he could say anything else, Lynsey darted from the office to inform a disappointed Morganna that she would be going with her. Despite the initial pushback, Morganna shrugged, seemingly happy to be the centre of attention, and minutes later, she, Lynsey, and the camera crew were headed to New Scotland Yard, ready for yet another explosive press conference that would live long in the memory.

Thankfully, the rain had finally relented.

As the press gathered in neat, organised rows in front of the podium, Commissioner Sarratt looked out from the glass doors of New Scotland Yard, wondering just how the morning would play out. The sun cutting through the clouds was a nice surprise, meaning the interested gaggle of journalists would be in higher spirits. As planned, the news of Sam Pope's attack on Wainwright had spread through the media like wildfire, and now all of them were there, ready to hear from her and the man himself.

The brave Admiral Wainwright.

The veteran, who'd dedicated his life to protecting his country, who'd stood up to Sam Pope and had won.

As she stood, hands clasped to the base of her spine, Sarratt knew the time to change her mind was dwindling.

'Sometimes, you need to do what is sensible as opposed to what is right.'

The words ran through her mind once more. If things didn't go to plan, then her career was over.

Potentially her life.

But gazing out at the people, and beyond them, the city, Sarratt was reminded of the oath she'd taken. Of the commitment she made to uphold the law, and to serve the good people of this country with integrity and respect.

Sometimes sensible didn't matter.

As the seconds ticked down, she heard the commotion behind her, and a round of applause as Admiral Wainwright stepped through the security barriers. His face was painted with a dark shade of purple bruising, and his heavily bandaged hand was strapped to his chest with a sling. Sarratt didn't turn to look at him.

He didn't deserve her respect.

Dressed in his finest military wear, the admiral certainly knew how to make an impression and would no doubt milk his victory for every last drop. Outside, the excitement grew, as the reporters had noticed them both, and cameras flashed, trying to capture candid moments between two of the most powerful people in the city.

'Good crowd,' Wainwright said with a grin. 'Why don't you run along and be a good little warm-up act.'

Sarratt finally turned, greeting the admiral with glare.

'After this, we are done.'

'No, Commissioner. *You* are done.' Wainwright took a menacing step forward and leant towards her ear. 'Let's not lose sight on who's *really* in charge here.'

Repeating the threat to underline his position of power, Wainwright stepped forward and pulled open the glass door and gestured for her to take the lead. The press would capture it as a moment of chivalry, but Sarratt knew what it was.

It was the march towards the death of her career.

With powerful strides, and her head held high, Sarratt marched towards the podium, greeting all the reporters with a smile. The red lights on the cameras told her she was being broadcast live to the nation.

'Good morning.' She spoke confidently. 'Last night, Sam Pope was arrested after a heinous attack on Admiral Nicholas Wainwright's safehouse. The Chief of Defence Staff had been put under protection when intel led us to believe that Sam Pope would make an attempt on his life.'

Sarratt paused, allowing the excitement to wash through the crowd before she continued.

'Our intel was correct, and after an unfortunate incident which resulted in a number of casualties, Sam Pope was apprehended by the Metropolitan Police and taken into custody. He remains on twenty-four-hour lockdown, and the legal proceedings will begin in due course.' Sarratt cleared her throat. 'Despite sustaining severe injuries, the Chief of Defence Staff would now like to address you all. Thank you.'

Sarratt nodded to the reporters and then turned to make her exit. As she passed Wainwright, he leant in close.

'Thank you, Henrietta. That will be all.'

He continued towards the podium, his threat lingering in Sarratt's ear. As he approached the microphone, one of the reporters in the front row began applauding.

Then another.

Soon, the applause spread through the entire group, and the admiral basked in the adulation, unaware of one reporter who was shuffling through the pack, heading towards the production team responsible for the conference.

Wainwright held up his one good hand for silence, and then leant forward, exaggerating the discomfort he was in.

'Thank you,' he said warmly. 'That was quite unexpected, but very much appreciated. This is not my victory. This is a victory for the Metropolitan Police. This is a victory for the United Kingdom. And this is a victory for every civilian who lives in this great nation.'

Another, more muted applause rang round. Wainwright looked out at them all. The people who would now look at him with such reverence, who would write paragraph after paragraph about how he, a man who had served his country with such distinction, was the one to bring down its most dangerous criminal.

He spoke into the mic, but the feed had cut.

Nobody could hear him.

Wainwright scowled, tried again, and when he couldn't

be heard, he shot a deathly glare towards the production team who were standing by.

Sarratt watched on, her arms folded.

It was now or never.

As Wainwright had made his way towards the podium, Lynsey had excused herself, shuffling past Morganna who seemingly didn't care. She'd secured her spot in the front row, had her own Dictaphone pointed towards the hero of the hour, knowing full well her cameraman had the best shot.

What Lynsey wanted to do wasn't her concern.

As a groundswell of support erupted through the crowd of her peers, Lynsey weaved her way through them, offering apologetic smiles until she reached the small, makeshift booth where the audio team was seated. The third-party company had a longstanding relationship with the Met, and was often called upon to set up press conferences and other speaking events. It was an easy gig for them, and the two men looked beyond bored as Wainwright began to speak.

Lynsey draped her arms over the booth and smiled.

'Please, step away from the equipment,' one of the men said half-heartedly as he turned to her. When he saw her striking smile, he seemed to snap to attention. 'Sorry, love. But we're working here.'

'I can see that,' Lynsey said with just a hint of flirtation. Massaging a fragile, male ego had been a skill she'd learnt long ago. 'I'm from the BBC.'

'Good for you, darling,' the other man piped up, as he puffed on his vape. 'But we're not, so please, go back to the group.'

Lynsey kept her eyes on the man who was offering her a playful shrug.

Behind them, Wainwright was droning on about victory.

Lynsey reached into her jacket pocket and handed the man a USB stick.

'This is to celebrate the achievement of the admiral,' she lied. 'By order of Commissioner Sarratt.'

The other man stood and swiped the USB stick from her hand and frowned. He then looked over towards the podium, where Wainwright was basking in his own brilliance. To the side, Commissioner Sarratt, who had spoken to him earlier that day, gave the technician a confirming nod.

'Right,' the man said, a little confused. 'We weren't made aware of this and—'

'She thought it would be a nice surprise.' Beckett shrugged, still with just a hint of playfulness. 'Unless you want to tell the head of the police that you don't want to?'

'No, no.' The man waved her away. 'Give me a sec…'

As the grumpier of the two began fiddling with the setup, the other offered Lynsey a biscuit, which she turned down.

She'd also be turning down the obligatory offer for a drink, no doubt.

The elder gentleman tapped a few buttons, and behind her, she heard a few groans of discontent as Wainwright's microphone shut off. All eyes span towards the booth, and Lynsey stepped away nonchalantly, rejoining the masses, who were waiting on bated breath.

Wainwright went to speak again, but nothing.

'Come on,' Lynsey uttered under her breath, just as the man pushed in the USB stick and played the audio file.

Suddenly, the tinny sound of rainfall echoed through the speakers, causing a wave of confusion to crash over everyone. Wainwright threw up an agitated hand, cursing to the side when suddenly, a recorded voice boomed through the speakers.

Confess.

All the reporters looked to each other, unaware of who's voice it was. Lynsey knew.

Morganna knew. So did Sarratt.

And as the colour quickly drained from Wainwright's smug, wrinkled face, it appeared he did too.

It was Sam Pope.

What?

The second voice was unmistakably Wainwright's, and all eyes fell back to the admiral, who had frozen in shock. Sam had never held him at gunpoint.

It had been a recording device.

Confess.

To what? Just take the shot.

Wainwright snapped back into the moment, and he yelled angrily towards the booth for them to shut it off. Sarratt stepped forward, her eyes glued on the two technicians, and she shook her head.

Confess to it. All of it.

Wainwright looked out to crowd, as the respect, and adoration was morphing from confusion to disgust.

Fine. Fine. I, Admiral Nicholas Wainwright, ordered the murder of Ruth Ashton.

A cacophony of gasps erupted from the crowd as the truth began to flow from the speakers. Wainwright took a few steps back, wondering how quickly his old legs could take him. He flashed a glance to the side and noticed the police officers who had taken up their positions on the side of the stage.

And Balikov?

Balikov? He was a smart man. He saw which way the wind was blowing and what needed to be done. Had you not stopped him, then we would have burnt this country to the ground and rebuilt it without the feckless, weak youth of today dictating what and how we did things. It would have been a better country for it.

The shock was quickly turning to outrage, and Wainwright could feel every strand of power that was once in his remit, being plucked from his hands with every word.

And how many would have died?

Even after an intense and gruelling fight through Wainwright's personal army, there was still a nobility to Sam's voice. The crowd had cottoned on to who was interrogating Wainwright, and both Lynsey and Sarratt could see the narrative being rewritten in front of their very eyes.

As could Wainwright, whose own eyes were now filled with terrified tears as his confession continued to blast out into the street.

As many as needed. Whatever it would have taken. But you, you, Sam, you stopped it. You ruined everything, and once you kill me, you will rot in a prison for the rest of your life. Now…take the fucking shot.

Slowly, the police officers began to diverge onto Wainwright, and the man who had strode out of New Scotland Yard just minutes before like a conquering hero, now looked like nothing more than an old, beaten man.

Sam's final words out of the speakers underpinned everything.

I'm not going to kill you.

The reporters all turned to each other, all of them realising they'd been chasing the wrong story. Lynsey watched from the back of the crowd, feeling an overwhelming sense of pride in what had happened. Sam had explained to them just how much trouble Wainwright wanted to plunge the country in and he made it clear that killing the admiral would only make him a martyr.

They needed to expose him.

They needed the truth.

As she heard her peers discussing the heroics of Sam Pope, she felt her eyes watering. Never had she wavered from her belief in the man. Sam had saved her life a few years ago, but hearing his voice boom through the speakers, after going through an unimaginable war with Wainwright, he still had the clarity of vision to not kill the man.

To seek justice.

As Lynsey dabbed at her eyes, she watched as the police officers read Wainwright his rights, arresting him for the murder of Ruth Ashton and for his terrorist activities. Wainwright didn't fight back. His shoulders were hunched, and all the calmness with which he'd run the task force had gone.

He was a puppet master who had just had his strings cut.

As the officers turned to march him back towards New Scotland Yard with metal cuffs around his wrists, Commissioner Sarratt stepped forward.

Shoulders straight.

Head held high.

A beacon of integrity.

Wainwright looked at her with hatred, and Sarratt fixed him with a wry smile as she leant in.

'Let's not lose sight of who is *really* in charge here.'

Wainwright's eyes bulged, and as he tried feebly to struggle against his restraints, the officers shuffled him away from their boss and off to face the rest of his life behind bars. Sarratt took to the podium, where every reporter was calling out over the other, all of them desperate to know what was to follow. Sarratt knew the stories would be sensational, that her own competency and judgment would be questioned.

But overall, justice had been served.

Before she began to take questions, she looked across

the sea of eager faces and her eyes locked with Lynsey, standing at the back, a smile across her face.

They shared a nod.

They had done it.

And with that, Sarratt took her first question, and got on with the unenviable task of clearing up a seismic catastrophe.

'Wow.'

Sutton dropped back into her seat, watching on the television in her front room as Wainwright was slapped in cuffs. Beside her, with an icepack pressed to his head with his right hand, and his left arm hanging in a sling, was Sam. He watched, emotionless, as Wainwright's treachery was displayed for the watching world.

As justice was served.

When they'd sat in the same room a few evenings a go, Sam had laid out his plan.

All three of the women didn't give him a chance in hell. Wainwright would have more security than the royal family, and they'd be waiting for him. Sam had been aware of the risks, but he made it clear that the only way for all this to be over, was for Wainwright to face the law.

Killing him would make him a martyr.

And it would justify Wainwright's mission against Sam.

Slowly, but surely, all of them had got on-board and Sutton had waited been distracted all day at work. DI Gayle had even checked on her at one point. But sure enough, as the news had filtered through of the incident in Crawley, Sarratt had reached out to Sutton to let her know that Sam was coming her way.

Beaten and battered, Sarratt had intercepted Sam's arrival at Mitcham Police Station, along with James

Murray. She'd told the officers that there had been arrangements made for such dangerous criminals, and the young men were not going to argue with the head of the Met.

Sarratt let Murray return home.

And then she personally drove Sam to Sutton and had thanked him for what he'd done.

Sam had slept soundlessly all night, and now, as he recovered on her sofa, Sutton couldn't fathom how someone so reviled by the press, and someone who was capable of such destruction, had such a good heart pounding in his chest. As they watched Wainwright get marched towards his fate, Sutton rested a hand on Sam's knee.

'You did it,' Sutton said with a smile.

'We all did,' Sam replied. And then, with a grunt, he pushed himself off the sofa and then shuffled painfully to Sutton's kitchen. He returned the ice pack to the freezer, popped a couple of paracetamol, and then lifted his jacket from her chair. Sarratt had acquired it from James Murray's locked office, and had returned it to him in Mitcham Station, complete with his identification. Sutton stood, confused.

'You're leaving?'

'You're a detective, Jess,' he said softly. 'I can't thank you enough for what you've done. But this grace period from Sarratt will only extend so far, and as long as I'm here, you're breaking the law.'

Sutton walked towards Sam, and she pushed up onto her tiptoes and planted her lips on his cheek. Painfully, he wrapped his good arm around her and pulled her in for hug, ignoring the searing agony from his body. As he pulled back, Sutton blinked back a tear and forced a smile.

Sam reached up, held her chin between his thumb and index finger, and smiled as he spoke.

'Thank you.'

Sam struggled into his jacket and then limped to her front door. Sutton glanced to the screen, where Sarratt was now addressing the press, and then called after Sam.

'It is over…right?'

Sam didn't say anything. He just smiled and pulled the door closed behind him.

The fight was never over.

CHAPTER THIRTY

The smell of fresh coffee wafted from the bedside table, and James Murray slowly opened his eyes. It had been a few days since Wainwright had been exposed on national television, and since then, Murray had followed the story with interest. Already, the leading journalists in the country were pressing down upon the government to expose all those who were in cahoots with Wainwright, and sure enough, the confession of Michael Hartson, the former Minister for Civil Service soon came to light.

Once again, it was Sam who had delivered it.

Commissioner Sarratt had stopped by one evening to thank Murray for his help, and they called a truce on the escalating tension that had threatened to boil over. Ultimately, they'd both been under the oppressive thumb of Wainwright, who had wanted Sam dead to hide his shameful betrayal of his country. Sarratt did take a moment to chastise Murray for his complicity in the death of Ruth Ashton, but as Wainwright had organised the hit, and Jensen had pulled the trigger, there was enough wiggle room for Murray to walk away from it.

The guilt, however, would last a lifetime.

Surprisingly, there was no guilt whenever his mind wandered to Jensen. They had fought together on countless tours when they'd served, and Fabian had been the first man he'd called upon when he started Guardian. But over time, the idea of a flourishing business hadn't appealed to Jensen, and the man had been willing to betray Murray to take control.

Wainwright had threatened the safety of Murray's family.

And he'd have only done that if Jensen had agreed to pull the trigger.

As the rain peppered the bedroom window of his five-bedroom house in North Barnet, Murray pushed himself up in his king-size bed and lifted the mug of coffee. The bedroom door was open, and he could hear Jasper and Oliver bickering downstairs at the kitchen table, with Jasper mocking his little brother's poor performance on whatever video game they'd become obsessed with.

Murray didn't know.

He wasn't around enough to know.

That was going to change.

As he sipped his coffee, he lifted his tablet, and began typing out an email to his accountant, outlining his intentions to close down Guardian as a business entity, and he was seeking financial advice on the best way forward. Most likely, he'd get a panicked phone call sometime later that day, with his accountant keen to keep the cash cow breathing.

But Murray had made up his mind.

Building a business that prided itself on ruthless efficiency and one that dealt in either lead or blood didn't hold the same appeal anymore. Not when he'd finally seen the type of people he'd been protecting. As he tapped away on the screen, he didn't notice the figure in the doorway.

'Morning, handsome,' Becky said with a smile. In her hand was a plate, with two slices of Bovril-covered toast.

Murray's favourite.

'Hey, babe.' He smiled as she stepped into the room and handed him his breakfast. 'Thanks.'

'What are you doing?' She dropped lazily onto the bed next to him.

'Just work stuff,' he said vaguely. The less Becky knew about his line of work, the better, and she agreed. Only this time, she didn't seem so disinterested.

'Is it to do with what's going on with that guy? The admiral?' she asked. She knew he'd been working with Metropolitan Police, and the news was rife with the story of Sam Pope bringing down the leader of the military.

Murray chuckled.

'You could say that.' He took a bite of his toast before he continued. 'But no. I'm actually thinking about stepping away from it all.'

Becky sat bolt upright.

'Excuse me?'

'Guardian. I'm shutting it down,' Murray said, with a clarity of thought that made him feel genuine happiness. 'I know it's brought us a good life and god knows what I'll do instead, but I—'

She didn't let him finish.

Becky launched forward and threw her arms around her husband, and buried her head into his shoulder. Taken aback by her reaction, Murray gently stroked the back of her hair and held her.

Her response told him everything he needed to know.

This was the right decision.

He held her for a few minutes, and eventually she pulled away. As she composed herself, Oliver appeared in the door.

'Dad, Jasper won't let me have a go on the PlayStation.'

Instantly, Jasper appeared behind his young brother to protest.

'How about we get out of here?' Murray offered, looking at Becky who grinned. 'There's got to be something fun on in town.'

'Can we go bowling?' Oliver asked, hopping from foot to foot with excitement.

'You betcha,' Murray said, swinging his legs out from the bed and taking another bite from his toast. 'Work can wait. Let's go and have some fun, eh? Now both of you, go, and get dressed.'

They both mockingly slammed their heels together and saluted.

'Yes, sir.'

The boys often mocked his military background, but Murray always took it as a compliment. Although they didn't fully understand what he'd done, or for that matter, what he did now, they were always quick to show his medals to their friends and ask him if he did similar things to what they did on their video games.

As he watched them run off through the house, he felt an overwhelming sense of pride, and then turned back to the en suite bathroom. As he did, he caught Becky smiling at him.

'What?' he asked.

'Nothing. It's just this feels like the old you.' She stood up, walked towards him, and gave him a kiss. 'Are you sure about this?'

'More than anything.' He held her hands. 'There's a lot more good I can do in this world. And I'm sick of dealing with the worst of it.'

He lifted her hands and kissed them before heading to

the bathroom. Smitten, Becky watched her husband walk away as she spoke.

'What's changed?'

Murray stopped. It was a big question that had a long, blood-soaked answer. He turned to her and flashed her the same smile he did all those years ago on their wedding day.

'Let's just say I bumped into an old friend who made a pretty good point.'

And with that, Murray disappeared into the bathroom and began getting ready for the first day of the rest of his life.

As had become their Sunday tradition, Sarratt and her husband and had loaded up the car and taken the short drive from Horsell to Brookwood. It was less than five miles, and took them around the outskirts of the town of Woking, where they would park up in the vast, muddy car park for visitors to Brookwood Country Park. Their German shepherd, Lance, came bounding out of the boot as Sarratt opened it, and both she and Jordan slid on their wellies to deal with the thick, muddy trail.

The morning was brisk, carrying the threat of a downpour, but their raincoats would act as a layer of protection. They interlocked their gloved hands and followed their eager dog along one of the windy paths that veered into the woods. Despite his appearance, Lance was a soft, gentle dog, and once the other nervous dog owners saw how friendly he was, they let their own dogs off the lead, and the owners forced small talk as their pets ran freely through the mud.

Jordan spoke eagerly and at length about the new menu he was concocting for his restaurant, buzzing off his recently awarded Michelin Star.

It was music to Sarratt's ears.

After a week that had seen her authority challenged, her position and her very well being threatened, it was lovely to breathe in the fresh air and hear about something else for a change.

Not Sam Pope.

Not the needless death of Ruth Ashton.

Just normal life.

As Jordan spoke, Sarratt linked his arm and pressed her head to his shoulder, the bobble on the top of her woolly hat tickling his nose. They laughed, passed through another passage of trees, and stepped out towards the beautiful canal. The waters were calm, and the sun that sliced through the cloud shimmered across the surface.

It was a picture of beauty.

Sarratt took a few steps forward, her toes on the edge of the embankment, and she stared out over the water.

She'd told her husband everything. From the threats from Wainwright, to providing a wanted vigilante with the weapons he needed to bring him down. Jordan, as always, had listened without judging, and when she finally broke down in tears having put Wainwright behind bars, he'd offered his shoulder.

And some more wise words.

'Fuck being sensible, eh? You'll always do the right thing. It's who you are.'

Those words now echoed in her mind as she gazed out across the water. The British countryside was a thing of beauty, something she believed went under-appreciated by the nation. But as she took in the beauty of her surroundings, she wondered what would have happened had Wainwright's alliance come to pass.

The country was indebted to Sam Pope.

As commissioner of the most powerful police service in the country, she could never say that out loud. Her role dictated that despite his efforts in bringing down Wainwright, she still couldn't just allow a rogue soldier to dish out justice where the system failed. She'd explained that to him when she'd driven him to Sutton's flat, promising him she'd try to give him as much leeway as possible.

As ever, he answered like a hero.

'You have a job to do, Commissioner.'

But she was swiftly realising that to deal with the myriad of shit that McEwen had promised her, she'd need to bend her role to make it fit in with reality. Nobody could affect change on the scale that she wanted by following the patterns of their predecessors.

Sarratt didn't want to be just another name on the list.

Another seat in the chair.

She wanted to make a real difference, and over the past few months, those two monumental victories had come from being associated with Sam.

By doing things outside of the box.

'Hey, babe. You okay?' Jordan called back as he followed Lance down the pathway.

'Give me a few minutes, okay?' Sarratt smiled, and Jordan gave the thumbs up and then chased after their excitable hound. Sarratt pulled out a cigarette, breathed in the smoke, and let it filter from her mouth. She'd promised Jordan she'd quit, but today was a day of relaxation.

Tomorrow, she'd be back in her office, smartly presented, overlooking a city that needed more help than ever.

But that was tomorrow.

Sarratt finished her cigarette, stubbed it out in the mud, and then turned to catch-up with her husband. As she marched around the stunning lake, she felt a renewed sense of pride and purpose, not just in her role, but in herself.

She was the one who was in charge.

And she wouldn't let anyone, no matter how powerful, tell her how to run the Met.

Later that afternoon, as Lance lay asleep under the table of the cosy, countryside pub where they frequented for the best roast dinner Sarratt had ever had, Jordan ordered two glasses of champagne to the table. Confused, Sarratt took hers, and expected to celebrate Jordan's award of a Michelin Star.

He held up his glass to her.

'To you, Henrietta. For doing the right thing.'

She smiled back the tears, clinked her glass, and took a sip.

For once, she was excited to get back to London.

She was ready to do some real good.

EPILOGUE

'You still look like hot shit.'

Murray laughed as he dropped down next to Sam, who rolled his eyes at his former comrade's words. There was truth to them. His arm was still in a sling, although Sam was beginning to experience some mobility in it. His ribs were still a constant, inhibiting hum that would catch him unaware whenever he made the simplest of movements. The cuts and bruising on his face were fading, but as he sat on the steps outside Trafalgar Square with his hood up, Sam looked like he'd had one rough night after the other.

'Thanks,' he finally offered. Murray held a cup of coffee in each hand and had a heavy holdall draped over his shoulder. He handed one of the cups to Sam, and then gratefully placed the bag on the step below. 'Going somewhere?'

'That's not for me,' Murray replied, and took a seat next to Sam. 'Look, Sam, I just wanted to—'

'You don't have to apologise,' Sam said firmly. 'You had a job to do, I get it.'

'To be fair, I did try to get you out of there safely. You

know, before I found out what a piece of shit the admiral was. Oh, and before you knocked me the fuck out.'

The two men chuckled.

Two old soldiers recounting their battles.

'Yeah, sorry about that. Needs must.'

'Hey, don't apologise.' Murray sipped his coffee. The wind whipped around them, and he was thankful for the heat of his drink. 'If anything, you knocked some sense into me.'

'Yeah?'

'Yes, sir. As of yesterday, Guardian is no longer a trading entity. I'm done.' Murray nodded to hammer home his point. 'Fuck knows what I'm going to do now. Becky thinks I should go into teaching.'

Sam let out an involuntary laugh.

'Now that, I'd like to see.' Sam chuckled again. 'But good on you, James. Turning over a new leaf is a big thing to do.'

'Well, in the spirit of turning over a new leaf, I thought I'd donate to the cause.' Murray set his coffee down. 'I got my tech guy, Ranjit, to erase any traces of Ben Carter from the systems we used to try to find you. We were the only ones who were aware of it, but there's no footprint in the Met database at all about your identification. Ranjit even told me he tightened it up for you. Says it's bulletproof.'

'Well, thank him for me.'

Murray began fumbling in the inside of his jacket.

'One other thing. Over the years, we worked for some pretty shady people. I can't say I'm proud of it, but what's done is done.' Murray pulled out a card. 'Except one client. He never gave me a name. He never gave me a reason. I had Ranjit run the card through the databases, and although there wasn't much in the way of names or locations, there was some pretty shady shit associated with this.'

He handed Sam the card. It was a smooth, black design, with one word typed out in the middle in an elaborate font.

Veilmont

'What's this?' Sam asked, looking up from the card.

'We figured it was some sort of organisation. Or a code word.' Murray shrugged. 'Like I said, there isn't much of a footprint. But on the dark web, there're a few sinister links. Nothing we wanted to get involved with. Whatever it is, there's enough power behind it to keep it completely in the shadows. Meaning there aren't many people who can go after them.'

Murray turned and looked Sam dead in the eye. The message was clear, and Sam smiled. He tapped the card on his hand and contemplated his next move.

He could have just handed it back to his friend, thanked him for the coffee, and then walked off to be swallowed by the city.

Just walk away from it all.

He'd done enough.

But as he tapped the card, he wondered just how dark those stories were, and if so, how many people had been hurt by this word.

How many people couldn't fight back?

Sam knew what his answer was, and he tucked the card into his pocket.

'I'll look into it,' he said, and then stood up, finishing his coffee. Murray reached for the bag and slid it across to Sam with his foot. 'What's this?'

'A parting gift.' Murray smiled. 'Call it a donation to the cause.'

Sam leant down and unzipped the sports bag. It was packed with weapons and ammunition.

Glocks.

Grenades.

An assault rifle.

His own personal arsenal.

'Wow,' Sam said, zipping it back up and hauling it up over his right shoulder. 'You shouldn't have.'

'There's a location and a code in there for a storage container in Berkhamsted,' Murray said as he stood. 'In case you need to replenish.'

Sam held out his hand to his former comrade. Life had taken them down very different paths, but fate had bound them together once again. Murray had a home to go home to. A family to love and a life to live.

Sam had a path of his own.

Murray took Sam's hand, shook it firmly, and then pulled him in for a hug. After a few moments, he stepped back, patted Sam on the shoulder, and nodded.

'Give em' hell, Sam.'

Sam smiled and turned away. As he walked down the steps of the famous monument, the heavens opened, and the rain began to fall. With an arsenal of weapons swinging from his shoulder, his body begging for mercy, and a new target in mind, Sam headed towards the nearest Underground station, knowing that for him, the fight would continue.

Someone *had* to fight back.

GET EXCLUSIVE ROBERT ENRIGHT MATERIAL

Hey there,

I really hope you enjoyed the book and hopefully, you will want to continue following Sam Pope's war on crime. If so, then why not sign up to my reader group? I send out regular updates, polls and special offers as well as some cool free stuff. Sound good?

Well, if you do sign up to the reader group I'll send you FREE copies of THE RIGHT REASON and RAINFALL, two thrilling Sam Pope prequel novellas. (RRP: 1.99)

You can get your FREE books by signing up at www.robertenright.co.uk

SAM POPE NOVELS

For more information about the Sam Pope series and other books by Robert Enright, please visit:

www.robertenright.co.uk

ABOUT THE AUTHOR

Robert lives in Buckinghamshire with his family, writing books and dreaming of getting a dog.

For more information:
www.robertenright.co.uk
robert@robertenright.co.uk

You can also connect with Robert on Social Media:

f facebook.com/robenrightauthor
◉ instagram.com/robenrightauthor

COPYRIGHT © ROBERT ENRIGHT, 2024

All rights reserved. No part of this publication may be reproduced, stored in a retrieval system, or transmitted in any form or by any means, electronic, photocopying, mechanical, recording, or otherwise, without the prior permission of the copyright owner.

All characters in this book are fictitious and any resemblance to actual persons living or dead is purely coincidental.

Cover by The Cover Collection

Edited by Emma Mitchell

Proof Read by Martin Buck

Printed in Great Britain
by Amazon